LIVING RIGHT

LIVING RIGHT

Laila Ibrahim

ISBN: 0692555099
ISBN 13: 9780692555095
Library of Congress Control Number: 2015917180
Flaming Chalice Press, Berkeley, CA

A strong America must also value the institution of marriage. I believe we should respect individuals as we take a principled stand for one of the most fundamental, enduring institutions of our civilization.

Congress has already taken a stand on this issue by passing the Defense of Marriage Act, signed in 1996 by President Clinton. That statute protects marriage under federal law as the union of a man and a woman, and declares that one state may not redefine marriage for other states.

Activist judges, however, have begun redefining marriage by court order, without regard for the will of the people and their elected representatives. On an issue of such great consequence, the people's voice must be heard. If judges insist on forcing their arbitrary will upon the people, the only alternative left to the people would be the constitutional process. Our nation must defend the sanctity of marriage.

The outcome of this debate is important, and so is the way we conduct it. The same moral tradition that defines marriage also teaches that each individual has dignity and value in God's sight.

President George W. Bush
State of the Union, 2004

SUNDAY, FEBRUARY 15, 2004

The house was quiet when they got home from brunch. *Josh must still be sleeping*, Jenn thought as she threw in a load of laundry. Then she checked the answering machine. Her mom had called to say that her friend Mary had seen Jenn on the news. *Guess this is my fifteen minutes of fame.* Jenn smiled. Then she was immediately ashamed for being arrogant and admonished herself, *I didn't set out today to be on the news but to do the work of the Lord.*

She climbed the beige-carpeted stairs to check on her teenager. His was the middle bedroom, adjacent to the kids' bath. She tapped quietly. No answer. Opening the door slowly, she peered into the dark room and immediately a foul stench hit her. After her eyes adjusted, she saw the cause: vomit speckled the side of Josh's navy-blue comforter, ending in a puddle on the ground. *Oh, poor honey*, Jenn thought. He'd entirely missed the garbage can she had left in the night. Dead asleep, likely he hadn't even noticed he'd been sick. Fortunately, he was on his side, so she wasn't worried that he'd inhaled his vomit.

She went to the bathroom to get washcloths and towels to wipe up the mess. As she approached the bed, she said, "Josh, it's Mom. You threw up while you were sleeping. I'm going to wipe you down."

He didn't stir. She rubbed the damp terry cloth against his slack mouth. No movement.

"Josh," Jenn said a little louder, her pulse speeding up.

She shook him gently and then urgently. "Josh!" He didn't respond.

"*Josh!*" Jenn yelled and shook him hard. His head flopped back and forth. His breathing was shallow. A wave of adrenaline shot through her body, putting every cell of her body on high alert. "Josh, wake up!"

Dear God, help my son. Jenn ran to the wooden banister overlooking the living room and called for her husband. "Steve!" Her voice was ragged and sharp, pushing down the rising force of hysteria.

Without waiting for an answer, she rushed into her bedroom, grabbed the cordless receiver, and dialed 911. *Pick up. Pick up. Pick up!*

"Hello, what is your emergency?" the dispatcher asked.

"My son," Jenn spoke in a rush. "He isn't breathing very well, and he won't wake up."

"What's your address?" the dispatcher asked calmly.

"Forty-four ninety-nine Sparrow Court, Dublin, California, 94568," Jenn replied. "Off of Hawk Way."

"How long has he been unresponsive?"

"I don't know. We just got home."

"How old is your son?"

"Sixteen. Please send someone now," Jenn begged. "He needs help. He threw up while we were at church. We left him for just a few hours, and when we got back, he was like this."

The dispatcher asked, "Do you see a bottle near him?"

"What?"

"Has he taken any pills?" the woman asked in a flat voice.

"No!" Jenn was shocked. "My son doesn't do drugs."

"An ambulance is on the way."

"Thank you!" A small measure of relief washed over her. "Thank you so much."

"Keep him on his side in case he vomits again. Otherwise, don't move him."

"We won't," Jenn said. "Thank you. Tell them to hurry, please."

"I'll stay on the line with you until they arrive. Someone will be there soon."

"Thank you."

Jenn went back to the banister and screamed down to the large, cathedral-height space, "Steve. Steve!"

"What?" He came out from the kitchen and looked up at her, his blue eyes wide with concern.

"Josh won't wake up. I just called an ambulance. Wait for them outside," Jenn commanded. "Wave them down so they know where to come."

"What are you talking about?" He rushed toward the stairs. "What's going on?"

"I don't know. Please, just wait for them. Outside," Jenn begged. Steve hesitated, his eyes on the bedroom door behind her. "Steve, please."

Steve turned to go outside and Jenn went back into Josh's room. Standing over his bed, she searched his face for some hint that he was about to wake up, but his eyes remained closed, with no hint of awareness or response. Her chest hurt. She took a deep breath, trying to control her fear. She knelt by her son and brushed his brown hair back from his cold, clammy forehead. Something was really, really wrong.

"Great physician, Lord Jesus Christ," Jenn prayed out loud, "please restore Josh to full health; Lord, if You save him, You'll be glorified through his life. Lord Jesus, please take care of my Josh. Guide the hands of the paramedics, doctors, and nurses that will—"

Suddenly Steve led two tall men into the room, one thin and the other broad, dressed in identical blue shirts. Jenn scrambled away from the bed to give them space to work.

"Hello? Hello?"

Jenn startled at the voice coming from her hand. It was the 911 dispatcher on the phone.

"They're here," Jenn said in a rush into the receiver.

"OK. Best wishes to all of you," came the steady voice.

"Thank you," Jenn replied automatically and then hung up.

Jenn grabbed onto Steve's arm, wanting the connection with him, as the paramedics bent over their son, working calmly and efficiently. The thin one tipped back Josh's head and leaned over his face. The other searched for a vein in his arm and then inserted an IV needle. He attached wires to Josh's body and connected them to a machine. Numbers came up on a monitor: 110, 93, 73/41.

"What does that mean?" Jenn whispered to Steve without taking her eyes off of the bed.

"I'm pretty sure one hundred ten is his heart rate, which is high. Ninety-three is the oxygen level in his blood. That's low. And the seventy-three over forty-one is his blood pressure—way too low. Oh, Jenn. Praise God you found him." She could feel Steve trembling.

"I didn't give him a hug," Jenn whispered. She blinked back tears.

"What?"

"I wouldn't hug him. Last night when he threw up. I was afraid I'd get sick. I could have...hugged him—" Her voice broke. "And I didn't."

"Oh, Jenn. He knows you love him," Steve reassured her. "That single lost hug won't matter."

Jenn shook her head slowly. "Of course it matters. What if he...?" Her voice broke. Her mind flashed to a brain tumor. She'd recently read about a teenager who fell into a coma in the night and never woke up. What if her Josh was gone just like that?

An EMT interrupted her thoughts. "We'll take him to Eden. One of you can come in the ambulance."

"What's wrong with him?" Jenn asked, desperate for a reassuring answer.

"I don't know, ma'am," the paramedic said. "But he's stable for transport."

The other EMT squeezed a gurney into the room. Obviously experienced, they were well synchronized as they transferred Josh's floppy body out of his bed. Jenn noticed the stain on the navy-blue comforter. The matching washcloths and towels were in a heap on the sage Berber carpet. Just a minute ago, she was going to clean it up, and now that didn't matter at all.

Steve pulled gently on her arm, leading her out of the way. Rachel was right outside the door in the hallway, her blue eyes wide, and her white skin pale.

"Mom, what's wrong with Josh? What happened?" Her voice was high and tight.

Jenn shook her head. "We don't know. He's going to the hospital. He's unconscious. We'll find out more soon." She hugged her daughter and talked to her husband at the same time. "Who should be in the ambulance with him?"

"You go," he replied. "Rachel and I will drive. Should I call Pastor James before we leave?"

Jenn nodded. "Sara, too—she can start a prayer chain. And let Lindsay and Mark know we won't be there for dinner tonight. I can't believe this is happening."

The EMTs carried Josh down the curved stairs. Jenn and her family followed close behind. Jenn was so shaky with nerves that she leaned on the oak railing for support; her hands trembled as she grabbed her purse and cell phone. Jenn, Steve, and Rachel stood on the sidewalk watching the two men load Josh into the back of the ambulance, then both climbed in with him, put all the equipment around his body, and watched the monitors once again. The big one said something to his partner. The thin one nodded and took out a long plastic straw. He tipped Josh's head back a bit and opened his mouth. Jenn watched him shove the tube down her baby's throat. She clutched at Steve.

He put his arm around her. "They're intubating him!" he exclaimed. "That's not good."

Her stomach dropped further. "Why are they doing that?"

"He's really not breathing right," Steve explained, his voice strained.

A chill went down Jenn's spine. "Praise God we found him when we did," she replied. *Lord, Your will be done, not mine.* Though she desperately hoped that the Lord's plan included healing her son.

The bigger EMT climbed out after Josh was settled into the ambulance and pointed to a seat for her. Steve squeezed Jenn's hand good-bye. She stepped onto the high bumper, started to shift weight onto her leg, but her foot slipped off because she was so shaky. After wiping her sweaty hands on her flowered skirt, she grabbed the handle hard, determined to join Josh. As she moved up and forward, she was grateful to feel Steve's hands on her hips, steadying and supporting her. Once she was in the back, she crouched over to a small jump seat and buckled up. Josh lay totally still across from her. The thin EMT sat right by his side.

"Ready?" the driver shouted, and then the metal doors slammed shut with a loud clang.

Jenn looked for Rachel and Steve through the cloudy window, but they were gone. She suddenly felt scared and alone. She closed her eyes, took a deep breath, and then looked over at her sick son.

He showed no awareness of the violations to his body. His head flopped a little with every bump. Jenn's throat tightened reflexively at the tube coming out of his throat. It looked like it was choking him, though she knew it was doing just the opposite. The hiss of oxygen filled the ambulance. His arms were belted tight to his side, the black straps contrasting with the white sheet that covered his body. She wanted to touch him, to let him feel that he wasn't alone, but he was too far away.

Jenn heard a steady, too-fast beep from the heart monitor and glanced at the numbers on the machine. His blood pressure was a little higher now: eighty-six over fifty-two. His oxygen read ninety-nine. Her mind flitted through all the possible causes. She could think only of horrible reasons for him to be like this: meningitis, a seizure, a brain tumor, a stroke.

God is watching over him. I trust in the Lord. God is watching over him. I trust in the Lord, Jenn intoned to herself over and over again on the long ride to Castro Valley.

◆ ◆ ◆

At the hospital, Josh was pulled out in a rush. No one said anything to Jenn. She was uncertain what she should do but ran after the gurney as it was wheeled through the automatic sliding glass doors and into an ER bay. The paramedics spoke to the medical staff while she stood by.

A person in light-blue scrubs walked up to her with a clipboard in his hand. "You're the mother? Does he have any medical conditions we should be aware of?"

Jenn shook her head silently. Her throat was tight.

He looked up from his clipboard and repeated the question. "Does he have any medical conditions we should be aware of?"

Jenn cleared her throat. "Sorry." Of course he hadn't seen her head shake. "No. Well, last night he threw up in the middle of the night. I heard him once just after midnight. I thought it was just a bug. When we got home from church there was vomit by his bed."

He looked back at his clipboard and wrote something down without saying a word.

"Did you find an empty bottle near him?"

"No."

This time she was more prepared for that question.

"Does he have any history of drug or alcohol abuse?"

"No." Jenn was emphatic.

He wrote again. "Is he depressed, or does he have a history of depression?"

"No."

"Has he had a head injury lately? A fall or a blow to his head?"

"Not that I know of. He's on the basketball team at Dublin High."

The man finished writing and turned away. Jenn looked at Josh. He was half hidden behind the doctors and nurses and other medical staff attending to him. She watched, feeling helpless. She wanted to tell them to be careful, to make sure they were doing the right thing, to think before they acted. But she just stood back, because they had done this many times before, while she had no idea what to do for her son except love him. And pray.

She caught snatches of words, some of which passed right by her while others caught in her brain like flies in a spiderweb: *CBC*, *blood cultures*, *chest X-ray*, *head CT*.

Staff came and went, and then suddenly the room cleared except for one middle-aged nurse. Josh looked vulnerable in the bed. The breathing tube taped to his cheek covered the lower part of his face, and wires connected his chest to nearby machines. His basketball camp T-shirt, the one he slept in, was cut down the middle. The yellow sleeves still covered his upper arms, but the rest of the shirt bunched sideways at his ribs. Jenn felt paralyzed. Was she allowed to touch him?

She looked at the nurse with a question in her eyes. The woman gestured to Jenn to come over.

"This side is easier—no IV," the nurse said with a Filipino accent, pointing to Josh's right. "You can touch his hand and the top of his head."

Jenn came to Josh's side and took his hand. It felt moist and flaccid—as if he weren't even there. She bit her lip to stop from crying.

"You did good," the nurse said kindly. "It's not easy to be in this situation. A lot of the time we have to take the parents out. He's stable. Now we watch. We'll make adjustments as we need to. He'll be transferred to the ICU soon."

"What's wrong with him? When will he wake up?" Jenn asked.

Gently the nurse replied, "I don't know. We have tests to run. Dr. Aziz will explain more when your son is settled. He's writing orders now."

The woman's words scared Jenn more than the ambulance ride. "Josh is going to be fine, right?"

"Dr. Aziz will tell you more."

"But…what…?"

The nurse shook her head. "There's nothing more I can tell you. We don't know what's causing him to be unresponsive, so we can't predict. We'll know more in twenty-four to forty-eight hours. I'm sorry I don't have answers, but I'll take good care of him—I promise. We all will. We're good nurses at this hospital."

Jenn felt light-headed, like she might faint. She grabbed the bed rail, leaned against the bed for support, and said a prayer. *Lord God, I trust in Your wisdom and love. I give Josh over to You. I know You'll care for him because You love him…*

Jenn's prayer was interrupted by the vibration of her cell phone. It was a text from Steve: *Update please.*

Jenn looked at the nurse. "It's my husband. He wants to know how Josh is doing. What do I say?"

"Tell him the truth. Your son is stable. That's good. You can join him in the waiting room, if you like."

"No. I'm not leaving Josh." Jenn was certain. "Steve will understand. Can I call him?"

The nurse shook her head. "Sorry. No cell phones in here, but you can text."

Jenn sighed. She hated texting, but she didn't want to leave Steve hanging. She slowly pressed the numbers on her keypad—4-4, 3-3, space...—over and over until she typed out: *he is stable. pray.* And she hit Send.

◆ ◆ ◆

The staff sent Jenn away while Josh was being transferred to the intensive-care unit. Joining Rachel and Steve in hard plastic chairs in the waiting room, she answered her husband's and daughter's questions as unsatisfactorily as the nurse had answered hers. She'd calmed some since she found Josh, but her body was still on alert, as if the slightest thing would get her heart racing again.

Feeling fidgety, she pulled out her phone as a distraction. There were three missed calls and a new text message. Lindsay had called twice and her mom once. She pressed the button to see the unread text from Lindsay: *Can I bring u dinner?*

That's so sweet, Jenn thought. Lindsay was one of Jenn's greatest blessings. They'd been best friends since Sara and Rebeccah, Lindsay's eldest child, were in the church nursery together. Their kids were like cousins, and their families ate together most Sunday nights.

Jenn said to her husband, "Lin's offering to bring us dinner. What should I say?"

Steve shook his head. "I love them, but I can't handle seeing anyone right now, even them. Tell her thanks. One of us can run out for something later. Or get food from the cafeteria."

Jenn texted Lindsay back, but she wasn't ready to talk to her mom. She would be full of questions Jenn couldn't answer and want reassurance that she couldn't offer. Instead, she attempted to center herself in prayer, to be an example of faith to her daughter, and to find a place of comfort. But really she just ached to be at Josh's side. Her mind kept flitting to images of him: vomit pooled by his mouth in bed, his floppy head jostling as they put him in the ambulance, a tube sliding down his throat. She stood up. Rachel looked up at her, her brow arranged in a question.

"I just have to move," Jenn explained. "I won't go far." She paced in the waiting area while Rachel and Steve flipped through old magazines. She watched the clock intently, but it never seemed to change. Her phone rang—Sara.

"How is he? Do they know what's wrong with him?" their eldest child asked in a rush.

"He's stable enough to be moved to the ICU. We're waiting for test results."

"I want to come to the hospital now. I'll take BART to Castro Valley. Dad said to ask you."

"And miss class tomorrow?"

"I don't care about school!" Sara declared. "Part of why I picked Cal was so I could be home for the important things. It matters that I'm there, too."

Jenn was touched by the passion in Sara's voice. "You know he's unconscious. He won't even know you're here."

"I'll know."

Jenn's throat tightened up. She'd be grateful to have Sara here. "OK," she agreed. "Call us when you get to the station. One of us will come."

"Thanks, Mom. I love you. Tell Josh I love him—even if he's asleep." Jenn heard the emotion in her daughter's voice.

"I will. Love you, too."

She walked over to Steve and Rachel. "Sara's on her way."

Jenn looked at the clock again. It had been forty minutes since she left Josh. They said the transfer would take half an hour. Her anxiety revved up with each passing second.

Jenn said to Steve, "This is taking too long. What if something's wrong?"

Steve took her hand and pulled her down to the chair next to him. "Jenn, we're all scared for him, but leaping to conclusions based on nothing is pointless."

"It's just where my mind keeps going. I feel so much better when I'm with him."

"Let them do their jobs," Steve reminded her.

"Family of Josh Henderson," a nurse called from the desk.

Jenn rushed to the station with Steve and Rachel trailing behind. "We're here."

"Only two at a time in the ICU," the nurse explained. "You can trade off."

Jenn was crushed. "Can we just have a few minutes with him as a family? Just in case, you know…" She couldn't go on. Her eyes welled up. Steve put an arm around her. "I'm sorry…" Jenn began.

"You don't have to apologize," said the nurse. "No one wants to be here."

Jenn gave a shaky nod. The nurse explained, "I'll let the three of you go back. They'll probably kick one of you out. Be calm and really quiet, and you might get ten minutes together."

"God bless you. Thank you," Jenn said.

"He's in bed six," the nurse told them.

"Thank you very much," Steve said as they were buzzed through.

Jenn took Rachel's hand as they walked down a short, bright hallway. She hated to be so emotional in front of her daughter, but it was hard to be a strong and confident mom in this situation. The ICU was an open room with rows of beds separated by curtains. Josh lay in the third bed to the right. His color looked better, but he seemed just as small and vulnerable as he did in the emergency room.

A young white nurse with bleached-blond hair introduced herself. "I'm Jessica. I'll be with Josh until this evening."

"How's he doing?" Steve asked.

"He's stable. So far, so good," the nurse replied. "Were you told he's only supposed to have two people at the bedside in the ICU?"

Jenn's spirits sank. She took a deep breath to calm herself. "We want to say a family prayer over him," she pleaded. "Then we'll go. Well, some of us will go."

The nurse acquiesced. "OK. Five minutes?"

Jenn nodded. She smiled at Rachel and gave a thumbs-up. Her youngest child's eyes were red and puffy. When had she started crying? Jenn hugged her close and murmured soothing words into her hair. "He's going to be OK. I have faith…in God and in the doctors."

"Thank Jesus we came home when we did," Jenn said to both Steve and Rachel. "Lord Jesus is looking out for Josh, for all of us. Who knows what would've happened if we had stayed out longer."

"Is…Is…I'm so scared," Rachel said. "How could this just happen with no warning? What's wrong with him?"

"We don't know, honey," Jenn said, pushing aside her worst thoughts. She wanted to offer some comfort to her daughter, so she explained, "The doctors will know more soon."

Just then a middle-aged man with dark complexion, hair, and eyes walked up. "I'm Dr. Aziz. I'd like to update you." He glanced at Rachel. "Can we speak in private?" Just that question scared Jenn.

The doctor led the parents to the other side of the curtain, giving them a small veneer of privacy.

"What's wrong with Josh?" Steve questioned.

"We don't yet know what's causing your son's condition," Dr. Aziz explained. "But we've stabilized him. We pumped his stomach and drew blood. The lab should have results soon. He's getting fluids to increase his blood pressure and keep him hydrated. We'll know more in a few hours. Has he been sick?"

"He threw up last night. That's the first we knew of anything," Jenn replied.

"Does he have a history of drug abuse?"

"No!" Jenn replied. "Why do you people keep asking me that? He's Christian. He does not use drugs."

"I'm sorry, ma'am. We want to rule everything out. Most of the time, with a presentation like this, it's an intentional or unintentional drug overdose," Dr. Aziz said. "I'm not saying that's the situation with your son, but we haven't ruled it out. We're looking into infection, medication, and diseases or disorders. When I have more answers, I'll find you. You don't believe he has a concussion or has had trauma to the head recently?"

Steve shook his head.

"Did you give the nurse your phone number? For updates."

"If you have something to tell us, you can find us in here," Jenn said more sharply than she meant to. "One of us will be right by our son's side the entire time he's here."

"Thank you, Doctor," Steve interjected evenly.

"Yes, thank you." Jenn sighed. "Sorry I'm so upset."

"This is a difficult situation," the doctor said calmly. "I'm on until eight o'clock tonight. Hopefully I'll be back with some results before I leave."

The family gathered around Josh, and Steve spoke aloud a prayer asking for wisdom for the doctors, healing for his son, and faith for his family. Jenn concentrated intently. Then Steve took Rachel back out to the waiting room.

◆ ◆ ◆

A nurse put a chair by the hospital bed for Jenn, a very welcome gesture of support. The constant beep of the monitor was oddly comforting. Jenn stared at it as if it were a video game. She prayed for Josh's pulse to slow down and his blood pressure to go up. It wasn't much, but she knew to ask for that. She startled whenever the blood-pressure cuff filled up without warning. In contrast, Josh didn't notice it at all. He lay there oblivious to his surroundings, with an IV in his arm and a tube of oxygen down his throat.

Jenn held Josh's hand and sang quietly into his ear. She started with the lullabies she had sung to him as a baby and then moved on to his favorite church hymns. When she got hoarse from singing, she sat up and studied his face. It had changed so much. All traces of baby fat were gone. His dark lashes and eyebrows were thick and healthy, and stubble covered his skin. She didn't realize he needed to shave every day. When did that happen? Her thoughts were interrupted by a tap on the shoulder.

Steve stood over her. "We got some dinner when we picked up Sara. Rachel has a burrito for you. You sit with her and eat; Sara can come in when you go out."

"Can you just bring it to me?" Jenn asked.

"Rachel needs a little time with you, and Sara wants to see Josh," Steve countered.

Jenn was so focused on Josh that she was being selfish. She shook her head. "Of course," she said as she stood up. "We're going to get through this, right?"

"Of course we are," Steve replied. "And so is he."

She reached for Steve's arm. "Are you sure? Do you know deep down that God does not want him home yet?"

"I'm sure of it. I feel it in my bones. Josh has something he's called to do on earth. He hasn't done it yet, so it's not his time to go home."

Steve's words were a balm to her soul. His certainty filled her with confidence. Jenn nodded and gave Steve a long hug. Then she forced herself to break away to find her daughters.

◆ ◆ ◆

When Jenn walked through the double doors into the waiting room, Sara was standing right there. Her blond hair was pulled back into a messy ponytail, and she didn't have any makeup on. She looked close to tears. Jenn opened her arms wide, and Sara melted against her body. After a few breaths, Sara broke away.

"How's he doing?" her older daughter asked.

"He doesn't look too bad, if you ignore the tube coming out of his mouth," Jenn explained.

"OK. I'll just look at his gorgeous hair," Sara joked weakly as she was buzzed through.

Jenn looked around the harshly lit waiting room for her third child. Rachel sat alone, flipping through a magazine on her lap, unconsciously picking at the skin on her thumb. Jenn felt a welling up of sympathy for her youngest. This situation was hard enough for her to deal with as an adult. It had to be overwhelming to a fourteen-year-old.

"What'd you get me?" Jenn asked casually as she sat down.

Rachel looked up, startled. "Oh...hi, Mom. Chorizo with everything. We know what you like."

Jenn smiled as she took out the shiny, aluminum-wrapped meal. It was warm and substantial in her hand. She hadn't realized the comfort one could get from a burrito.

"How's Josh?" Rachel asked, hope and fear in her voice.

"Same," Jenn replied. "Stable. Whatcha reading?"

"*National Geographic*." Rachel turned the magazine so Jenn could see the spread of marine animals. Images of penguins, sperm whales, and dolphins filled the pages. Rachel pointed to a page. "Aren't they adorable?"

Jenn nodded with a smile. "You've loved penguins since that trip to the Monterey Aquarium when you were four."

"What's not to love? They're cute, and they waddle, and they cuddle with each other. They're the best animals ever."

"It's been too long since we've gone to the aquarium...Maybe we could go over Easter break."

Rachel perked up. "Really?"

"No promises, but..."

"Josh'll be fine by then, right?"

Though Jenn had her fears, she didn't share them with her daughter. "There's no reason to think he won't be. He's in the Lord's hands. Just keep on praying for him."

Rachel leaned her head against Jenn and went back to the magazine. Despite the pit in her stomach, Jenn ate the burrito. She wanted to say the perfect words to her daughter, to reassure her that their lives were not turned upside down irrevocably, but she couldn't offer Rachel something she wasn't certain of herself. As hard as she tried, she couldn't imagine an innocuous explanation for Josh's illness. While she desperately hoped he could be cured with an antibiotic or some simple medicine, her mind kept flitting to a brain tumor. She knew it was dramatic, but it was her biggest fear.

After eating most of her dinner, Jenn texted Sara to trade back. When she got to Josh's bedside, Steve's brow was furrowed. Jenn's heart skipped a beat.

"What's going on?" she asked. "What happened?"

"Dr. Aziz stopped by before his shift ended," Steve explained. "None of the tests show anything that would cause this."

"That's bad?" asked Jenn.

Steve exhaled deeply. "He says this profile is entirely consistent with an overdose of sleeping pills."

"That can't be it; you know that, right?" Jenn insisted. "There's no reason for him to take sleeping pills. Where would he get them?"

"I don't know." Steve changed the subject. "It's late. Rachel needs to get home. Do you want to stay here tonight or be with the girls?"

"I can't bear to leave him. Can I please be the one to stay? I'll call you right away if there's a change," Jenn promised. "Is that OK with you?"

"That's fine." Steve rubbed his head. Jenn felt a rush of gratitude for her husband.

"Rachel asked me if she has to go to school tomorrow. I don't think so. What about you?" Jenn asked.

"No," Steve answered. "It's one day of ninth grade. I doubt she could concentrate anyway."

"I can't believe this is happening."

"Me neither," Steve agreed. "Do you want me to bring you back some other clothes for the night?"

Jenn looked at her church outfit: flowered sheath, hose, and blue flats. She wasn't comfortable, but it didn't matter. She pulled the small gold hoops off her ears and slipped the gold bangles from her wrist. She shook her head. "I'll be fine; just take these."

Steve kissed his son's forehead. Then he put his hand over Josh's brown hair and stared down at him. Tenderness welled up in Jenn. Steve stepped away, his eyes moist, gave her a long hug good-bye, and left.

Once again she was alone with Josh and the sound of beeping machines. Jenn was finally ready to contact the outside world. She dialed her childhood number in Orange County. The Southern California suburb she grew up in had no defined urban center except, perhaps, for Disneyland. In sharp contrast to her current home in the San Francisco Bay Area, Orange County was a center of conservative political and religious values. Jenn had made peace with being a conservative in a liberal bastion, and there was a lot she preferred about the Bay Area, including the weather, the food, and the traffic.

On the third ring, her mother picked up. "What's wrong? Sara asked me to pray for Josh, but she didn't say more than that." Her mom sounded as worried as Jenn had expected.

At the sound of her voice, Jenn's eyes welled up. "Oh, Mom. Josh was passed out when we got home from church. I'm at the hospital with him."

"Is he OK?"

"They don't know what it is," Jenn explained. "He's still unconscious."

"Josh is sick? Really sick?"

Jenn nodded even though her mom couldn't see her. "The doctors are running tests. We should have answers in a few hours. I don't want to worry you, but I know you'd want to start praying for him."

"Oh, honey, of course. I'm so sorry. For you and for our Joshy. The prayer chain has already been started."

Jenn felt a sweet comfort from her mother's words. "Thanks, Mom. That means a lot."

"What's his doctor's name? We'll include him in our prayers."

"Dr. Aziz. At least for now. A new one will come on soon."

"That's not a Christian name, is it?"

"No, Mom. But he seems like a fine doctor." Her mom's not-so-subtle biases always rubbed Jenn the wrong way. Jenn chalked it up to age, but it was hard to hear and even harder to know how to respond.

"We'll pray for the Lord to guide all his doctors to find what's wrong with Josh and for Josh to be strong in mind, body, and spirit. Josh knows the Lord's love so deeply. I know he's being held by Jesus right—"

Jenn's phone beeped. She looked at the screen. It was her home number.

"Mom, I'm getting a call from Steve or one of the girls. I have to go. I'll let you know when we learn more. I love you. And tell Dad I love him."

"Will do, honey. And don't you worry. God's going to fix Josh right up."

Jenn accepted the other call.

Steve's voice came through: "It's me."

"There's no change," Jenn said.

"I searched Josh's bedroom," Steve explained.

"Why did you do that?" Jenn asked, upset though she didn't know why.

"I had to be certain. Are you sitting down? This isn't good."

"You're scaring me."

"I didn't find anything in his room, so I searched all the trash cans. I found an empty bottle of Ambien in the garbage outside."

A hot wave passed through Jenn. "Dear Lord! Where could he have gotten that? What doctor would give a sixteen-year-old Ambien without permission?"

"It wasn't made out to him," Steve explained gently. "It's yours."

Jenn's stomach lurched. "Mine?"

"The bottle was empty. Do you remember how many were left in it?"

Her brain buzzed. It was hard to think. "From our trip to France last summer? For the flight?"

"Jenn," Steve pushed her, "how many pills were in the bottle?"

"Most of them. I only took three: one for each flight and one to sleep the night we got there. How many were in the prescription?"

Steve paused and then replied, "It says thirty."

Adrenaline coursed through her veins, and she started to shake. "Josh took twenty-seven sleeping pills?"

"You have to tell the staff right away," Steve instructed.

"Why would our son do that?" Jenn questioned her husband. "Why would our Josh hurt himself?"

2

Jenn flipped the channel to Fox News, her morning cooking companion. The news floated in the background as she pulled out ingredients—eggs, bread, OJ, sausage, yogurt, protein powder, and frozen blueberries—and placed them on the beige soapstone countertop. She knew what everyone in her family liked for breakfast and took pride in starting their days off right.

The eggs, sausage, toast, and OJ were for Steve. He preferred his eggs over easy but didn't like to get in a rut, so every few days she scrambled them. Today was a scramble day.

Sara and Josh liked smoothies. This morning would be blueberry-banana but only for Josh, a junior at Dublin High. Sara, a freshman at UC Berkeley, came home only on the weekends, though lately she'd been staying on campus many Friday and Saturday nights, too, coming home only for church on Sundays. Jenn didn't like to use frozen, but her kids liked berries, and there weren't any fresh this time of year.

Rachel was her picky eater. Youngest kids seemed to go either way: flexible or fussy. Rachel went finicky. She ate white toast with sweet butter and strawberry jam for breakfast. A few times a year, she would get in a Frosted Mini-Wheats phase, but right now she preferred all white bread, all the time. Jenn had hoped that her tastes would expand now that she was in high school, but they hadn't so far.

Jenn thought through her day while she cooked. Thursdays were spacious because she didn't carpool. She'd meet Lindsay for their walk in the neighborhood at half past nine. After that she'd run her errands: first the dry cleaner's and then Walgreens, Jo-Ann Fabric, and Safeway. She never shopped for groceries anywhere else, out of loyalty to Steve's employer. She might even take herself out to lunch. Something else was on her errand list, but she couldn't remember what it was. She ran through her family in her mind, finally getting to Wynnie, their golden retriever. Then she remembered they needed dog food and added Pet Food Express to her mental list.

"Breakfast!" she yelled up to her family. Josh arrived first. Her middle child took after her, with the Mediterranean look that some people of French descent shared. They had the same brunette hair and dark-brown eyes with olive skin that tanned easily. Before she and Steve had had kids, she'd thought their sons would take after him and their daughters would resemble her. But it went the other way: Josh looked like her, and the girls had Steve's Scandinavian features: golden-blond hair, blue eyes, and pale skin.

"Do you know what time we have to leave for your game tomorrow?" Jenn asked.

"Coach wants the drivers at three," Josh replied.

"I'll be there."

"Thanks, Mom."

Jenn smiled at her son. "Of course."

Rachel walked in and asked, "Did you sign my paper for the field trip to the Lawrence Hall of Science?"

"There's an envelope by the computer with the form and a check. Let me know if they need drivers. It didn't ask for them on the permission slip."

"I think they got a bus, but I'll tell Ms. Ahn," Rachel replied as she pulled her long hair into a high ponytail. Then she grabbed her toast and started to leave.

"Sit, Rachel," Jenn commanded. "Your dad will be down in a sec. You have time for a prayer before school."

On cue Steve walked in. Even after nineteen years of marriage, her heart swelled when she saw him. God had chosen well when He put Steve in her path her junior year of high school. They were true partners in this life, both doing their roles to make their family strong. He had never disappointed her. They all sat down, reached their hands around the table, and formed a precious connection.

Steve prayed, "Dear Lord, thank You for the night's rest You gave us. We accept this new day as a gift from You. May we use it minute by minute to do Your will. Help us to treat everyone kindly, fairly, and thoughtfully and to know that there is nothing we can't handle with You. In Jesus's name we pray. Amen."

"Amen" echoed around the table.

Rachel grabbed her toast, kissed her parents good-bye, and left.

"Did you make a reservation for Saturday?" Josh asked. The kids were insisting that Steve take Jenn out somewhere nice for Valentine's Day…without them.

"Yep," Steve replied. "Seven o'clock at McNamara's Steak House." Steve wiggled his eyebrows. He loved a good steak.

Rachel yelled from the study, "Mom, it's not here! I'm going to be late!"

"What's not where?"

"My permission slip!"

"Look again, Rach. On the right side of the keyboard."

"I can't find it!"

Jenn sighed and went into the study. She spotted the envelope immediately.

Pointing, she said, "Right there, Rach."

"Oops. Sorry, Mom. I thought it would be a big envelope."

"I swear you couldn't find—" Jenn stopped herself. Insulting Rachel's observational skills wouldn't help her daughter to mature.

Rachel shrugged and rushed out.

Josh was asking a question when she sat back down to breakfast. "Can we go to *Catch that Kid* on Saturday?"

"What's it rated?" Jenn asked.

"It's PG, but at youth group Pastor James said it's wholesome."

Steve said, "If he says it's appropriate, then sure. Who are you going with?"

"Just Sara and Rachel. You know...a sister-brother Valentine's thing," he said with a wry smile.

"Sounds fun," Jenn said. "Any requests for dinner? I'm shopping today."

Immediately Josh replied, "Fettuccine Alfredo. And Caesar salad."

"Yum," Jenn agreed. "Pasta it is. With some chicken—protein, you know."

Josh laughed. "Yes, the all-important protein." He cleared his plate, kissed Jenn on the head, and headed out.

"Can you take in my blue suit today?" Steve asked.

"It's already on my list," Jenn replied. "I'm getting ribbon for the welcome team at church. I'll swing by the dry cleaner's on my way."

"You're really getting involved with the welcome team," Steve commented.

Jenn shrugged. "It's creative and helpful to the church. I love knowing I'm guiding new Christians to a deep relationship with Jesus. Pastor James asked me to be the chair next year."

"Are you going to say yes?"

"If you don't mind," Jenn said. "We meet during the day, so it won't affect the family too much."

"Not at all. It's good for you to do things outside the family."

◆ ◆ ◆

After cleaning the breakfast dishes, Jenn went to her room to pray, with Wynnie following close behind. Jenn got comfortable in her favorite chair in the corner. It was covered in a blue and tan plaid fabric that brought the colors together in the room.

The Bible on the little table next to the seat was a gift from her mother on her wedding day. The holy book had been her grandmother's, given to her on *her* wedding day. Jenn felt God here. She closed her eyes and took in the warmth of the sunlight streaming through the window, like a blessing directly from the Holy Spirit. Her body and mind calmed quickly. Then she spoke silently to her Lord.

"God, thank You for the power of the Holy Spirit. I ask that Your presence fill me with wisdom and revelation so that I may follow You, love You, and serve You entirely. Bind up all distractions and show me Your will for me. In Jesus's name I pray. Amen."

And then she listened. Some days God spoke clearly to her, and other days she didn't hear anything. Some days her mind wandered to her to-do list, and others she could really listen. Today she was focused, and God was quiet. She took that as a sign that her life was on track. Jenn got up, put on her walking shoes, put a leash on Wynnie, and set out to meet her best friend.

Twice a week, on Tuesday and Thursday mornings, Jenn and Lindsay met for a walk, usually in their suburban neighborhood, but sometimes they hiked at Marshall Canyon. Dublin, named for the Irish city, had bright-green rolling hills in the winter and spring. Once it stopped raining, they turned golden brown, reminding her of the hills of her childhood in Orange County.

They leaned on each other for support in all things and most especially in guiding their kids in righteous living. Both women would have preferred Christian schools, but neither family could afford that on one salary. They were a team, fending off the secular influence of public schools.

"How's your dad?" Lindsay asked.

"Much better," Jenn replied. "He's still tired, but the antibiotics knocked out the bronchitis."

"Mark's leaving for OC tonight, so he can be there when his dad gets the stent tomorrow. Guess we're hitting the sandwich-generation time of life."

"Yeah," Jenn agreed. "When did we start worrying about our parents as well as our kids? I feel like a stereotype sometimes."

"Me, too!"

"Let me know how I can help when Mark is gone."

"Thanks, honey." Lindsay smiled at her friend.

Jenn switched topics. "I'm getting ribbon for the welcome board today. Do you think crosses are too much?"

Lindsay shook her head. "As far as I'm concerned, there can never be too many crosses! Or too much glitter."

They both laughed.

◆ ◆ ◆

"Steven!" Jenn called out. "Steve! Come quickly!"

Josh ran into the room, his face filled with concern. "Are you OK?"

"Please get your father," Jenn said urgently.

"He's next door—returning something to the Engs. Should I get him?"

The news that had upset her so much still played in the background, and she shook her head. "No, it can wait a few minutes."

"What's the matter?" Josh asked.

Jenn gazed at her son. He looked so afraid. She exhaled with a sigh. "I'm sorry to worry you," she said. "It's just something on the news. Gavin Newsom is mocking marriage."

"Who?" Josh's eyebrows knit together in a question.

"The mayor of San Francisco is giving out marriage licenses to homosexuals. Remember the sermon from a few weeks ago? Pastor was talking about just this. It's a blatant political attack on family values."

Josh gave her a blank stare.

"Honey, you don't need to worry. This doesn't affect you."

She stood up and embraced her son, savoring the feel and smell of him, this fleeting physical connection that came more rarely since he hit adolescence. Each hug felt precious.

When she released him, she said, "After I'm done with the dishes, let's register you for the ACT and SAT, OK?"

Josh nodded and mumbled something noncommittal before he left.

A few minutes later, Steve came into the kitchen. "Josh said you want me?"

Jenn pointed to the TV. "They're breaking God's law in San Francisco, not to mention state and federal laws too."

Steve turned to the TV. He opened his arms, inviting Jenn in. She leaned against his chest, her face turned toward the television. The screen showed a crowd of people around city hall in San Francisco, activists screaming at supporters of traditional marriage. More than three hundred homosexuals had been given marriage licenses during the day. City leaders planned to keep giving them out on Friday, too. Jenn felt torn up inside. Marriage was between a man and a woman for the purpose of creating a family. These people wanted to destroy the most basic foundation of society. Attacks on Christian values were going too far.

"It's just wrong, and so close to our home," Jenn said. "We need to do something to stop it. Should I call Governor Schwarzenegger?"

Steve shrugged. "I suggest we pray on it, Jenn. God will guide you."

They stood watching arm in arm until the next commercial. Then Jenn let go of Steve so he could get back to his project.

Fox went on to other stories, but Jenn fixated on the attack on marriage. A few weeks ago, Pastor Williams had given a sermon about the harm homosexuality brought to good families. He called on each congregant to stand up for children who were being led astray from God's purpose by homosexual activists and to take up the fight to preserve marriage.

When she finished cleaning, Jenn went upstairs to talk with God. "Lord," she started, "You know about the tragedy in San Francisco. You know Massachusetts has already succumbed to the forces of secularization. What is Your will for me to protect marriage? May Your Holy Spirit cleanse me from my sins and bind up any distractions so that I may hear Your will clearly. In Jesus's name I pray. Amen." And then she listened, focusing on the question, *What is Your will for me to protect marriage?* again and again until the answer came. Clear as a bell, she heard, "Love My children." *Love My children.* It was so simple. Then the image of Pastor James floated into her mind. Peace floated into Jenn like the soothing waters of a warm bath. She smiled to herself. As always, God guided her well when she took the time to listen.

◆ ◆ ◆

Jenn found Steve in the garage and told him about her conversation with God. "He said to love His children and then sent an image of Pastor James. It's pretty clear, don't you think?"

"Seems like Pastor James is your next step," Steve said. "Call him up and offer your hands for this ministry. You've been looking for a little more to fill your time now that Rach is in high school. I think you're being called."

"You think so?" Energy rose in Jenn. "To do what?"

Steve shrugged. "I don't know. Write a letter? Make phone calls? Pastor will have ideas. You know he saw the news tonight and has a heavy heart, too."

Jenn felt an odd stirring. For twenty years Steve and her children had been her primary focus. The four of them would always be the center of her life, but they just didn't need her much anymore. The number of hours a week she spent caring for her children kept decreasing. She made them food, drove the car pool, and signed permission slips, but that hardly took any time at all. She rarely helped with homework and never tucked them in at night. Rachel even wanted to do her own laundry.

Sara lived in Berkeley most of the time now that she was in college. Jenn had eighteen more months with Josh at home; two years after that, she'd have an empty nest. It was unsettling. Steve had been encouraging her to find more activities at church to fill her time. It looked like defending family values just might be the next step on the path God was opening for her. "Love My children." *I can do that,* Jenn thought.

"In the morning I'll call Pastor James to offer my hands for this ministry." Jenn was excited. This felt right. She was being given an opportunity to protect her children and so many others. "Thanks, hon."

She went inside to call Lindsay. As Jenn hoped, her best friend wanted to be part of this fledgling ministry, too. Everything was falling into place.

3

Pastor James was thrilled to hear from Jenn. He asked to meet with her and Lindsay that very morning. He wanted to make a plan right away, since time was of the essence. After drop-off, Jenn swung by for Lindsay and drove them both to church.

Pastor James ushered Jenn and Lindsay into his office—tight quarters with a light maple desk and three chairs from Scandinavian Designs. A large plain wooden cross hung on the wall.

He'd been the associate minister at their congregation for four years, and Jenn had taken a liking to him immediately. Fresh from seminary, he had a contagious enthusiasm for spreading the gospel of Jesus Christ and gifts in working with the youth of the church. Jenn felt bad for him that he had yet to get married, but she assumed God would bring his mate to him before too long.

Pastor James started their gathering with a prayer and then jumped right in: "You're here because of the travesty in San Francisco."

Jenn nodded. "God wants me to do something. I'm here—we're here—to ask for your direction."

"I prayed for God to send me followers for this work, and He sent me you," Pastor James said. "I can feel the Holy Spirit right here in this room!"

Jenn flushed. Pastor James's confidence confirmed that she was on a righteous path.

"You tell us what to do, and we'll do it." Jenn looked over at Lindsay for affirmation. Her friend smiled and nodded.

"God wants us to witness publicly," Pastor James said.

Public witness? She hadn't been expecting that. Jenn thought she might start a prayer chain or make some phone calls. "In Dublin?" she asked.

"Oh no. San Francisco," he declared with a grin, looking like an eager little boy.

"You want to lead us to San Francisco?" Jenn asked.

Pastor James shook his head. "Sadly, I have a wedding tomorrow. You'll have to go without me."

"Us?" Lindsay asked.

"With your husbands and children. Invite the whole youth group and their parents. It will be an opportunity for our teens to take a stand for their faith, guided by their parents." Pastor James's face glowed with excitement, but Jenn's stomach did a flip. This was more than she had bargained for. She didn't want to refuse Pastor James but didn't see herself leading public ministry.

Lindsay asked, "You want us to drive to downtown San Francisco with our children?"

"Obviously we need to pray for this unlawful and immoral activity to stop immediately," Pastor James replied. "But I understand they are going to continue through the weekend unless they get a court order that forces them to stop. We need to get there now. If God doesn't end this, He wants us to witness—in person. This is an opportunity to teach people about the love of our Savior."

Jenn looked over at Lindsay. "Are you up for this? With our kids and husbands?"

Lindsay reminded her, "Mark's in Orange County for his dad's heart procedure. What about Steve?"

"He'll come. He cares deeply about family values." She turned to Pastor James. "Are you sure Lindsay and I are being called to do this? I've never organized a witness." Jenn wanted to be certain this was God's path for her.

"You've been to witnesses?"

"Of course. Practically every week in high school and college."

"I asked God to send me servants, and you called less than five minutes later," Pastor James replied. "He's speaking clearly."

Jenn's heart fluttered like a moth; she felt a little sick. She wanted to do God's work but had never thought something like this would be His plan for her. All the reasons not to do this flit through her head: it was too much work, she didn't know how, and her kids might be resistant. But for some crazy reason, even though it made no sense, she was excited. She turned to Lindsay. "We'll do this together, right?"

"Of course," Lindsay agreed. "You and me—every step of the way."

Pastor James leaned forward and beamed at them both. "I can't wait to tell the deacons about your decision. I can plan with you until nine forty-five, and then I have a pastoral call. Mrs. Bartley is in the hospital with pneumonia."

Pastor James jumped right in with instructions. He explained how to make signs, handed them a list of people to call, and told them to wear their church T-shirts to better keep track of one another—and tell people whom they were representing.

Before they left, Pastor prayed over Jenn and Lindsay—the power of his words seeped into her body and soul, leaving her feeling calm and tingling, in the way that good prayer did.

◆ ◆ ◆

"Steve, I just got out of the meeting with Pastor James," Jenn spoke into her cell phone from the church parking lot.

"How'd it go?"

"He wants us to lead a witness in San Francisco—tomorrow!"

"Us, as in…?"

"You and me and Lindsay. Mark's out of town."

"Oh yeah, his dad's stent," Steve remembered. "Has Lindsay heard from him?"

"They're talking right now." Jenn looked over at her friend and studied her face. "I'm gonna say it went well; she looks too happy for bad news. But how about it? You, me, Lin, and, well, the whole youth group, in San Francisco tomorrow?"

"Are you serious, Jenn?" Steve sounded doubtful. "Tomorrow?"

"Pastor James was very certain God is calling me to this ministry." "What do you think?"

"I'm nervous," Jenn stammered.

"We don't have to do this, you know. Just because Pastor James wants you to doesn't mean you have to say yes."

The thought of not doing it just felt wrong. She really wanted this. "I can't explain it, Steve, but I know Pastor James is right. I'm being called. We might save someone's soul. Remember when we were in college and we witnessed together? I knew I was doing God's work. This feels like that. I want us to do this as a family. To show our kids this part of faith."

Steve was quiet. Jenn waited for his answer. She looked down and noticed the black asphalt under her feet. She started to feel silly and was about to say never mind when Steve spoke up. "OK, Jenn. We'll spend our day witnessing tomorrow. Just let me know what you need me to do."

"Thanks, Steve!" Jenn did a little happy dance. "Can you cut the wood sticks for the signs when you get home?"

"You're the boss," Steve said, and they hung up.

A few minutes later, Lindsay snapped her phone shut. Her father-in-law had come through the procedure just fine, and Mark agreed they should witness for traditional marriage even though he couldn't be with them.

"We're really going to do this!" Lindsay squealed.

"Yes, we are!" Jenn replied. She felt more excited and purposeful than she had in so long. Her days had become so routine. Her life was in a nice groove, but it bordered on being in a rut. This was something new and meaningful.

They drove to Safeway to pick up food for bag lunches. Jenn would make sandwiches and pack them up with fruit and chips. Lindsay agreed to bake cookies. Rather than get disposable water bottles, they'd ask everyone to bring their own. But they picked up a few spares in case someone forgot.

At Office Depot they bought tagboard, glue sticks, and staples. After that they picked up wooden strips from Home Depot. They spent the afternoon at Jenn's house, printing out the slogans that

Pastor James suggested and gluing them onto the tagboard. In the evening Steve would cut the wood, and Jenn would staple the signs together.

At four Jenn had to get over to Dublin High to drive for Josh's game. She scribbled a note to Rachel and headed out the door. She waved Josh over to the car when he came to the parking lot. He leaned against the driver-side door to talk to Jenn through the window.

She told Josh about her meeting with Pastor James and then explained the plan for the next day. "We'll meet at Dublin BART at nine tomorrow morning. We're inviting everyone from the youth group—parents, too. Sara's going to meet us at the West Oakland station. Hopefully we'll get at least ten kids to go with us. And some parents. After the game I'd like help making calls."

"Sorry, Mom. I can't go with you—game tomorrow," Josh stated matter-of-factly.

"You'll have to miss this one," Jenn replied. "Sorry."

"What?" Josh exclaimed. He pushed back from the car, looking incredulous. "You want me to miss my basketball game for this? No, Mom."

Jenn wasn't surprised that Josh was upset since he was very loyal to the team. "Josh, you have to pick God over everything else," Jenn patiently explained.

"Does Dad know you're forcing me to miss a game?" Josh challenged.

"We made this decision together," she told him. She worked to keep her voice calm. "Our family is being called. He has a plan for us. You may not know why this is so important right now, but someday you will."

"Coach doesn't like excuses," Josh explained. "He might cut me from being a starter."

"Your coach claims to be a Christian. This is his opportunity, and yours, to show faith. It's easy to say you are faithful when you don't have to make a sacrifice. You have to walk the talk if you're really a soldier for Christ."

Then Jenn gave him the look. Josh looked like he wanted to keep arguing, but instead he hit the car door with the palm of his hand and walked away. Jenn didn't like the attitude, but she took it as frustrated consent.

◆ ◆ ◆

Over dinner that night around the table, Steve said, "Congrats on the win today, Josh. Mom says you played well."

Josh shrugged modestly, but Jenn saw the small proud smile on his face.

"Next year you guys are going be a force. I think your team might go all the way," Steve said.

"Coach says so, too," Josh replied. "That would be awesome."

"I think I got some great shots of the game. I'll get them printed out Monday. What did Coach say when you told him you would miss the game tomorrow?" asked Jenn.

"He said he's proud of me. So you're right," Josh said. "He hates gay people more than he loves basketball."

"Honey, we don't hate homosexuals!" Jenn exclaimed. She was shocked to hear something like that come out of Josh's mouth. "Don't ever think that. We want to help them find their way back to righteous living."

"But what if they can't?" Josh asked.

"They can, if they accept that our Lord Jesus Christ died for their sins," Jenn replied. "All we have to do is recognize that and live by His rules. It's very simple. Are you worried about someone who's homosexual?"

Josh shook his head.

"There's a bunch of gay kids at Dublin High," Rachel said with a shrug.

"How do you know?" Steve asked.

Rachel replied, "They wear rainbow pins."

Jenn felt herself get warm with anger. "I don't know why the school encourages these things." She shook her head. "It's unfair to those children. Do you talk to them?"

"Of course," Rachel said. "They're just kids. I'm not going to call them the F word or anything."

"The F word?" Jenn asked.

Josh sighed and rolled his eyes. He sounded annoyed when he said, "*Faggot*, Mom. The F word is *faggot*. Kids who are out get called that all the time."

"That's horrible!" Jenn exclaimed, shocked. "And exactly why we're going to San Francisco: to fight for the souls of those children, every one of them."

Rachel burst in. "I think it'll be fun. I love going to San Francisco—the tall buildings, the shops, the wacky people."

"This isn't about fun, Rachel. This is about witnessing and standing up for family values," Jenn said.

"That doesn't mean I can't have fun while I'm doing it," Rachel retorted. "*Now* can I join MySpace—to tell people about the witness? A bunch of the youth group have it. If kids see other kids are going, they'll jump right in." In her my-parents-don't-know-much tone of voice she said, "It's called social media, you know."

This wasn't the first time Rachel had brought this up. Jenn looked at Steve with a question in her eyes. He raised an eyebrow. She guessed they were on the same page about letting her make this step, but she wanted her daughter to know they were taking this decision seriously. "Dad and I will pray on it and let you know. Are you sure Pastor James thinks it's in keeping with our Christian values?"

"He said so; I promise!" Rachel said. "At youth group he told us he researched it, prayed about it, and decided it was a great way for us to 'stay connected to each other in Christ.'"

"I want you two to make phone calls to the youth group tonight," Jenn said. "I will, too."

"Sure," Rachel replied.

Josh shook his head. "I have to study."

Annoyed that Josh was fighting her about this, Jenn stared at Steve, giving him the talk-to-your-son look.

Steve spoke up. "You can take fifteen minutes from your night to make a few phone calls, Josh. Those kids look up to you. Show some leadership."

"It's Friday night," Jenn said. "Your studying can wait. This is the moral issue of our time. I'll use our home phone. Josh, you can use your cell phone, and Rachel can use mine. It's worth the minutes."

Josh didn't look happy, but he sighed and nodded. He muttered, "What are we supposed to say?"

"We'd like them to join us as we take a stand for marriage and family values. They can meet us at the Dublin BART station. Dad and I will be with you the whole time. And Lindsay too, so we have enough adults, but encourage parents to join us. I'll bring signs and food for everyone, but they should bring their own water bottles. Try to get a head count. And, Rachel, we'll let you know about 'my place.' That might be just perfect."

"MySpace! Capital M-y, capital S-p-a-c-e. With no space between the *My* and the *Space*."

Jenn laughed. "MySpace. Got it. I stand corrected. Let's do this soon so we can start our video at eight. OK?"

The kids nodded. They knew this routine.

"Who's picking tonight?" Steve asked.

Rachel pointed at her brother. "Josh, so I guess we're watching something *StarWars...*"

All eyes turned to Josh. He shook himself out of his thoughts. "Ummm," he said while his family waited, "I'm feeling *Empire Strikes Back*–ish."

"I'll make the popcorn," Jenn said.

"Duun, dun. Dun, dun, dun, duuun, duuun," Steve hummed the familiar theme song.

4

The phone rang at six in the morning. That couldn't be good.

Jenn sat on the edge of her bed and picked up the extension on her nightstand.

"Hello?"

"I'm so sorry!" Lindsay's voice came through the line in a rush. "I can't come with you. Melanie threw up all night. With Mark out of town, I can't leave her to go to SF."

Jenn's spirits sank. She needed Lindsay and Steve today. Leading a witness was a big stretch for her.

Lindsay went on. "Rebeccah and Michael still want to come. Is that all right?"

Jenn sighed. "Of course. God has a reason for all things. He's just reminding us we aren't in control."

"I just talked to Mona. She's going and can step up however you need her to. And I'll send the cookies with the kids."

"Thanks for getting a sub for yourself. Give Melanie my love. I'll pray that she feels better soon. We'll take good care of Rebeccah and Michael."

Jenn forced herself to slow down enough to make their usual Saturday breakfast: pancakes from Grandma Mary Alice's recipe, fruit salad, cheesy scrambled eggs, and bacon. And white toast with sweet butter and jam for Rachel. After grace, Rachel told them about her dream from the previous night, set in the movie *Catch that Kid*. It involved a lot of hiding and running. Jenn was distracted, making mental lists of what she needed to bring, afraid she was missing something. Despite her preoccupation with details, she noticed Josh wasn't shoveling away his usual quantities and hardly said a word.

"Are you OK?" Jenn asked him.

He shrugged. "I have a headache."

"Oh, honey. Why didn't you say so?" Jenn said. "I'll get you some ibuprofen before we go."

They finished breakfast, cleaned up, and rushed out of the house with bags of food and signs. They were waiting at the entrance to the station by eight forty-five. No one else was there. Jenn felt foolish standing by the entrance with bags of food. What if no one else showed up? All this preparation would be for nothing. *Not nothing*, she reminded herself. Her family was standing up for their faith.

"If it's just us, we'll have plenty to eat," she joked to her family, covering up her embarrassment while trying to keep up the energy. Rachel passed the she-thinks-she's-so-funny look to Josh but didn't say anything.

Ten minutes later, eighteen teens and four adults surrounded Jenn in their bright-blue church T-shirts. Jenn sighed with relief; her church family had come through. Now she worried there wasn't enough food. They only had twenty-five bag lunches. If anyone else showed up, she'd have to send Steve to get more food. The turnout was amazing with such short notice. The excitement in the group was palpable. The kids were chattering away in small clumps, divided mostly by grade. Parents asked her how they could help. She assigned them to groups of teens, handed them bags of food, and outlined the general plan. This was going to be a great day—an important day—in their family's life and the life of the church.

Boarding in Dublin on a Saturday morning meant a nearly empty train. Jenn pointed the group to the back half of the second car. Even though there was plenty of room on the train, the kids squeezed in three or four to a two-person seat, with some sitting on laps, like piles of happy puppies. The adults filled in around them protectively. Jenn and Steve took the sideways seats on the end. After everyone settled in, she stood up and spoke to the group as the train rattled past Castro Valley.

"Thank you all for being here today." Jenn beamed at the group. "We're going to San Francisco to save souls for Jesus. I'm proud of all of you for giving your time on a Saturday for this holy work. Pastor James is sorry not to be with us today, but he told me to tell you that we're all in his prayers."

Jenn choked up as she looked at these faces. Each person there was a gift from God. "He instructed us not to speak to the activists while we're there. If someone tries to speak with you, just look away," she said slowly, emphasizing each word. "Our signs speak for themselves. We're not engaging in arguments. We want to appear calm, confident, and full of faith. No, not appear that way. We want to *be* that way: *be* calm, *be* confident, and *be* filled with spirit."

Jenn asked each of the kids which sign they wanted: "No same-sex marriage—ever," "Adam and Eve, not Adam and Steve," or "Save traditional marriage." The "Adam and Eve" one was the most popular by far. Jenn was impressed with how responsible and respectful everyone was being. Years of being in church together meant she trusted these kids and adults to take care of one another once they stepped off the train. For now, they could simply enjoy one another's company.

Only a few people got on at each stop until the Fruitvale station in Oakland. There a large crowd pushed onto the train, filling up the remaining seats. Four women were left standing in the open space in front of Jenn. Jenn looked them over without making eye contact. Each wore a rainbow of some sort. One had a hat with a rainbow over the words "I can't even think straight." Another had a T-shirt with a rainbow that said, "We're not in Kansas anymore, Toto." Two of them had matching rainbow pins on their backpacks. The rainbows were a clear sign of where they stood on the issue of traditional marriage. Jenn hated that the homosexuals had stolen the rainbow, a symbol of God's covenant with Noah and promise to all Christians. Clearly the people were going to city hall in San Francisco too, but for the other side. Jenn felt a pit in her stomach.

The one in the hat leaned into their group, whispered, and pointed. Four heads turned at once to look at Jenn's kids.

The tall, blond woman with the Toto shirt said, "Hell no!" She leaned forward, looking ready to fight. Jenn's heart started to beat faster. She grabbed Steve's arm and subtly tilted her head toward the foursome.

The hat woman put a hand on her friend. "Don't engage. They aren't going to ruin this day for us. Let's go." She jerked her head sideways and walked down the aisle, followed by their two friends.

The blonde watched her friends leave and then looked back at the teens. Jenn squeezed Steve's hand. He patted her leg, letting her know he was right there. She could feel him starting to stand up to defend their group when the woman left to join her friends.

Jenn looked at her kids. Their signs were turned around. She didn't blame them. She expected hostility once they were off the train, but on it? Toward teens? She prayed, *God, watch over us and keep us safe as we do Your holy work.*

"That was close," she whispered to Steve.

"I'm glad one of them had some sense," Steve said.

"Do you think we'll be in danger in San Francisco?" Jenn asked.

"Not if we don't fight back."

Jenn nodded. She smiled reassurance at the teens who were looking at her. Josh wasn't one of them. His head was leaned against the window, and he stared out at the view, not talking to anyone. Michael said something to him. Josh shook his head while he kept gazing out. Jenn checked her watch. The ibuprofen should kick in soon.

She looked for Rachel. She was sitting on Jamie's lap chatting away with her friends. That girl took everything in stride and made friends with whoever was near. Jenn never worried about her. She laced her fingers with Steve's and leaned her head against his shoulder. He squeezed her hand and kissed her hair. She took a deep breath to slow her racing heart. Steve's presence calmed her. This was a marriage. Lifelong companions in Christ.

Before they got to West Oakland, Jenn went to the door. Once the car stopped, she straddled the gap so Sara could see her. It was hard to stay at the entrance of the train with people pushing past her to get into the car. She scanned past the crowd getting on but didn't see Sara. They had agreed that she would get off her train from Berkeley and wait for them to arrive in West Oakland. They should have made a plan for which car they would be in. Jenn had had no idea it would be this crowded.

She kept watching, but her oldest child wasn't anywhere to be seen. Jenn didn't want Sara going into San Francisco by herself, but she wasn't sure what to do if she couldn't find her daughter. It was too late to get all these kids off the train, but she hated to leave her own child behind.

"Mom!"

Suddenly Sara was right there, and relief passed through Jenn. They stepped into the car.

"Hi, honey." Jenn hugged her daughter close as the doors slid shut and the train jerked away from the station. "Are you OK?"

"I'm fine, Mom." Sara gave her an incredulous look. "Why wouldn't I be?"

◆ ◆ ◆

After Powell station, most of the travelers on their train stood up. They politely made their way toward the doors, squeezing close together. Jenn didn't want to miss their stop, but she also didn't want the kids to get lost in the crowd, so she told them to get ready but stay put. She watched as the crowd shuffled through the bottleneck of the doors, a stream of people constricting, like water squeezing past large boulders. She signaled the group, and they joined in at the tail end of the crowd moving off the train. Jenn straddled the gap to stop the doors from closing until the last of her crew made it off the train. As soon as she stepped onto the platform in San Francisco, the doors swished closed behind her.

The Civic Center station was even more packed than West Oakland. People in colorful clothes rushed by. They carried flowers, balloons, and signs. Someone walked past with a white cake topped with two brides in full white dresses. A young child sat up high in a backpack, and another was pushed past in a stroller. White-haired men holding hands shuffled to the escalator. A musician with long hair and a full beard played an accordion with the case open for tips. Shiny coins and a few bills sat on the red velvet lining.

"Go to the wall!" Jenn shouted. "We'll stay down here until everyone clears out." She leaned over to Mona. "Can you take up the rear? Make sure all the kids are in front of you, OK?" Mona nodded.

The teens whispered and gestured at the colorful crowd while they waited for the platform to clear. Jenn and Steve led the group to the escalator. At the top she saw a sign for UN Plaza straight ahead. Pastor said to look for Grove, so they went the other way. Steve led them through the exit gates and down the hallway to a staircase marked Market and Seventh. Jenn shrugged and turned back around.

"Down there," she said to Steve, pointing to another green sign down the dirty marble corridor. Steve nodded.

"Sorry, guys," Jenn said. "More choices than we realized."

They wandered through the underground maze, searching for the way out. Jenn took a breath to calm herself. Just getting outside was an exercise in patience. After many wrong turns, they finally found an exit labeled Civic Center/Grove.

As she rode up the long escalator, Jenn heard loud noises from the street above. She closed her eyes and prayed for strength. She opened her eyes and looked up through the tunnel of the escalator.

A pigeon flew across the white building shining in the sun above her head. She laughed. It wasn't a dove, but sometimes God had to use what was available. He was reminding her whose work she was doing.

Jenn's faith restored, at the top she quickly moved away from the escalator so she wouldn't block the way. Grungy homeless people sitting on the sidewalk shook paper cups at her. She ignored them and hoped they would leave her kids alone. This was why she hated coming to San Francisco, especially by BART. She waited for Mona to step off the moving stairs.

"Come on," Jenn said, hoping she sounded more confident than she felt. She slid her hand into Steve's and walked quickly along the dirty sidewalk, littered with fast-food wrappers and spots of who-knew-what ground into the cement, until they came to the plaza across from city hall. The beautiful domed building loomed ahead of them. As they waited for the light to change, she watched kids on the play structure on the corner of the plaza. She was surprised to see them. Young children didn't belong in the Tenderloin neighborhood.

They crossed Hyde Street and made their way through the center of the plaza between leafless, gnarled trees and tall flagpoles. White news vans topped with satellite dishes surrounded the plaza. Jenn stopped the group directly across the street from the majestic building. It was hard to believe this beautiful, traditional city hall was the center of an attack on family.

A long line snaked out the front door and around the corner. People moved through the crowd singing, giving out flowers, and generally celebrating. A female couple walked out of the door holding hands. They were around thirty years old, dressed in flowing outfits that were identical but in different colors: one bright fuchsia and the other teal blue. They had white flower leis around their necks. At the top of the stairs, they raised their clenched hands high into the air. Tears flowed down their cheeks, and huge grins covered their faces. The crowd cheered for the ecstatic couple.

Rachel pulled on Jenn's arm and spoke into her ear her own thoughts out loud: "They look so happy."

Jenn nodded. They did look happy. She hadn't expected to see such pure joy. She was taken aback by the sight.

The group, her group, looked at her. They needed direction. Jenn pointed to the ground. They would stay right where they were, standing on this side of the street, and respectfully hold up their signs. They would not engage in arguments or debates. Then they could return home, back to their lives, where people did not look so happy after sinning.

◆ ◆ ◆

Couple after couple came out in the same way: hands clenched over their heads to the cheers of the crowd. They were dressed in all sorts of ways: Two men in suits. Two men in shorts. Two women in wedding gowns. One woman in a wedding gown and one woman in a tuxedo. Two women in shorts. On and on it went. Some had children with them. Some carried signs. Some were old, older than Jenn's parents. Some looked as if they were barely eighteen. Most of them had tears in their eyes or even running down their faces.

Jenn had expected to see people angry and shouting like on the television. Fox News didn't show these ordinary-looking people so full of emotion.

Her kids were clustered into little groups, talking with one another, their signs held up. She was relieved to see Josh engaged with his friends. Jenn considered leading them in a song or chants but thought that maybe their presence was enough. She checked in with Steve, who agreed that they didn't need to draw any more attention. They got a few glares, and a few people took their pictures, but no one tried to talk with them. Jenn noticed some of her kids turned away from the cameras.

Jenn pulled out her camera.

"Really, Mom?" Josh questioned her.

"We'll be glad to have a record of this day. I won't take shots of people across the street. Just us, in our shirts."

He shook his head but didn't challenge her further. Most of the kids were willing subjects. Rachel and Jamie were outright hams. Jenn managed to corral them into a group shot just before lunch. She knew that even the kids who grumbled would clamor to see the pictures once they were developed.

Jenn and Steve got out the bagged lunches. There was a choice of turkey and Swiss or PB and J. Each paper bag held a mandarin orange, carrots, and two chocolate-chip cookies, courtesy of Lindsay. There was just enough.

"You think of everything!" Mona said, clearly impressed.

"Not really, but thanks. All those years as a room parent prepared me for this! We wanted today to be a positive, spiritually uplifting experience for all of us. Warriors for Christ need energy for the battle!"

As they were eating, a newsperson approached them. Jenn recognized Ken Brown from Channel 4.

"Can I ask one of you a few questions? On camera?" he asked.

Everyone looked to Jenn. Suddenly the stakes were totally changed. She hadn't anticipated something like this. *A news interview?* Jenn looked at Steve. She pantomimed, *You or me?* He pointed to her emphatically. She interpreted his attitude to be *You got us in this. This is yours.* She nodded. *Lord be with me*, she prayed to herself. Jenn finished chewing her bite of turkey sandwich and wiped the crumbs off her face.

"How can I help you?" she asked. She sounded confident, but her pulse raced. She'd never made a public stand for her faith before. This was her chance to reach more people with Jesus's message of salvation. She hoped she was up for the challenge.

The newsman looked over at the cameraperson, waited for a signal, and then asked in a formal voice, "As you can see, most people are excited for these couples, but you seem to have a different opinion. Can you tell us why you're out here protesting these marriages today?"

Jenn's mind went blank as she searched for a good answer. She started out nervously, "Well, Ken, the Bible calls these relationships a sin—an abomination. As President Bush said in his State of the Union Address, 'A strong America must value the institution of marriage.'"

Jenn felt the teens watching her. She took a deep breath, and the Holy Spirit entered her body, sending a chill down her back.

Jenn continued, more calm and confident, "Our nation must defend the sanctity of family from homosexual activists. The definition of marriage has not changed in two thousand years. One man and one woman. It's very clear."

"I see you brought some young people with you today."

Jenn smiled. "Yes, these are members of our church youth group in Dublin. We're out here today standing up for the children. It's their future we're fighting for. These teens leaped at the chance to take a stand for their values."

As she spoke, a crowd gathered around them. One person started to chant, "We're here. We're queer. We're married. Get used to it!" Other voices joined in until there was a loud chorus yelling at them. The camera panned to the chanting crowd and then turned to scan Jenn and the kids. The kids huddled in close. Jenn felt trapped. She grabbed Steve's hand. The chanting continued louder and louder.

"What do you have to say to this crowd?" Ken Brown shouted to Jenn.

She stared at him. Her mind was completely blank. She frantically searched for the right words; then she remembered her prayer. "God loves them. Salvation is theirs if they live according to His laws."

The reporter signaled to the crew. "That was perfect," he said, back to a casual tone. "Thanks. You'll probably be on the five o'clock news and maybe again at eleven."

The chanters dispersed as quickly as they had gathered, once the camera was turned off. Jenn let out a breath. Apparently, it was over, and they were safe.

The sudden quiet was unsettling. The kids, all in one mass, stared at Jenn. Various expressions covered their faces. Some looked scared, others excited, and one or two as though they might cry. They needed her leadership to break the tension and instill faith.

"Everyone OK?" she asked as she scanned the group. They all nodded. "Well done, all of you!" Jenn said to them. "You handled that situation perfectly. I'm so proud of you! We'll stay just a few more minutes and then go home. If we make the news tonight, we really will have furthered God's message."

The tension visibly left the group. They spread out and clumped into small clusters. She could see them rehashing the moment with dramatic expressions on their faces. She scanned for her kids. Josh was with a group but looking over at the steps of city hall. Sara had her arms around Jamie, who looked shaken up.

"Mom, look at this." Rachel handed her a quarter sheet of paper with a rainbow border and a heart with an X through it at the top. It read:

What if you're <u>judging</u> your sister, child, cousin, uncle, friend, or coworker?
Gay people are four times more likely to attempt suicide and twice as likely to succeed as straight people. Are you sure this is the message you want to send to your loved ones?
PFLAG
Parents, Families, and Friends of Lesbians and Gays

"Where did you get this?" Jenn quizzed Rachel.

Rachel pointed. "One of them handed it to me."

Jenn was furious that these people were trying to tell her daughter that their church was causing anyone harm.

"Rachel, no one we know is choosing the homosexual lifestyle. These people are terribly misguided. Don't let them confuse you. We came out today to save people. Do you understand?" Jenn asked forcefully.

Rachel nodded. Jenn crumpled the paper and dropped it in the recycling.

She'd done what she set out to do. The witness was a success by any measure.

She didn't understand why she felt so horrible.

5

"I think we really furthered the Lord's message," Jenn told Pastor James when he called that evening. She sat on the family-room couch telling him about the day. Whatever strange feelings she was having in San Francisco had vanished on the ride back to Dublin. The group was tired but proud to have been a voice for Christian values. The kids were bubbling with excitement on BART. "Channel Four News even interviewed me! Steve said I did fine, so I don't think I embarrassed us."

"Oh, Jennifer, that's amazing!" Pastor said. "Were you wearing your church T-shirts?"

"Of course!"

"I'm going to launch our phone tree as soon as we hang up. Our congregants will want to see your good work for our Lord."

Jenn's heart soared. Her church was going to learn about what she had done. Lin called a few minutes later.

"How did it go?" her cheerful voice came through the line.

"It was amazing!" Jenn said. "The kids were strong and faithful."

"Were people hostile toward you?" Lindsay asked.

"It was scariest on BART but not at city hall. Well, except during the interview."

"What interview?"

"Oh, Channel Four asked me a few questions." Jenn tried to sound casual. She suddenly felt bad that Lindsay was left out.

"Wow!" Lindsay exclaimed.

"I'm so sorry you missed it," Jenn replied. "I wish we'd done it together."

"Me, too."

Changing the subject, Jenn explained, "I've got to go. Steve and I are eating out tonight. I really didn't leave enough time to get ready. See you tomorrow?"

"If we all stay healthy."

"How's Mel?"

"Better. I think it's a twenty-four-hour thing. She's kept everything down since eleven o'clock."

"I'll pray for the rest of you to stay well," Jenn said, and hung up. "Josh!" she called.

"What?" he asked, coming into the family room.

"Can you record the news? Nana wants me to send it to her."

Josh started to say something but just nodded and got to work with the remote.

Jenn rushed upstairs, threw on her favorite red dress, and fixed her makeup. She didn't look her best—after the day in San Francisco, she could have used a shower—but she was ready to go in time to make their reservation.

◆ ◆ ◆

"I'm proud of you." Steve smiled. He sat across the candlelit table, dressed up in Jenn's favorite suit. The steak house was packed with couples for Valentine's Day.

"Thanks!" She grinned. "You know it wasn't just me."

He shrugged. "But you went out on a limb today. *You* spoke to the news. I could feel you living God's purpose."

Jenn's eyes welled up. "Remember that witness I told you about when I was sixteen? The one my parents made me go to and that I resisted, but in the middle of it I felt the Holy Spirit so intensely? The moment I decided to dedicate my life to Christ?"

Steve nodded.

"Today was like that. At first I was embarrassed to be taking this public stand in the face of hostility. But then the Holy Spirit carried me, and I knew God wanted me on this path even though it made me uncomfortable." Jenn gave Steve an embarrassed smile. "Do I sound prideful and arrogant?"

Steve shook his head and smiled. "Proud but not prideful. Sometimes God brings you to the front. You know it's His glory and not yours that matters."

"I do."

Steve pulled out a box wrapped in red foil.

"Oh, Steve!" Jenn exclaimed, even though Steve usually got her something for Valentine's Day.

"Josh helped me pick it out."

Curious, Jenn took the box. It was heavy. Underneath the shiny paper was a Nikon D70, a digital SLR.

Jenn's hand covered her mouth. "Oh my goodness. Steve! Thank you."

He smiled at her. "It has six point one megapixels!"

"I know this was expensive. Are you sure?"

"I've seen you checking them out for a long time. You deserve it."

"I can't wait to learn all about it!" She leaned around the table to give her husband a kiss.

◆ ◆ ◆

When she got home from dinner, Jenn was shocked and excited to see the number "26" blinking on their answering machine. They'd never had so many people call them at once. She hit Play. Her brother Tim's voice came out of the speaker. "Jenn, Mom told me you got on the news tonight. Congrats! From all of us. We'll have to catch up soon. It's been too long. Jessie says, 'Hooray for Jenn!' *Beep.* Hi, Everyone. It's Hannah from Valley Preschool. We saw Jenn on the news tonight. You looked and sounded great, Jenn. Thanks for standing up for marriage. *Beep...*" It took her nearly half an hour to get through them all: lots of people from church, her cousin Jonah, and parents from Dublin schools and soccer left her congratulatory messages. Jenn did not expect or want this kind of attention, but if this was God's plan for her, she would do her best to be a gracious and faithful soldier for the Lord. It was too late to call people back, but she could do that tomorrow. After she listened to her messages, she checked her e-mail, not something she normally did at night. Her inbox was flooded. When the kids came home from their movie, she was still sitting at the computer.

"You're still up?" Rachel asked, surprised.

Jenn rolled her eyes and made a chagrined face. "I'm listening to messages and reading e-mail. How was the movie?"

"Great!" Rachel said.

Jenn looked at her other children.

"I liked it," Sara said. "It was cute."

Josh shrugged. "It was good, I guess. I'm tired. I'm going to bed."

"How's your head?" Jenn asked.

"Fine, I guess. Not great."

"Take something so you can sleep. But be sure to eat something first so you don't throw up from it."

Sara asked, "How long are you gonna stay up?"

"I don't know. Until I get through the e-mails. Good night." Her kids kissed her cheek, and she turned back to the screen.

By the time Jenn got to bed, Steve was snoring quietly. She had trouble falling asleep because she was so energized from the day. Each time she started to doze off, scenes from San Francisco popped into her mind. Faces of people chanting around her got her heart racing and startled her awake. As she lay in bed with images streaming through her head, Jenn heard the awful sound of retching down the hall. She rushed out of bed to the kids' bathroom and turned the handle. The door was locked and wouldn't open.

"It's me. Are you OK?" she asked, wondering which of her kids was sick.

Josh opened the door. He looked pale and clammy.

He croaked, "I just threw up."

"Oh, honey. I'm sorry. Maybe you have the same thing as Melanie. Something's going around. No church for you tomorrow."

Josh nodded feebly. She walked him to his room and tucked him back into bed. They had decorated this space together a few years ago, the summer between sixth and seventh grades. Out went the

Buzz Lightyear bedding, and in came a plain navy comforter and matching curtains. She had heard that boys never cared about their rooms, but Josh went shopping with her when he'd outgrown his childish taste. He had an opinion about how his room should look. Jenn liked to redecorate each part of the house every five years. It kept things fresh and up to date. Soon it would be time to redo this space again. Time did fly. It was a cliché but so true.

Jenn brought the garbage can next to the bed in case Josh threw up again in the night and got him a glass of water. When he was settled, she prayed over her son: "Great physician, Lord Jesus Christ, please restore your servant to full health. Dear God, remove all fear and doubt from his being by the power of Your Holy Spirit, and may You, Lord, be glorified through his life. In Jesus's name I pray. Amen."

"Thanks for taking care of me." His eyes welled up.

"Of course, honey. I love you—to heaven and beyond. I'm not going to give you a hug, because I don't want to get sick. If you need anything in the night, come get me." She blew him a kiss.

"I love you, too. You know that, right? Even though I don't say it or show it so much anymore. I still do!"

"I know, Josh. Really, I do." Jenn said. And it was true. It was right for a young man to distance himself from his mother. She didn't *like* it, but she accepted it as part of God's plan.

◆ ◆ ◆

The next morning, Jenn poked her head in to say good-bye to Josh before they left for church. He was sleeping peacefully, so she didn't disturb him. He looked so sweet and vulnerable. She wrote him a note and left it against the water glass so he would see it as soon as he opened his eyes: *Text if you need anything. I'll have my phone in my pocket. We'll come right back.*

Jenn, Steve, Rachel, and Sara climbed into the car. They'd drop Sara off at the BART station on their way to church. She missed a day of studying to witness yesterday, so she was going to school to study. God would understand. No one succeeded at a top-rated university without a sacrifice.

Understandably, Jenn was proud of Sara's academic achievements. She'd gotten into Williams, Vassar, and Pomona as well as the top UCs. Jenn had encouraged Sara to consider Christian colleges, but she hadn't applied to any. When Sara accepted the offer from UC Berkeley, Jenn was thrilled, and she'd encouraged Sara to simply commute from Dublin. Jenn had stayed with her family when she attended BIOLA, the Biblical Institute of Los Angeles. Steve had, too. But unlike Steve, Jenn didn't regret living at home during those years. He wished he'd had the full college experience and wanted that for their kids. Jenn didn't understand the attraction of being crowded into a small space with other eighteen-year-olds, but she knew that she had to start giving her children more leeway to make their own choices.

Steve pointed out that Sara was a great kid and that they could trust her to live out their Christian values wherever she went to school, which she demonstrated with her choice to reside in Freeborn, the substance-free dorm. Jenn was grateful that was an option, even at U.C. Berkeley.

When they walked into the church sanctuary, the praise band was already playing. People gave her hugs and high fives. It took longer than usual to walk to their favorite section: close to the front on the right. Many congregants waved from across the sanctuary. Jenn felt like a celebrity.

"Everyone thinks what we did is so cool, Mom," Rachel said. "Way to go!" Rachel held up her hand for a high five.

Jenn shrugged and slapped her daughter's hand. She was proud but didn't want to be boastful. It was hard to know how to behave. She waved and thanked and hugged people as modestly as possible. She felt bad to be getting all this attention when Lindsay had done as much as she had to get ready for the witness. She reminded people that the kids and Lindsay should be praised, too.

During the pastoral prayer, Jenn was surprised to be called to the front. When Pastor James put his arm around her, she blushed and put her face in her hands. Then she composed herself and looked out at the crowd.

"We all say we want to do God's work in the world," Pastor James spoke out to the congregation. "This woman, Jenn, is a shining example for all of us. Yes, she serves on the welcome team for our congregation, but that is not all. On Thursday morning I saw the horrifying images of marriage being mocked in San Francisco. That night I asked God to send me a messenger, and who called first thing the next morning? This woman! She didn't hesitate to put her faith into action. She took time out of her busy life to organize our teens to stand up for our Christian beliefs. We are in the middle of a war for the soul of our country. Each of us must be soldiers for

Christ." He faced her and put his hand on her head. "God blesses you, Jenn. He is blessing you for your gifts to our community and to the world. In the name of Jesus, we bless you."

Jenn's eyes filled up. She hadn't expected recognition. She certainly didn't organize the protest for this kind of attention. But it was nice—very nice. For as long as she could remember, she'd wanted to be known as a good Christian. Or rather, to *be* a good Christian. Her primary goal in life, besides being a good mother and wife, was to be a faithful representative of Christ on earth. And in this moment she knew she was doing the Lord's work. The Holy Spirit filled her chest and moved inside her. A chill ran down her back as the energy swirled through her body.

◆ ◆ ◆

As they walked from the sanctuary to the car, Jenn called home to check on Josh.

"He's not answering," she told Steve. "Should we go straight home?"

Steve shook his head. "He can call us if he needs us. That's the beauty of cellular phones. Most likely he's sleeping and will enjoy the quiet a bit longer."

They went to Mimi's for brunch. The children had grown up with this tradition, ordering pancakes and hot chocolate each Sunday after worship. It was strange to have just one child with them, but Jenn knew she'd better get used to it. Josh was making it clear he didn't want to stay in the area for college. She'd be lucky if he stayed in California—he was exploring East Coast colleges. They decided that if he got a good scholarship, she and Steve were going to let him go that far. In theory she should be glad to have her kids fly the coop, but she'd just as soon have them nearby forever.

6

EIGHT HOURS LATER
THE AFTERNOON OF SUNDAY, FEBRUARY 15

Jenn pushed the red call button. Her heart beat fast and hard as adrenaline coursed through her body once again. She shook as she waited. Her head was so crowded with questions that it felt like it was full of static.

"Can I help you?" a young nurse with light-brown skin and high-lighted hair asked.

Jenn took a deep breath. "My husband... Josh's father. At home he found an empty bottle of sleeping pills. We suspect Josh may have taken some. Well, a lot."

The nurse nodded slowly. "OK. Do you know what kind of pills—over-the-counter, prescription?"

"It's Ambien. There were twenty-seven pills in the bottle, and now it's empty." Despite herself, a tear slid down Jenn's cheek.

The nurse patted her shoulder. "I'll get the attending. Dr. Prud'homme is on right now. This explains a lot."

Jenn was forced to wait for the new doctor to come to speak with her. She stood up and paced by Josh's hospital bed, forcing herself to take deep breaths. *Why? Why? Why?* ran through her head. She reminded herself, *It's best that we know what caused him to be like this*...and then she prayed, *God, please remove the Ambien from Josh's bloodstream.*

Jenn stopped pacing when the attending doctor stepped past the curtain. Dr. Prud'homme looked like she was in her mid-forties, with pale skin and brown hair pulled back into a ponytail. She looked kind enough but didn't bother with any pleasantries after introducing herself.

"From a medical point of view," the doctor said, "this is good news. Ambien moves through the body fairly quickly, causing very little damage at that dosage. He should start to wake up about fifteen hours after he took it. It's most likely he'll have a complete recovery within twenty-four hours. He'll need to be evaluated by a psychiatrist to ascertain if he is an immediate danger to himself or others before he can be discharged."

"A psychiatrist? Really?"

"With all due respect," the doctor said slowly, "your son attempted suicide today."

That word was like a slap to the face. "You don't know that. Couldn't it have been at mistake?" Jenn asked.

"I'm obliged to have him evaluated before he goes home," Dr. Prud'homme said firmly but with compassion. "The psychiatrist will determine his mental state. I'm sorry. I know this is hard to hear."

Jenn watched the doctor walk away. She was so stunned she could hardly breathe. Her body trembled. Suicide? She forced herself to take deep breaths. She considered what could possibly be bothering Josh so much...College? Kids felt so much academic pressure, but he was a great student. Girl problems? Jenn didn't know about a special girl, but that might be it. Boys usually kept that sort of thing private from their parents.

Pregnant! The word leaped into Jenn's mind. What if he'd gotten someone pregnant? That would go against all of their values. He might think his life was ruined.

"Dear Lord Jesus," Jenn whispered, "it's my will to surrender to You everything that I am and everything that I'm striving to be. I offer You my life, mind, body, soul, and spirit and all my hopes, plans, and dreams. I surrender to You my past, present, and future.

"I offer You the life of my son, Josh. I know he is in Your…"

Jenn started to sob, tears pouring down her face. Fear and sadness and hopelessness overwhelmed her; she couldn't continue her prayer. More than ever she wanted to feel the Holy Spirit, but she felt empty. This was punishment. Last night she went to bed full of ego and pride. And tonight her entire life was turned upside down.

◆ ◆ ◆

Past midnight, Jenn slept in the chair next to Josh. Her head rested on the bed, and she held his hand as they dozed. She woke up when he suddenly pulled away. Despite being groggy and half-asleep, she was relieved that he was coming around and glad for the chance to finally speak to him directly, to find out if her fear was true.

"Josh?" Jenn said quietly.

His eyes were still closed, but he reached for the tube coming out of his mouth and pulled on it. Jenn took his hands and said calmly, "Leave it, Josh. It's there to help you breathe. Stay still."

He yanked his hands away from Jenn's grip and clawed at the plastic on his face, his features contorted. Ignoring the panic that started to rise in her, Jenn blocked him with one hand and pressed the button for the nurse with the other. Then she wrapped her hands around each of his wrists and used all of her weight to push his arms into the bed. He fought against her, grunting and thrashing. He twisted from side to side. Jenn wanted to yell for help but resisted. Josh stared up at her, desperation and anger in his eyes.

Jenn repeated her words, trying to soothe him. "Josh, it's a tube to help you breathe. Leave it. If you stop fighting me, I can let go of you."

Josh glared more intensely and pushed harder against her. It was horrible to see him like that. Panic rose in Jenn. She closed her eyes to hide from the intense anger on his face.

"Can I help you?" a voice broke in the private chamber of her mind. Jenn opened her eyes to see a new nurse. The woman took in the scene and pushed a button on the wall. Suddenly a team of people rushed into the room. One of them pushed Jenn aside to take over restraining Josh. Jenn stood back and watched. Josh yelled and grunted around his breathing tube. "Ugh, uhh. Uhh!" Jenn felt her heart twist in sympathy. When the medical staff stepped back, Josh's arms were tied down at the sides of the bed. He fought against the restraints, but he couldn't get free. He looked at Jenn, panic shining in his eyes.

"Mmma. Ughh." More garbled, desperate sounds.

"This is your treatment?" Jenn challenged the nurse. "You're going to leave him tied like an animal?"

"The tube needs to stay in," the nurse said. "I know he looks like he's awake, but he's not. He's actually having a nightmare right now. Soon he'll drift into a different sleep state and calm down. He won't remember this tomorrow. See...He's starting to leave REM."

Jenn looked at her son. He had stopped jerking against the restraints. Josh's eyes got softer; then they closed. He blinked them open and shut a few times; his grunts turned into murmurs. Soon he looked deeply asleep. Jenn breathed a sigh of relief.

She asked the nurse, "How long does he have to have the tube?"

"We'll remove it when he's breathing on his own for thirty minutes. We've been stepping down the oxygen. He's responded well so far. By midmorning the tube should be out, if his numbers stay good."

"This is a nightmare—for both of us," Jenn mumbled.

The nurse said kindly, "I'll pray it'll be over soon...for both of your sakes."

"Thank you," Jenn replied. "That means a lot to me. Thank you very much."

◆ ◆ ◆

Just past two in the morning, Jenn woke with a start. Josh was awake and fighting against the restraints again. Jenn stood by the bed to soothe her terrified, disoriented son. She sang his favorite hymns, prayed out loud, and rubbed his brow. Eventually he drifted off to sleep again.

She inhaled deeply to calm herself. She was nervous and jumpy. *God, give me the strength to get through this night.*

Jenn took her son's hand. It felt warm and dry. He was there, in his body, in a way he hadn't been earlier that day. Relief passed through her. She took in his face, and then her eyes traveled down his long body. He took up the whole bed. In her head she'd known her son would be a man someday, but in her heart it was shocking that Josh was now more of a man than a boy. That little child she used to carry in her arms was in there somewhere, sort of, but also he was gone.

He'd been the cuddliest of her babies. As infants the girls liked to be held, but as soon as they could crawl, they were off. But Josh was happiest in someone's arms until he got to be too big to hold. And she indulged him in that for as long as possible, because she enjoyed it, too.

Jenn bent over and kissed Josh's hand. She rested her face by his hand. Her chest swelled with love.

She considered their options if she was right about a baby. Could he finish at Dublin High? Only if Josh and his new family lived at home. She'd agree to that. Would Steve? In her mind she started rearranging their house. If Josh and his family squeezed into the downstairs study, they'd have some privacy. The desks could be moved into the family room. It would be crowded but manageable. She could be with the baby during the day while the kids finished high school.

Suddenly she had a nauseating thought: what if the girl's family was pressuring her to have an abortion? That would kill Josh. She looked at him again. He would be devastated to know that his lust led to the destruction of a life.

"God, please let me be wrong. If I'm right, open their spirits so that they may do Your will on earth. In the name of Your Son, I pray. Amen."

Jenn whispered into Josh's ear, "Whatever you've done, Josh, I forgive you. Daddy will forgive you, too. But most important, God will forgive you. He already has. He gave us His Son so that we could be cleansed of our sins. Open your heart, and you will feel His love." A tear slid down her cheek. She wanted to do so much more, to fix whatever it was that Josh had done wrong. She wanted him to know that he didn't have to carry his burden alone.

But, she reminded herself, the best thing to do in this moment was to rest. So she forced herself to put her head down on the bed and use her favorite trick for falling asleep when she was anxious: she counted backward by sevens starting from one hundred, starting over again whenever she realized she was ruminating. After nine restarts she fell asleep.

She dreamed with her cheek resting against their nestled hands. Each time Josh woke up through that long night, she comforted him, trying to believe that this nightmare would be over soon.

At eight, Jenn's buzzing cell phone woke her up. It was Steve, letting her know that they were at the hospital. Exhausted and bleary-eyed, Jenn clumsily texted that she would come out.

When she looked up from her phone, Josh's eyes were open wide. He started to roll to his side, but the restraints stopped him. Jenn started to soothe him, but he didn't fight. He sank onto his back with a deep sigh. He was awake, for real now. Relieved and tired, Jenn took his hand. She resisted the urge to question him. There'd be time for that later.

"It's been a long night, hon," Jenn explained gently to him. "They tied down your arms because you were pulling out your breathing tube. But you made it through. Things are going to get better from here." Jenn bit her lip to stop herself from tearing up. "Dad wants to see you. Sara and Rachel, too. I'm going to go trade with him. I'll let the nurse know you're awake and you won't tear out the tube. She'll untie you."

She squeezed his hand, kissed his head, and pulled away to leave, but he held on tight. He struggled to speak but only made grunting sounds. He tried a few more times, frustrated and desperate to say something.

"Just a minute; I have a pencil and paper." Jenn dug around in her bag.

She placed a pencil in his hand and held a piece of scrap paper close to the tip. Josh's fingers shook as he scrawled out the letters: *S…o…r…r…y.* Jenn looked at her son. Tears rolled out of the corners of his eyes, down the sides of his face, and onto the bed.

"Oh, Josh," Jenn said, anguish in her voice. "Me, too! I'm so sorry that you couldn't tell me how desperate you were. I failed you, honey, but we'll get through this. Together. I have faith. And so does Dad. The whole church is praying for you. God will forgive you for whatever you've done."

Josh turned his head away and closed his eyes. Jenn gently wiped his face, since he was restrained.

"I'm so sorry, honey."

The nurse walked up and matter-of-factly said, "Change of shift. No visitors for about fifteen minutes."

Jenn looked at Josh. It was heart-wrenching to leave him like this. He tried to say something but then returned to the paper when he realized she couldn't understand him. He wrote *OK* in large, shaky letters.

"We'll talk more. You know, when..." Jenn pointed at his breathing tube.

He gave a slight nod. Then she kissed his head and left.

◆ ◆ ◆

"You look like you hardly slept," Steve said as they hugged good morning.

"It was a long night. How about you?" Jenn asked while giving first Sara and then Rachel a hug. Her youngest daughter kept her arms wrapped around Jenn.

"I slept OK," Rachel said. "How's Josh?"

"He's awake and calm. His arms were restrained in the night, and the tube is still in, so he can't talk, which is pretty awful. Hopefully the nurse will untie him now and take the tube out soon, because he's breathing fine on his own. I had to leave during change of shift, but I told him you were coming."

"Tied down?" Rachel asked, her face pinched in disgust.

"He kept trying to pull the tube out when he was dreaming," Jenn explained. "It sounds like it'll be there for a few more hours. I'm sure a doctor will tell us more soon."

They chatted for a few more minutes until Josh's nurse came through the double doors. She was heading home, which meant they could be with Josh again.

"Can I see him?" Rachel asked.

Steve looked at Jenn. She raised her eyebrows and gave a quick nod.

"Sure," Steve said to Rachel. "First Rachel and Sara? Then we'll trade out. Jenn, do you want to go home? Take a nap or a shower?"

Jenn shook her head. "I'm not ready to leave him." Her voice cracked. "I'll go grab some food and then wait out here."

After the girls went back, Jenn said to Steve, "I've been racking my brain for why he'd do this, and I've only come up with one reason that feels right. He got someone pregnant...and she wants to get an abortion!"

"What?" Steve exclaimed.

"What else could bother him so much? Obviously, I didn't ask with the tube in his mouth. We'd help him raise the baby, right? They could live with us?"

Steve rubbed his face and took a deep breath. She knew it was a lot to take in. Jenn gave him a minute to think.

"We'll do whatever needs to be done to make this right, whatever *it* is." Steve sighed and shook his head. "Let's wait to talk to him until he gets home, agreed?"

"Agreed," Jenn said. "I need some coffee."

"Do you want company?"

"Only if you want the joy of a hospital cafeteria early in the morning," Jenn teased lamely.

"In that case I'll pass," Steve said. "I'll just wait here until it's my turn to go in."

"We're gonna get through this, right?" Jenn said.

Steve nodded. "We will, but I just wish I knew what *this* really was."

"Agreed," said Jenn. She squeezed Steven's hand and walked away, hoping their faith would see them through this crisis.

◆ ◆ ◆

It was disorienting to be out here. The rest of the hospital felt vast compared with the cocoon she had been in with Josh all night. Jenn walked down to the cafeteria even though she had no appetite. The food choices felt overwhelming. She settled on a banana and coffee. Standing in line, she was acutely aware of the people around her. She wondered whether anyone else here was going through what her family was. Her gaze flicked across the array of faces of many ages, races, and sizes.

Some were dressed in business clothes, chatting with their colleagues. A few people were in scrubs. She spied a couple at a table. Their red-rimmed eyes told her they weren't here for work. Somehow it made her feel better knowing she wasn't the only person in pain.

A text came through while she was paying for her food. She couldn't manage to juggle it all, so she waited until she finished with the cashier, set the food on a table, and then pulled out her phone.

They're taking out the tube! Steve texted.

Jenn's chest leaped in excitement. That was a great sign. She texted back, *Thank the Lord.*

She walked back to the reception area, where she found Rachel sitting alone.

"How is he?" Jenn asked her daughter.

"Mom, he looks so much better. Just like Josh. Well, maybe like he had the flu or something. But so much better. The nurse said she'd bring him a tray. After he eats and goes to the bathroom, he can leave."

"Really?" Jenn asked.

Rachel shrugged her shoulders. "That's what I heard her say to Dad."

Jenn's stomach unclenched. Soon they would all be home and this would be behind them.

She flipped through old magazines, including the one with the penguins and sperm whales that Rachel was reading last night.

Ding. A text came from Steve: *He's sitting up.*

Ten minutes later Jenn's phone chimed again.

Want to trade? Steve texted.

She replied, *Yes.*

Jenn left Rachel to join her son and oldest daughter. She felt nervous as she walked down the shiny corridor. She'd never felt uncertain around Josh, but she'd never been in a situation like this before. He was sitting up with Sara on the bed right next to him. He laughed at something his sister said. He looked better but also so vulnerable, like a little boy.

A sad smile passed over his face when Josh saw her. Jenn leaned past Sara to give him a hug. He wrapped his arms tightly around her and held on for a long time.

"I'm sorry," he whispered in her ear. "I'm so embarrassed."

She pulled back and looked him in the eye, putting her hand on his cheek. "I'm glad you're all right now. We'll talk more at home.

Just know that I love you. So much. We'll get through this together, with our Lord's guidance and love."

Josh gave a small nod.

A middle-aged white man in a lab coat walked through the curtain and introduced himself. He told them he was the psychiatrist who would be doing Josh's evaluation. Jenn knew this was coming, but it still felt strange. Dr. Post went through a few questions in front of Jenn and Sara and then asked to speak to Josh in private.

Sara and Jenn went out to the waiting room. Jenn was anxious, thinking about what the doctor was asking and how Josh might be answering. After twenty minutes Dr. Post found Jenn and Steve in the waiting area. They walked to a corner of the room so Rachel and Sara couldn't overhear their conversation.

"Your son is cleared to go home." A wave of relief passed through Jenn. "I've written a prescription for an antidepressant. It can take a few weeks to fully take effect. I want to see him next month. Call my office to make an appointment." The psychiatrist handed them two cards. "Here's the name of a therapist. You may choose your own, of course, but Kyle is excellent in this kind of situation, and I recommend him highly."

Jenn was dazed. Josh on antidepressants? Seeing a therapist?

"Are you sure he's depressed?" she questioned the doctor. "He's a great student. A student athlete. He's responsible and respectful."

"Actually, those are the kinds of teens we see here most often. They deal with enormous stresses, and it becomes too much. Josh talked to me about social pressures, especially the overwhelming demand to get into a good college. He said he's been unhappy for some time."

Jenn asked, "He didn't give you any other reasons he might be upset?"

"This was just a screening. The goal is for the antidepressant to give him the floor he needs to handle whatever pressures he is dealing with in a more constructive way than wanting to end his life."

End his life. Those words hit Jenn like bricks to the belly. She looked at her husband with a silent question.

Steve said, "Jenn, we're going to do what the doctors think is best."

"A combination of talk therapy and medication is indicated," the doctor said, "and generally very successful."

"And prayer," Jenn said, recovering her voice. "We'll be praying with and for our son."

The doctor nodded. "Your family is welcome to supplement the recommended treatment however you see fit. I'll see you in my office in four to six weeks. Call if you need anything in the meantime."

7

The family filled the Land Cruiser. Jenn kept turning in her seat so she could see the kids in the back. It was sweet to see Josh sandwiched between Rachel and Sara, with Sara's head leaning against his shoulder.

Jenn was a jumble of feelings. There was an elephant in the room, so to speak. She'd never really understood that saying before, but now she did. They were being smothered by something huge that none of them were mentioning but all of them felt.

Normally the kids were chatty in the car but today they were quiet. Rachel stared out the window, not paying attention to anyone. Sara spoke softly into Josh's ear. He gave a small smile that looked like a lot of effort.

Jenn urgently wanted to think of something to say to make things seem normal again. She racked her brain and finally came up with something. "Rachel and I think we should have a family trip to Monterey soon. We haven't been to the aquarium in a long time." She struggled to make her voice sound casual.

"Can we go to the Santa Cruz Boardwalk, too?" Rachel asked.

"That sounds like fun," Steve said.

"Maybe over Easter break?" Jenn suggested, grateful that Rachel and Steve were enthusiastic.

"Mine's not the same as yours, you know," Sara said.

Jenn gave Sara a questioning look.

"My break is in March," Sara explained. "It's not at Easter; it's the middle of the semester."

Jenn was deflated. "Of course." Jenn nodded. "I guess we can wait until summer."

"No, you go without me," Sara replied. "My schedule probably won't line up with yours, even over the summer."

That was unsettling, but it made sense. Jenn hadn't thought through all the changes college would bring to her family. Soon Josh would be gone. Maybe they'd never have a family vacation again. That was unacceptable.

"We can go to Monterey without you, but we have to take a family vacation this summer. All of us. Agreed?"

"Sure, but I won't know my schedule for a while. Everyone says I need to take a summer class if I want to get out in four years."

"Let's look at the calendar when we get home."

"I won't know what summer session I get until registration in May. Something will work out, Mom, but we can't plan now."

Jenn sat back with a sigh. Her attempt at creating a lighthearted distraction with a trip had backfired. Josh hadn't participated in the conversation at all, and she hadn't succeeded in bringing them together around a vacation. They sat in silence on the rest of the drive home.

As they parked in the garage, Jenn said, "Josh, take a rest before dinner. Do you want company?"

"No, Mom. I want to be by myself," Josh replied. He looked wiped out just from the ride.

"Oh, your room..." Jenn stopped. "I forgot. It's a mess."

Steve broke in. "Rachel and I took care of it."

"What's wrong with my room?" Josh asked, his brows knitted in a question.

"The paramedics…and vomit. Your comforter is ruined," Steve said. "I threw it out. There's a blanket on your bed."

Their son looked horrified. "Sorry, Dad."

Steve replied calmly, "It's OK, Josh."

"Let's talk later," Jenn suggested. "You rest. I'll get dinner ready."

◆ ◆ ◆

After they all ate, Jenn and Steve sat down with Josh in the living room. He sat on one side of their beige sectional sofa, while she and her husband sat on the other. He looked small under the tall cathedral ceiling. She usually loved this more formal space, but now that they were here, she was sorry they weren't having this conversation in the family room.

Their son looked exhausted and frightened. Jenn felt jumpy. She wanted them to say the right thing so that Josh would trust them with whatever was going on. He had always hated disappointing them, more than most kids. Ahead of time they had agreed that Steve would take the lead.

"Josh, we want to understand what happened," Steve said, sounding measured and thoughtful. "We're confused. Very confused. Can you tell us what you were thinking? Were you trying to end your life?"

"No. I wanted to *stop* thinking…about everything. I just wanted a break."

Jenn was suddenly angry. "A break?" she asked. "Twenty-seven sleeping pills for a *break*?"

Josh hung his head and mumbled, "It was stupid, I know. I'm so ashamed. I won't do it again. I promise."

Steve asked, "Is there something you've done that you're ashamed about?"

Josh grabbed a down pillow and hugged it to his stomach. He muttered, "I don't know."

Steve explained, "God can forgive you, whatever your sins. You know that, right? Tell us what's bothering you."

Josh mumbled, "Like I told that doctor, school pressure, college—" He stopped short. They waited for him to keep going, but he didn't say more.

"Josh, there's no taking back suicide. You can't fix it. It's permanent," Steve reminded him. "Your salvation is at stake."

Jenn took a deep breath to calm herself. She knew he was holding something back, so she probed gently, "Whatever is bothering you—grades, college, drugs, girls—can be fixed."

"I don't take drugs—I promise!"

Jenn noticed he didn't mention girls. "Whatever you might need a break from, it is nothing, absolutely nothing, compared with"—she chose her words carefully—"your relationship with God and our Savior. Do you agree?"

Josh nodded without looking up.

Steve said, "Does the Bible say you need to go to college?"

Josh shook his head.

"Your primary obligation is to take care of your soul. If school pressures are too much, then we need to dial back," Steve said. "Do you need to quit the team?"

Josh looked up, panic on his face. "No. Not that, please," he begged.

"Do you need to drop your APs?" Jenn asked.

"No. I'm not doing too much. I don't want to quit anything. That would only make it worse. I'd feel like more of a loser," he mumbled.

Loser! Josh felt like a loser? Jenn was shocked. "Honey, you aren't a loser! How can you say that?"

"I'm so different from everyone else. I pretend, but it's true."

"Because you're Christian?" she asked.

Josh looked between them. He gave a small shake of his head. "I...I can't. I don't know." He shrugged.

"Josh, your faith should be a source of pride," Jenn said sharply.

Steve placed a hand on her knee. She was coming across too harshly. She spoke more gently this time. "Josh, I'm sorry. I was just so scared. We love you. More than you can possibly know."

Josh looked at her and nodded, his expression flat. She had to get through to him.

"I know high school is hard. It will get better—I promise. Can you imagine what might have happened? Your sisters...us. Our lives would have been ruined..." Jenn stared at her son.

Josh nodded, tears in his eyes.

Jenn said, "Next time you feel like that, come to us. To me. With anything."

She let out her breath, looking at Steve and then back at Josh. No one said anything. Josh looked back and forth between his parents and then down at the ground. He seemed dejected. She desperately wanted more from him. She'd hoped to walk away from this conversation with a coherent explanation. She wanted him to tell her what was really going on in his head, but he sat there silently, offering them nothing. As much as she wished she could, she couldn't force him to talk. She racked her brain for the magic words to get him to open up, but nothing more came.

Finally Josh asked, "Anything else?" His voice and face were flat.

Steve replied, "You're not giving us anything, Josh, so we're going to follow the doctor's orders: medicine and therapy."

"And we want you to have counseling with Pastor James," Jenn explained.

Josh hung his head and put his hand in his hair. He grabbed at his roots. With his head still down, he mumbled, "Do I have to?"

"Yeah," Steve said, kindly but firmly.

Josh gave a single nod. "Can I go to my room now?"

Steve nodded as Jenn said, "I suppose."

Josh got up. "I really am sorry."

"We'll get through this, together, with our Lord's guidance." Jenn stood up to hug him. He stood so much taller than her that she doubted her arms were much of a comfort to him. She wished she could just cradle him and pray away his pain like she could when he was young.

Steve wrapped his arms around both of them. "God, help Josh to know that being Your servant is enough. Guide me and Jenn to shepherd him in his time of doubt and fear. Help him to surrender that he may fully know the grace that comes with Your love. In Jesus's name I pray. Amen."

They stepped apart. Jenn hoped the words were a solace and source of strength for their son, but she couldn't tell. His expression was blank.

Jenn asked, "Do you want to go to school tomorrow?"

"Can I have one more day?" Josh asked. "Please."

"Sure," Steve replied.

After Josh was out of earshot, Jenn asked her husband, "Do you think we got through to him at all?"

Steve replied, "He seems genuinely ashamed and sorry, but he didn't explain much, did he?"

"He's hiding something from us," Jenn said. "Did you notice he didn't deny anything about girls? I really think that might be it. It's frustrating that he's not being honest. I'm sorry I lost my temper. I'm tired and confused, but that's no excuse."

"You had a really rough night after a hard day."

"That was the most awful day of my life. I've never been that terrified."

"Me either, Jenn," Steve agreed. "You need sleep. We all do. Hopefully tomorrow will be a reset. You'll be more patient, and maybe Josh will be ready to talk to us. Everything might seem more normal."

"I sure hope you're right."

They all went to bed early that night.

◆ ◆ ◆

In the morning Jenn drove the car pool to school. It felt strange to leave Josh, but he wasn't alone; Sara was home. They were chatting in his room when she left. Maybe he would open up to her.

No one was downstairs when she got back. They had to still be in his room. She went upstairs to offer to make them breakfast. Jenn started to push open the door to his room but stopped when she heard panic in Sara's voice. Jenn stood by the door listening through a small crack.

"Josh, you have to tell them!" Sara insisted.

"I can't. They'll hate me," Josh said. "Do you hate me?" Despair dripped from his words. Josh was crying. He sounded miserable.

Jenn's senses went on high alert. Her lungs tightened as she stood outside the room, scared and confused.

"Oh, Joshy! Of course not," insisted Sara. "I'm afraid for you. I love you. I could never hate you. But you have to tell Mom and Dad. Have you told anyone else?"

"No." He sighed. "I tried telling Pastor James, but I got too scared. You're the first person I've told out loud. How can you not hate me? I feel so unclean...I hate me."

Josh had told Sara the truth. Jenn strained to hear more words, such as *baby* or *pregnant*, but their voices got too quiet. Her own heartbeat was so loud she couldn't hear over it. She started to push the door open but stopped herself. It would be better to ask Sara. Then she'd tell Steve, and they could make a plan before they spoke to Josh.

She had to calm herself. Jenn left her eavesdropping and sought the refuge of her prayer chair. God would guide her. In her personal sanctuary, she asked for strength and handed over her life and Josh's life to the Lord, where they belonged. She returned to her Savior. After she finished praying she was still on alert, but she felt much better as she was making her children breakfast.

"Special treat!" Jenn forced herself to say cheerily as she carried two smoothies into Josh's room. Josh's eyes were red, but Jenn didn't say a word about it. "You can have breakfast up here today."

"Thanks, Mom," Josh said. "But that's OK. We'll come down."

"I have to leave soon. Can you drive me to BART?" Sara asked. "I want to take the ten o'clock train."

"Sure, hon," Jenn replied. "I'll stop by Walgreens on my way home to get the pictures from the game and get your prescription filled."

"I don't want to take any drugs, Mom," Josh said, his voice full of emotion.

Give me strength, Jenn said to God. Out loud she said matter-of-factly, "Josh, I'm not happy about it, either. But the doctor was clear: medicine and therapy. Dad and I agree we're following the doctor's orders. I'll call the counselor he suggested when I get home." More gently she said, "You need something, Josh. They're the experts. We have to trust them."

In a flat tone, Josh conceded, "All right."

"Let's sign you up for the SAT today, too," Jenn said. As soon as the words were out of her mouth, she regretted them. "Sorry. Never mind. We can do that whenever you're ready. No pressure."

"It's OK, Mom," Josh said. But he didn't look OK.

That was so stupid. How could she have brought up college?

"When do you want to leave?" Jenn asked Sara.

"Nine forty-five, 'kay?"

Jenn started to say, "Fine," but then she realized they'd need more time since she wanted to asked Sara about Josh. "How about nine thirty? I want to get to the store before it gets too crowded."

Sara looked puzzled but just said, "I'll be ready."

◆ ◆ ◆

Jenn was preoccupied as she drove. In her mind she considered various ways to bring up the topic: *What's up with Josh?* or *I heard you and Josh talking; what's his secret?* or *I know Josh has a secret, and I know you know what it is.*

"Mom. Mom!" Sara's voice broke into Jenn's thoughts.

"What?"

"You missed the turn." Sara sounded annoyed.

Jenn looked at the road. She pulled over rather than make a U-turn.

"What are you doing, Mom?" Sara challenged. "I'm going to be late."

"Sara," Jenn said cautiously, "I heard you and Josh talking in his room this morning."

Sara's eyes got big, and she bit her lip. "So you know. Are you OK with it?" She looked scared and dubious.

"I don't know what...what 'it' is. I heard you say he should tell us something, and then I heard him crying. What's Josh keeping from us?"

"I can't tell you." Sara shook her head. "You have to ask Josh."

"Honey, clearly he needs help with his situation."

"He trusts me, Mom. I can't betray that. But please ask him. I told him to tell you." Suddenly Sara started sobbing. She put her face in her hands, and her shoulders shook. Sounds came out of her that Jenn hadn't heard since Sara was a preschooler. It broke Jenn's heart.

"Sara." Jenn put her arm around her daughter. "This is too much for you to bear alone. Please tell me. Daddy and I can handle it. Hand over this burden to us."

Sara shook her head but didn't look up.

Jenn started to bristle. "Sara, do you understand how serious this is? Your brother attempted suicide. If you know why, you have to tell us."

"I can't."

A hot wave of anger moved through Jenn. She'd never known Sara to withhold information from her. "You're taking his side against us?"

"I..." Sara tried to speak. Her voice caught. She took a jerky breath. "I...I'm scared, Mom. So scared."

Jenn's eyes welled up too. "Oh, honey...me too."

Sara pulled her seat belt loose and leaned against Jenn, crying onto her chest. Jenn wrapped her arms around her daughter, comforting them both.

"I don't understand," Jenn spoke softly into her daughter's hair. "Why can't you tell me?"

Sara pulled out of Jenn's arms. "I...just...He has to be the one to tell you. It has to be him. I want him to trust me, Mom, so he knows he can...Don't you see?"

"He can confide in me," Jenn told her daughter. "Why doesn't he know that? Is it a baby? We'll help raise it." Jenn stared at Sara for a reaction to her suspicion. There wasn't one. Maybe she was wrong. "Drugs? We'll take him to rehab. There are treatments."

Sara shook her head. Very quietly she said, "I'm not telling you. At least not yet. I told Josh to confide in you. And I begged him not to do anything stupid. I think he got the message."

Jenn sat back in her seat and let out her breath. She wiped her eyes and rubbed her face. Her life was unraveling and Sara knew what was going on with Josh, but wouldn't tell her.

Confused and angry, she sighed and started the car to get Sara to BART. In the parking lot, Sara said, "Mom, I'm not taking Josh's side *against* you. We all have to be on Josh's side. He needs each of us right now."

Jenn spoke sharply. "I never thought you'd keep important secrets from me. Now I don't know what to believe."

"I love you. You can believe that. And so does Josh. He's just confused."

"So am I, Sara," Jenn said. She watched her daughter walk away. She'd hoped this drive would give her answers, but instead she was more confused than when she left home.

8

At Walgreens Jenn acted as if everything were normal. The world went on despite her personal turmoil. She suspected the clerk gave her a knowing look after reading the prescription, but she didn't care. Exhausted even though it was only ten in the morning, she found the cold, hard chair in the waiting area a welcome break. Her eyes followed the black lines that divided the linoleum squares. The receptionist called Josh's name. Normally, Jenn leaped up the moment a prescription was ready. Today she just sat in the tacky plastic chair, avoiding going home until she made a plan for what to do next.

She decided to search Josh's room when she got the chance. She'd never rifled through any of her children's belongings, because she'd never felt the need. But Josh's life was at stake. He had a secret, and she needed to know the truth.

When she got home with the medicine and the photos, Jenn heard the shower running in the kids' bathroom. This was her chance. She rushed to Josh's bedroom, knowing he'd be furious if he caught her, but she was utterly certain of the need. She rummaged through his desk, going through each drawer, looking for anything that looked like a journal. She found a few notebooks, but they were all for schoolwork. Nothing journal-like was in the drawers of his bureau. She rifled through his nightstand and even under his mattress. Her heart caught at the sight of a LEGO Stormtrooper in his nightstand drawer. She paused for a moment, remembering the little boy who built for hours on end. She cleared her head and searched on but found nothing that would reveal his secret to her. Worried about being caught, she slipped out of his room the instant she heard the shower turn off.

Jenn went to the computer in the family room. She went to Google and typed in "How to monitor your kids on the Internet." She clicked on the first article from *Parenting* magazine. Reading through it, she learned about parental controls, MySpace passwords, and search histories.

Listening for Josh, she clicked on "History" and then again on "February 14," the night before Josh took the pills. A list popped down: yahoo.com, myspace.com, and so on. Nothing jumped out. She looked behind her to make sure Josh had not come down quietly. She went back another day and scanned down: Bank of America, Bank of America sign-in, Yahoo, Yahoo sign-in, MySpace, "How many sleeping pills can kill you?"

Jenn's stomach dropped. Her hands got instantly clammy, and her mouth went dry.

The next URL was a gay quiz. After that, another search query: "How do you know if you are gay?" What?! That wasn't what she was expecting to see—it was worse. Her heart squeezed so hard it felt like it might burst.

"Mom?" Josh's voice came from behind her.

She jumped and released the mouse. The search history disappeared. She quickly hit the Back button and was at the Google search page again. Jenn felt pounding in her chest. She hoped her face wasn't flushed. She took a deep breath and forced a calm expression onto her face. Then she turned around.

She looked at Josh and asked neutrally, "What?"

"I just want to tell you that you're right," he said. "I need to talk with someone—and you were right about the medicine, too. I'm sorry I was being difficult."

"I'm sorry too, Josh." Jenn kept her voice calm while her head and chest were exploding. "We only want what's best for you. We can't help you if you won't tell us what's wrong. Do you understand that?"

Josh nodded.

"Is there anything you want to tell me?" Jenn pushed. Maybe he would just come out with it. He looked like he wanted to say something. Unconsciously, she held her breath. She wanted his trust.

Josh shook his head.

She exhaled with a sigh. "All right. I'll call the therapist now," she told him.

"Can I use the computer?" he asked.

"What for?" Jenn asked, trying to sound casual.

"A school project. I have an essay on the Civil War due at the end of the week."

"Don't push yourself too hard."

"I won't."

"Let me just finish what I'm doing." Jenn turned back to the computer. Josh walked into the kitchen, and she closed the windows from her search.

Jenn walked carefully up the stairs, breathing deeply to fend off panic. Her world was coming apart more than she could possibly have imagined. Homosexual? Her Josh? It made no sense. She sat on her bed, her mind reeling as she considered what to do. Her whole body shook. Her immediate impulse was to ask Josh about the search.

But she didn't want to face the answer alone.

◆ ◆ ◆

Jenn's hands shook as she dialed Steve's work number. He didn't pick up. She went to her chair to pray: *Merciful God, by the power of Your command, drive away from my son all forms of sickness and disease. Restore strength to his body and joy to his spirit so that, in his renewed health, he may bless and serve You, now and forevermore. Please, God, help me to understand or at least accept the path You have put us on. In Jesus's name I pray. Amen.*

She felt a little bit better but not normal. Sitting on the edge of the bed, her leg jiggling up and down, Jenn dialed Steve again.

"What's up?" he asked on the other end.

"It's me." Jenn started to cry. "I'm sorry to bother you." Her voice was high and cracking. "I just don't know what to do."

"Did Josh hurt himself again?" Steve asked, panic in his voice.

"No, but I'm afraid he's going to. I overheard him and Sara talking about a secret. He was very upset. I wanted to know why, so I looked up how to spy on him on the computer. Last week he searched on Google about being…" She faltered. "About being *homosexual*"—she whispered the word—"and how to kill himself." Just saying it out loud made her feel ill.

Sounding confused, he asked, "Are you sure?"

"I'm sure I saw that search history," Jenn explained. "I'm afraid he thinks he's homosexual."

"What did you say to him?" Steve asked, his voice tight and controlled.

"Nothing. I was too upset. I wanted to calm down and talk to you first. What should we do?" The line was silent. "Steve? Are you there?"

"Yes, I'm thinking. You're sure he thinks *he's* the homosexual and he's not just looking on behalf of a friend?"

"No, I'm not certain of anything," she replied. "I haven't spoken to him. You think it might not be him?" Hope rose in her chest.

"Let's talk to him together when I get home. OK?"

"Mom!" Josh yelled up the stairs, startling Jenn. She wondered whether he'd overheard. She felt guilty but reminded herself that she was only helping her son.

"OK, together, tonight," Jenn told Steve. "Please leave early if you can. It's going to be hard to be with him and not ask him about this. Josh is calling, so I have to go. I love you."

"I love you too. Stay strong." Then he hung up.

Strong. Jenn did not feel very strong.

She took a deep breath to calm herself and draw in energy. Keeping her voice light, she yelled down to her son, "Yes?"

"Should I make myself lunch?"

"No. I'll be down in a sec, after I finish a phone call."

"Thanks, Mom."

He sounded just like her Josh, not like a…homosexual. It just didn't make any sense to her. He was devout and kind. Why would he possibly choose to be hurtful to himself and them? Jenn picked up the card on her nightstand and dialed the therapist's number.

She reached his voice mail. A kind, calm voice invited her to leave a message.

Jenn spoke into her phone. Her voice was shaky and weak. "Hi. My name is Jenn Henderson. I got your name from Dr. Post at Eden. My son…He thinks…My son. My son may have attempted suicide. We hope you can help him." She left her home and cell numbers and hung up.

She couldn't even admit that Josh had hurt himself on purpose. That was a phone call that Jenn had never made before and had never expected to make.

Dear God, give me strength.

◆ ◆ ◆

In the kitchen Jenn put on a calm face. She pulled out a can of tomato soup, Swiss cheese, and sourdough bread. Fox News ran in the background, but she didn't really listen to it as she made Josh's lunch. While she was cooking, he came in and set the table without being asked. He was such a thoughtful person; he couldn't be a homosexual.

She slid a golden-brown grilled cheese onto the plate in front of him and then set a bowl of warm red soup next to it.

"You made my favorite. Thanks, Mom." He looked like he was about to cry.

"Of course. You're my favorite son." She smiled, feeling teary herself. This was their long-standing joke. When he was younger, he'd always replied, "Aw, Mom, I'm your only son." He'd stopped saying that some time ago. When did that happen? There were so many little endings in her children's lives that it was impossible to track them all.

Today he just looked at her and shook his head with a small smile. He grabbed a half of the sandwich and dipped it in the soup. She watched as he took the first bite. She longed to say more but was at a loss for words. Instead she put her own lunch out and washed the pan in silence.

When she finished cleaning up, she came up behind Josh and wrapped her arms around his shoulders. He put his hand over hers. She leaned over and kissed the top of his dark-brown hair. She was full with adoration for her son. Could he feel the love she poured into him? She said a silent prayer: *Lord, heal my son in mind, body, and spirit. Help him, and me, to be the best instruments for Your will. Amen.*

Her cell phone rang from the other room. She gave Josh a squeeze and went to answer. It was the therapist.

"Thank you for calling me back," Jenn said.

"Of course," the kind, calm voice came through the phone. "Can you tell me a bit more about what's been happening with your son?"

"Yes. Let me get somewhere private," she whispered.

Jenn walked upstairs to her bedroom, closed the door, and sat on the edge of her bed. "Well, he...I don't...What do you want to know?"

"You mentioned an attempt at suicide. Is he stable now? Is he home? Tell me about that."

"On Sunday, while we were at church—we're Christians—he took twenty-seven sleeping pills. Ambien. They were mine from a trip last summer. I had no idea he would do that, or I would have thrown them out. We didn't know he was depressed."

"Has his mood changed recently?" he asked.

"He's been quieter, but he's sixteen. We expect him to tell us less, to be more private."

"Do you know what may be bothering him?"

"Well, he told the doctor at the hospital that school pressure was hard," Jenn explained. She started to leave it at that but then went on. It was hard to say out loud. "I also have a small idea that he might be confused…He might think he is homosexual." Jenn choked up a bit. She cleared her throat and took a deep breath to calm herself.

"What makes you think that?"

"On the Internet he did a search for 'How do you know you are homosexual?' You know, on Google. It's probably for a friend. I'm just telling you what I saw."

"Have you talked to him about this?" Kyle sounded curious.

"Not yet. I just found this today. His father and I want to talk to him together. He can't be homosexual. He knows it's a sin."

"I see," Kyle said calmly. "It makes sense why he might be troubled."

"Can you help him?" Jenn asked.

"I believe so."

Jenn felt relieved; her shoulders loosened, and her breath came easier. She hadn't realized it, but she was already attached to the idea that this man could fix her son.

Kyle went on. "We need to meet each other so he can decide if we're a good match. It's a very personal decision, working with a therapist. He needs to feel I'm the right fit for him. I assume you would like an appointment after school. I have time in my schedule on Thursday at four."

"He has basketball practice," Jenn explained. "Sorry to be difficult."

"It's no problem," Kyle replied. "I have morning appointments, and...I have Mondays at seven. Will that work?"

"Yes, thank you. Very much." Jenn's voice was high and tight, and she knew the therapist could tell she was upset.

"You're welcome. This is hard on all of you. It's natural to have strong feelings."

Jenn nodded even though he couldn't see her. She didn't trust her voice.

Kyle gave her his address and other details. By the time she'd collected herself, Josh had finished lunch. She found him in his room.

Jenn leaned on the doorframe. "I just spoke to Kyle Goss, the therapist. You have an appointment with him on Monday at seven." She hoped she sounded calm and normal, though she didn't feel that way.

Josh's eyes widened in alarm. "What did you tell him?"

Jenn paused to search for the right words. "I told him you were under stress, that you took a lot of sleeping pills, and that we're Christian. He seemed to think he could be helpful. He sounded nice, Josh. I think you'll like talking with him."

"I guess." Josh shrugged.

"I'll be downstairs if you need anything. Rachel will be home around three thirty. Lindsay's dropping her off today." She paused to say more, but nothing came. She felt a giant wall separating her and Josh. She hoped the conversation tonight would tear it down—or let her know that it was never really there.

Jenn made another of Josh's favorites for dinner: lasagna. While she cooked she ruminated over the previous forty-eight hours. She was so distracted that she nearly burned the onions beyond use. *Trust in the Lord. Stay calm*, she reminded herself. She wanted to finish dinner so it would be in the oven before Steve got home. The sound of the front door opening and closing told her Rachel was back from school.

"I'm in the kitchen," she called to her daughter.

"How's Josh?" Rachel whispered as she got close.

"Better. A lot better. We had a sweet day." She kept her voice light. She was not about to share her discovery with Rachel. "How was your day?"

"Not good. I was too worried about Josh to pay any attention. I know I'm going to fail my geometry test on Friday."

Jenn crossed to her youngest child and gave her a hug. This was turning her life upside down, too.

Rachel clung to Jenn. "Is he going to be OK? People at school asked. I didn't know what to say."

"Just say he was sick and he's better now. That's all. Did people hear he was in the hospital?"

Rachel nodded. "I guess James told his friends, and it spread."

Jenn's stomach churned. "I'm sorry, Rachel. It really isn't anyone's business. He'll be at school tomorrow. They'll see for themselves that he's fine."

"Is he? Really OK?" Rachel asked eagerly.

"I'm not going to lie to you," Jenn replied. "He's struggling with something big. But I have faith that God will heal him. Have you been praying for Josh?"

"I start, but I don't know what to pray."

"I'll give you my favorite. It helps me—a lot. Say it three or four times a day. Whenever you find yourself worrying about him, just say the prayer. Hand over your fear and sadness to the Lord."

Jenn went to the computer in the family room, typed out the prayer, and printed it for her daughter:

"Almighty and merciful God, dear Lord Jesus, by the power of Your command, drive away from my brother all forms of sickness and disease. Restore strength to his body and joy to his spirit so that, in his renewed health, he may bless and serve You, now and forevermore. In Jesus's name we pray. Amen."

Jenn's phone vibrated. She flipped it open and saw a text message.

Did u talk 2 josh? Sara texted.

Jenn replied, *Not yet. waiting 4 dad 2 come home.*

K ILY.

Jenn looked up from her phone and asked Rachel, "What does *ILY* mean?"

"I love you." Rachel laughed. "You're so cute, Mom." Then she went back into the kitchen for a snack.

Jenn was proud of herself for texting at all. And now she was supposed to remember what all these letters meant? It was hard to keep up with these new things.

9

Jenn occupied herself with cooking, laundry, and helping Rachel with homework while she waited for Steve to get home. Josh stayed in his room. *Don't borrow trouble*, she reminded herself each time the word *homosexual* popped into her head. She resisted the urge to check on him constantly and was glad for the excuse to see him to deliver clean and folded clothes.

Josh sat at his desk, doing schoolwork. He looked great, just like her boy. It wasn't obvious that he had been in the hospital, except a spark was missing from his eyes. He looked wistful or melancholy. Not really depressed—just subdued or maybe resigned.

"You OK, honey?" Jenn asked with a small smile.

"Fine, Mom," he said in a flat tone. "Thanks for doing my laundry."

Then his attention went back to his book. She wanted to hug him, to pour faith and energy into his body. She longed for the perfect prayer to bring her son back to his real self. But she didn't know one, so she just left.

◆ ◆ ◆

She heard Steve pull into the garage. Her heart skipped a beat. She was about to find out the truth. She held back from pouncing on him right away, instead waiting for him to find her in the kitchen. He walked in while she was loading the dishwasher and gave her a peck on the cheek; she hugged him with a sigh.

"Do you know what you're going to say?" Jenn asked, looking up at him from their embrace.

"More or less."

"Do you think he could be…?" Jenn couldn't even say the word. It hurt too much.

He shrugged but looked resigned. "Let's talk to him, and then we'll know where we stand. Or at least know more about where we stand."

"You think it's true, don't you?" she asked quietly.

"He's always been a little different. He never asked if he could date. That's strange."

Jenn's anxiety grew again. Pressure built at the back of her eyes. "I can't stand this anymore. I just want to know—one way or the other. Can we go talk to him now?"

Steve nodded, and Jenn led the way upstairs. Steve knocked and then walked in without waiting for an answer.

Josh was lying in bed on his back with his eyes closed. His lids opened, and his head tilted forward. After a brief glance at each of his parents, he put his head back down and pulled his comforter over his face. Jenn furrowed her brows at Steve. They walked to his twin bed, one on each side.

"Josh, sit up, please," Steve said. "We need to speak with you about something very important."

Josh didn't move.

"Joshua!" Jenn scolded.

His covers moved like he was shaking his head back and forth. This was totally out of character.

"Complete and immediate obedience, Josh," Steve said, which he hadn't done since Josh was little.

A small voice came from under the covers: "I can't. I can't look at you. I'm so ashamed of myself. I just want to die."

Jenn had never heard him sound so miserable. Her chest squeezed tight with empathy. She knelt by Josh and hugged him over the covers, but he just shrugged her off.

"If you really knew me, you would hate me," Josh mumbled under the blankets.

"Josh, we can never hate you," Jenn said. She looked at her husband. Tears were streaming down his face. The last time she saw him cry was at Rachel's birth. She took a deep breath.

God, hold our family in Your care during this time of struggle. Guide our son back to Your path. Amen. Jenn reached for Steve's hand, her own hand shaking. Steve sat on the bed, and their arms rested on the covers over Josh.

"We're going to help you, son," Steve said. "I've been doing research. There are cures."

Josh asked, "Cures for what?"

Steve said quietly, "Same-sex attractions. Homosexuality."

The word pierced Jenn.

Josh moaned. His body shook, and sobs came from under the covers. Like Steve, Jenn felt tears slide down her cheeks. She was glad Josh could not see them. They weren't being the model of strong, confident parents. Jenn was absolutely terrified for her son.

"Sara told you?" Josh asked, still under the covers.

He hadn't denied it.

Though she'd been expecting this, it was like a blow to her stomach. She resisted the string of questions swirling in her head: *How do you know? Are you sure? Who did this to you?*

Instead she explained, "I saw your Google search in the history on our computer. Well, first I heard you telling Sara that we would hate you if we knew your secret. I asked Sara to tell me, but she wouldn't."

"Who have you told?" Josh sounded desperate.

Gently she reassured him, "Just Daddy. I haven't told anyone else." Jenn felt weak all over. She couldn't believe she was having this conversation. What could possibly have caused her son to think he was homosexual?

"Don't tell anyone," Josh begged. "I'm so ashamed."

"We should speak with Pastor James," Steve said. "He loves you, Josh. He can be our guide for treatment. There are good cures. I have great faith you won't have to live with this for your whole life."

"Are you sure?" came a small but hopeful voice.

"I looked into it after Mom called me. It'll be hard work, and you have to be committed to a cure, but the websites are very clear that treatment is one hundred percent effective," Steve explained.

"I'm committed. You know I am. Right? I've been praying to be cured since first grade."

"First grade?" Jenn was stunned. "Since you were *six*?"

The covers moved in a nod.

"Oh, honey." Jenn started crying again. "Ten years! You've been living alone with this for that long? I'm so sorry." She bent and kissed the blankets over her son's head. Steve wrapped his arms around both of them, and they cried and rocked together.

Then Steve spoke: "God, in Your name I pray. Lord Jesus Christ, I put my son's life in Your hands, where it has always been. Please heal my dear son, Josh, of the affliction in his soul. Take away impure longings. Make him strong in mind, body, and spirit that he may live Your will on earth and in the hereafter. Amen."

A calm silence filled the room when the prayer was over. Jenn felt the Holy Spirit come into her body with each breath. She hoped Josh felt it, too.

"Pastor James can know," Josh said, still hidden under the blanket.

"Oh, Josh. That's a very wise and mature decision," Jenn said. "Would you like to tell him, or should I?"

"You."

"He'll want us all to come in for pastoral counseling. Will you speak to him?"

"Yes."

"That's great, Son. You're really showing your dedication," Steve said. "I know it's hard. I'm proud of you."

A sniffle came from Josh.

"Do you want to come?" Jenn asked Steve.

"Of course. First or last part of the day is best, but I'll make anything work."

"You already missed work on Monday," Josh said. "You can't miss any more because of me."

"Josh, your well-being is more important than work." Steve was clear.

Josh pulled the covers back. His face was blotchy and red and his eyes puffy. Jenn's heart twisted. He sat up and leaned back against his headboard.

"Are you sure?" he asked. "I'm sorry to be such a problem."

"I'm absolutely sure," Steve said to their son. "Nothing is more important than my children's souls."

Josh looked back and forth between Jenn and Steve. "You really don't hate me?" he asked, longing and desperation in his eyes.

The question broke Jenn's heart. To imagine that Josh had been living in fear of their disapproval all these years. They both shook their heads.

"We love you, Josh," Steve said, "and only want what's best for you. As a family, we're going to do everything to find a cure. Absolutely everything."

Steve spoke Jenn's deepest feeling out loud. For the first time in many days, things were falling into place. This was a test of their faith.

Jenn said, "Josh, we're going to work on this together, as a family. We'll come through this knowing God's love and Jesus's power more than ever."

Josh leaned forward. Jenn wrapped her arms around him, and Steve wrapped his arms around her. She didn't pull away until her son was ready to let go.

◆ ◆ ◆

Jenn hated to bother Pastor James at home in the evening, but this was an emergency.

His voice came through after the third ring: "Pastor James speaking."

"Hello, Pastor. This is Jenn Henderson. We're...having a family crisis—" And then her voice broke; she couldn't go on.

"Take your time. God's in no rush. I'm so glad you called. I'm ready whenever you are."

Jenn cleared her throat and took a breath. "Josh is concerned that he might be a—" The word caught in her throat. Saying it out loud made it too real. "—homosexual."

There was a distinct pause. "Oh, dear! I'm so sorry, Jenn. Is he acting angry or proud?"

"Not at all. He's very ashamed."

"That's good news. Great news indeed. Praise God! Has he acted on his feelings?"

"No!" Jenn was horrified. "Well, actually I don't know." She hadn't even considered the possibility.

"Has he mentioned that he has a...special friend?"

"No."

"We can find out together. I'd like you all to come in for some pastoral counseling. Right away. There are effective treatments. We want to prevent Josh from venturing into the homosexual lifestyle. Can you come in tomorrow at nine? I'll cancel my morning meeting."

Jenn was so grateful that she hardly had the words to express herself. "Thank you. Of course we'll come. What do we need to do?"

"Bring your Bible to my office. We're going to hand his life over to our Lord Jesus Christ. Josh is going to be an example of the healing power of faith in God and His Son."

Before bed, Jenn looked through the websites that Steve had mentioned. There were great Christian-based treatments. They spoke of complete transformation if you followed their program and surrendered your life to Jesus. It didn't take away Jenn's anxiety completely, but it was reassuring to know there was something that could be done to save her son.

◆ ◆ ◆

Josh looked nervous as they pulled into the church parking lot the next morning. The large modern church sanctuary was to the right. Church offices were straight ahead. Tension was thick as they walked on the straight cement path. Jenn noticed a small yellow crocus poking up among the plantings. She considered pointing it out to Josh but decided against it.

Instead, she said to him, "I'm proud of you, honey. This is the next step in your recovery."

Pastor James warmly welcomed them into his office. He was a very average-looking man: thin, medium height, mousy brown hair, and brown eyes. He gestured to the chairs in front of his desk, wordlessly inviting them to sit. Jenn directed Josh to sit between her and Steve so he'd feel their support from all sides. Pastor James settled into the chair behind his desk.

He began by addressing Josh. "Your mother tells me you're having homosexual feelings. Is she correct? Are you?"

Jenn was shocked that he jumped in so brashly. Josh stared at the desk and nodded wordlessly.

"Have you acted upon the feelings?"

Josh squeezed his eyes shut, and his face turned red. He looked so uncomfortable; Jenn was embarrassed on his behalf. She was relieved that he gave a quick shake of his head.

"Congratulations, Josh," Pastor James said enthusiastically. "The ability to refrain from the lifestyle is a strong indicator for successful treatment. Other indicators are family support and commitment and the intention to follow our Lord Jesus Christ."

That sounded good to Jenn. Josh had all those.

Pastor James continued. "Both your parents are here today. Strong family support. Check! Are you willing to do what you need to do to help your son with this affliction?"

"Absolutely, Pastor," Steve said. "A hundred percent. We'll do whatever it takes for Josh to return to righteousness."

Jenn nodded enthusiastically, wanting to show Pastor James her commitment.

"Josh, are you committed to living biblically?" the pastor asked.

Josh looked up. He stared straight at the man across from him and said clearly, "More than anything I want to be right with the Lord Jesus Christ. I want my shame to be gone."

"Well, you've come to the right place. We'll start with prayer. We'll end with prayer. It always comes back to prayer, to your relationship with the Lord. We'll pray in your home, in your room, in youth group. You'll be an example, Josh, for our whole community. You have a special calling: to show sinners who are less committed and weaker a true and righteous path toward God's love."

Jenn thought the pastor was putting too much pressure on Josh. Being an example for the whole community was a lot to ask of a teenager. She considered saying something, but before she could work out a response, Pastor James spoke again.

"Let us pray." He bowed his head and reached out his hands. The four of them made a circle of connection.

"Jesus, in Your name we pray. Lord, help Your child Josh to know he is not alone in his misery but rather that You love him deeply. Remind him that You do not condemn him for homosexual feelings and temptations and that You only ask him to desire a righteous path. Turn him away from homosexual lust and relations. Turn his thoughts away from a destructive course and toward a wholesome path. May Your servant Josh discipline his mind for Jesus as he disciplines his body for basketball.

"Lord, release Josh from the hold of the devil. Drive the evil from his soul. Jesus Christ, deliver Josh from his present state of mind so that he can be free to live a morally dignified lifestyle. Lord Jesus, uncover the deep needs at the root of Josh's same-sex desires.

"Lord, guide Josh's parents, Jenn and Steve. They are Your willing servants, no matter how hard the road. Dig deep into their souls that they may discover the cause of his homosexuality. They have failed You in some way, Lord. They are ready to do better. Forgive them as they repent of their sins. In Your name we pray. Amen."

Jenn felt the weight of the truth—they had failed as parents. She didn't know where they had gone wrong, but she fiercely committed to do better as they sat in silence in their sacred circle. Jenn gave Josh's hand a squeeze before they unclasped hands.

Pastor James said, "We can start on your recovery right now. I know this will sound harsh, but there are very clear steps that will lead to your healing. Josh, trade places with your father. Jenn, they need to work on their relationship. A proven factor in male homosexuality is desperate longing for connection with the male parent. Steve, I'm sure you did not intend for Josh to have a defensive attachment. It happens when fathers are not committed to their children. Josh needs to increase his masculinity by spending less time with Jennifer and more time with Steve participating in traditionally male activities."

Not committed to his children? Steve? Jenn was doubtful about Pastor James's thinking, but she was glad to have something clear and concrete to do to fix Josh.

"My dad's around as much as any of the dads," Josh pointed out. "Well, more, since he doesn't commute. And he coached my soccer team."

Steve said, "Josh, don't argue." He stood up and pointed to his chair. Josh slid over.

Pastor James explained, "Josh, I imagine you think you have a close relationship with your father. But you wouldn't be having these feelings if you truly did." Then he went on more gently. "As I said, this is going to be hard to hear. No family wants to know that they have damaged their child. But if treatment is going to work, you have to be committed."

"We are committed," Steve insisted. "It's just…well, you're right; it's hard to hear."

"Of course. This is a lot to take in," Pastor James said, kindly but firmly. "I'll tell you a few more things before our time is up. Then I'll give you a booklet and some other resources that you can take your time with at home."

Jenn's mind was reeling. Was she really too attached to Josh? He'd been special to her because he was the boy. But he and Steve seemed as close as any other father and son. Steve was much more involved than her dad had ever been, and her brother, Tim, wasn't homosexual.

"You will also need to find a cause of trauma," Pastor James went on. "Most likely sexual trauma. A babysitter, a grandparent, a teacher. Some male figure in his life sexually abused Josh."

Molested. The word stabbed at her. She felt sick. She had immediately thought that someone probably made Josh homosexual, and now Pastor James was confirming that belief. Jenn desperately wanted to know who had done this to her son.

"Nothing like that ever happened to me!" Josh declared.

"Most people can't remember," Pastor James replied knowingly. "But it is a fact that homosexual feelings are caused by sexual abuse. Did he go to childcare when he was young?"

"No, of course not," Jenn said. "I was home with my children, like I am now."

"Perhaps at a gym for a short time?"

"Yes, I took them to childcare at the gym," Jenn replied. "He always loved it."

Pastor James nodded. "Yes, some kids crave that attention, because it is missing from their male parent."

"They were all girls at the gym," Jenn said.

"The men hide in the back until parents are gone. They're very sneaky." Pastor James held up his hands and waved off more comments. "We won't be able to uncover this now. It will take a lot of time with a qualified counselor."

"We have an appointment on Monday," Jenn told him. She was hopeful she had done something right. "I got the name of a therapist from a doctor."

"Is he a Christian counselor? That's very, very important. I can't emphasize that enough. You do not want someone encouraging these thoughts...or behaviors." Pastor James shivered.

"I'll ask," Jenn said. "I hadn't even thought of that. This is very overwhelming."

"Prayer will help with your confusion. Nothing is as clarifying as prayer and building your relationship with Christ. He will take away these sinful thoughts and feelings, if you really believe in Him. The pamphlet I'll give you will have some specific prayers. You can't say them too often to shore up your faith. Prayer will be the wall of defense against Josh's unnatural lusts. And Josh," he added, holding up a finger, "pray as if your life depends on it, because it does."

Pastor James continued. "Josh, you are not alone in this struggle. Many young people have succeeded in being cured. I know you'll be one of them. I highly, highly recommend that you go to an Exodus or Resurrection Ministries program as soon as possible. You'll meet so many inspiring Christians. It will give you faith and strength like nothing else. Your family can go together. Do you have any questions?"

The three of them stared at Pastor James. Speechless, Jenn glanced at her son and husband. They looked as stunned as she felt. It was truly too much to take in. She felt sick and hopeless, back on the roller coaster of horrible feelings. The all-consuming combination of anxiety, sadness, and confusion threw her back to how she felt the day she called the ambulance. Josh was abused? She was too close to Josh? She and Steve had caused him to have homosexual attractions? They weren't praying right? It was hard to know where to begin. All the confidence she felt as a parent crumbled away.

Finally, holding in his emotions, Steve said tightly, "No. Thank you for your time."

"Of course. Let's end with prayer." They took hands. Pastor James began. "Almighty and merciful God, by the power of Your command, drive away from Josh all forms of sickness and disease. Guide Your son Josh in choosing Your Son over all other distractions. Bring the Holy Spirit into this family that they may root out the causes of trauma and evil that are infecting their lives and keeping them separate from Your love. In Your name we pray, Lord Jesus Christ. Amen."

Pastor James handed Jenn a pamphlet. When she opened up her bag to put it away, the sight of the Walgreens Photo Center envelope stopped her short. She started to pull it out but stopped, instead just following Steve out the door.

Once they were in the hallway, she told Josh and Steve she had forgotten something and went back to Pastor James's office. She tapped on the door and walked in after he yelled for her to come in.

He looked calm and unconcerned, like he had completely moved on from their conversation. With a shaky hand, she reached into her bag and handed an envelope to Pastor James, explaining, "Pictures, from the witness on Saturday. I made doubles because I thought you'd want them."

"Thank you, Jenn. You are so thoughtful! We'll get these up on our public-ministry board as soon as possible," Pastor replied. "God bless you."

10

Jenn held in her tears in the car. *Abused.* The word was a vise grip on her heart. How could she have been so oblivious and naive? She desperately wanted to reach back and grab Josh's hand, to apologize and ask for his forgiveness. But apparently that was part of the problem: she needed to discourage their connection. Holding herself back was his treatment.

"Jenn, I'll take you home," Steve said. "Then I can drop Josh off at school before I head to work."

Josh sat forward, poking his head between their seats. "I can't face school after that. Can I please just go home?"

"Of course," Jenn said.

Steve looked over at her. He shook his head, eyebrows raised. What was he trying to signal? That Josh should go to school after all he'd been through?

"Josh, you have to man up," Steve said flatly. "No more lying around feeling sorry for yourself. School. Practice. Home. And then youth group. You've got to get back in the game. Sorry, dude."

Jenn looked back at Josh. He looked ready to cry. He sat back hard against the backseat. "All right."

"Do you have everything you need?" Jenn asked. "Your lunch and backpack?"

Steve gave her a glare. Oh! She was doing it again. This was going to be hard. She was so used to caring for her son. Pulling back from that was going to be a huge adjustment.

◆ ◆ ◆

The phone was ringing as she walked into the house. She went to the family room to see who was on the line: her parents. It was probably her mom, since her dad rarely called. She wasn't ready for a conversation yet, so Jenn let the machine pick up.

Her mom's voice came through after the beep. "Jennifer, it's Mom. I'd like to know how Joshy is doing. Please call me when you can. You're all in our prayers, of course. My morning spirit circle is praying for all of you too. Love you. Call me back as soon as you can."

Suddenly exhausted, Jenn sank down on the sage-colored couch. Her eyes glazed, and she stared at the blank TV across from her. There was a slight reflection from the windows. She saw bits of dust on the screen sparkling in the sunlight. If she weren't so tired, she would hop up and clean it, but she just wanted to sit. Her mind was a jumble of thoughts. She wondered how Josh was doing… He'd probably just gotten to school. Hopefully Steve had walked him in, because he didn't have a note.

She considered calling Sara or Lindsay or Mom to let them know what Pastor James told them. It was difficult to believe Josh had been abused, but Pastor James was so certain. Her mind rifled through every adult they knew, every occasion when Josh was out of her sight. She thought about Thanksgivings at Steve's aunt and uncle's house. He used to take naps there alone in a room. Or

Christmas at their parents' house. Or gatherings at the Bishops'. Or church. The list went on and on. He'd been out of her sight hundreds of times before he started kindergarten.

To stop the thoughts, she tried praying but couldn't get in the right state of mind and spirit. Instead she turned on the TV, something she normally only did during the day when she was really sick. But she needed a diversion. She flipped the channels until she came to *Family Feud*. That would be distracting enough. When it finished, she considered getting up to do laundry but instead watched *The View*. In the middle of the show, the phone rang. It was her mom again. She sighed, turned off the TV, and picked up.

"Hi, Mom. How are you?"

"Fine. How is Joshy?"

"Josh is struggling. He's still struggling." She did her best to keep her voice even. "We had pastoral counseling today. It's good to feel the support of the church. I know it will help. And your prayers too."

"I'm sorry, sweetie."

"Me too, Mom." A tear leaked from Jenn's right eye. "It's laundry day. I have to get it finished before I get Rachel. Thanks for your prayers. We need them."

"Can't you tell me more about what he's struggling with? Specific prayers are more beneficial."

Jenn took a deep breath. "I'm having a hard time understanding, myself, Mom."

"I know I'm an old lady, but that just means I've seen a lot of life," her mother stated clearly.

Jenn smiled to herself. She hated to keep anything from her mom. Although she knew Josh wouldn't like it, she knew that her mom could be trusted with this. She said, "Well, Mom, he's struggling with homosexual thoughts."

"Oh, dear," her mom said slowly. After a long pause, she asked, "Are you sure?

"We're not sure of anything," Jenn said quietly. "We're getting treatment. Pastor James is confident that Josh is a great candidate for therapy."

"Well, that's good. I imagine it's from living so close to San Francisco. You may want to move back home, you know. Have him in an environment more conducive to Christian values."

Jenn rolled her eyes. Her mother had been trying to get her to move back to Orange County since 1987, the year Jenn and her family moved to Dublin. Of course she would use this opportunity to make her case yet again. "Good try, Mom."

"You can't blame me for wanting my kids close."

"No, I can't," Jenn agreed. "And now I'm starting to see things from your side."

Tenderly her mom said, "I'm sorry things are hard…for Joshy and for you. I love you both, very much."

"Thanks, Mom. I love you, too."

"We're praying for your family."

"That means a lot to me." Jenn's voice cracked.

"All things are possible with God."

"I keep reminding myself that He is walking right next to me."

"Yes, He is. God loves you, and Josh, more than we can possibly understand. Reach out to Him whenever you need comfort. And to me, too, dear."

"Thanks, Mom." Suddenly Jenn started to sob. "Mom?"

"Yes?"

"Pastor James says someone sexually abused Josh."

"What?" her mom questioned.

"That's a cause of same-sex attractions."

"Oh, honey. Are you sure?" Pain and confusion came through the phone.

"I'm sure he said it. It's made me realize that Josh was away from me hundreds of times when he was little. I thought I'd done such a good job with them. Now I know I didn't."

"Jenn, you and Steve are great parents. What does Josh say?"

"Josh doesn't remember being hurt, but Pastor says that means he repressed it or was too young," Jenn explained, her voice high and tight.

"I don't know that that's true. Pastor James must be mistaken."

"I wish you were right." Jenn felt sick inside with the enormity of telling her mom about her failure.

"I am right," her mom insisted.

It was sweet to hear that her mom had faith in her as a parent, even if Jenn didn't believe it anymore. "I'm glad you know, Mom. Don't tell anyone. OK? Not even Dad, please."

"Oh, honey, I won't. But your father won't condemn Josh, or you. God is the only judge. You know that, right?"

Jenn knew her mom was trying to be a comfort, but she wasn't succeeding. She didn't understand the secular influences that could pressure Josh into thinking the homosexual lifestyle was acceptable. Suddenly, Jenn was too overwhelmed to keep talking. She nodded and muttered something noncommittal. "I gotta go, Mom. Give Daddy my love. 'Bye."

Jenn hung up, not even certain her mom had said good-bye.

◆ ◆ ◆

After dinner, Steve took Josh and Rachel to youth group. Usually Jenn did the driving, but this way Steve and Josh had more time together. When Steve and the kids got home, Jenn waved from the family-room couch where she was watching *American Idol*. Josh ignored her and stormed upstairs, obviously upset. Steve and Rachel came into the family room.

"What happened?" Jenn asked, her brows furrowed with a question.

Steve shrugged. They both looked at Rachel for an answer.

"Pastor James asked everyone to pray for him," their daughter explained. "He said Josh has been having impure thoughts. Josh got so embarrassed that he turned totally red. What's Pastor talking about?"

"Oh, dear," Jenn said. She patted the couch, indicating that Rachel should sit next to her. Steve sat in the recliner.

Jenn eyed Steve. He eyed her back. She guessed he wanted her to take the lead on this one. She was hesitant to tell Rachel without asking Josh first; she'd already broken her agreement with him by telling her mom, but she didn't want Rachel hearing this from anyone else, so she plunged ahead.

"Your brother has been having some homosexual thoughts."

"Josh is gay?" Rachel exclaimed, her eyes wide with shock.

"No," Jenn corrected, "Josh is not a homosexual. He's confused. He understands this and is working on healing. Dad and I are getting him treatment."

Steve spoke up. "We don't want this to change how you feel about him. Josh is still a good person."

"In fact," Jenn said, "his honesty and commitment make me even more proud of him. If anything, you should have more respect for your brother, not less."

Rachel looked confused but nodded.

"Do you have any questions?" Steve asked.

Rachel asked, "Does Sara know?"

"Yes," Steve replied. "Josh confided in her first."

"Do Poppy and Nana know?"

Jenn reluctantly admitted, "I told Nana today. I asked her to keep it private for now."

"You did?" Steve challenged.

Jenn sighed. "It's hard for me to keep anything from my mom; you know that. She took it well. She's supportive."

"What about Grandma?" Rachel looked at Steve.

"I haven't told her," Steve replied. "And I don't plan to. She's not tolerant about these things. I'm afraid she'd write to Josh. He doesn't need harsh criticism right now."

Jenn was relieved to hear that. Her mom was one thing, but Marilyn's judgmental attitude would not be helpful to any of them.

"Does this mean he isn't Christian anymore?" Rachel asked.

"No!" Jenn and Steve said at the same time.

Jenn was shocked that Rachel was calling into question Josh's faith. He was as devoted as anyone.

Steve said, "Josh is committed to living his Christian values. I'm confident his faith will be even stronger after this test. Every Christian is tested, Rachel. We're all sinners. That's why Christ died for us."

Jenn stepped in. "As Christians we don't throw away the gift of the resurrection. Josh is choosing to devote his life to Christ. He's an example for all of us."

The phone rang. Jenn looked at the caller ID and sighed. It was Lindsay.

"I'm going to get this. I haven't updated Lin in a while." She picked up the cordless phone and walked into the living room.

"Michael just got home from youth group. He told me that we need to say extra prayers for Josh. What's going on? How can I help?"

The love and concern in Lindsay's voice cut through Jenn's numbness. Her eyes welled up. "Oh, Lindsay, it's a nightmare." Jenn needed Lindsay's full support more than ever in her life. Josh wouldn't understand, but she told her friend about their last two days. "I didn't tell you before now because that would make it real. But Pastor James convinced me that we need to face this head on."

"You know we're going to be there for you and Josh one hundred percent. Whatever you need, you tell me."

"Thank you, so much. We need your prayers. And please, please keep the specifics confidential. Josh doesn't want it spread."

"Of course." Then Lindsay suggested, "Let's have a prayer circle in his bedroom. All those powerful prayers will bring Jesus right there to strengthen his soul."

"Josh isn't ready for something like that. So public. He's very upset after youth group tonight."

"He doesn't need to be there. We'll do it while he's at school. Like a spring cleaning, he'll come home and just feel the godly spirit. I don't need to tell people the details. You know people will have heard that he's having impure thoughts. What sixteen-year-old boy doesn't? How about I arrange a series of prayer circles? Josh's room will just be the first stop."

Jenn considered the offer. Pastor James said that they needed to be fully committed. She knew she and Steve needed to be shining examples of godly commitment to their children.

"That would be great, thanks," Jenn agreed. "I'm so scared for him, Lindsay. He's so fragile. It's too much for a boy to have to deal with."

"God never gives us more than we can handle, Jenn. You know that."

"I keep telling myself He has a plan for us and I'm not to question. But it's hard. So hard."

"You're wise not to question," Lindsay reminded Jenn. "Trust in the Lord—and the power of prayer."

Usually those words were a comfort, but tonight they rang hollow. After Jenn hung up, she went to face Josh.

When she opened his door, he said, "I don't want to talk. To anyone. About anything." He was sitting on the edge of his bed, hitting his fist into his baseball mitt like he used to do with his fury when he was a little boy. What she had to tell him was just going to make him even angrier.

"Josh, I have to tell you something. You're not going to like it. I'm sorry. This is all getting out of hand," she explained.

Josh stared at her without saying a word.

She was worried, but she spit out the words: "I broke your confidence. I think a secret is more harmful than helpful. The devil lives in secrets."

Josh's eyes got big with anger. "Who did you tell?"

"Rachel asked us what Pastor James was talking about. I wanted her to hear it from us. And I want her to know what you're going through."

Josh glared at her.

"Lindsay called because Michael told her about youth group. She wants to support us. She's my best friend. I tell her everything. I asked her not to tell anyone else anything besides what Pastor James told the youth group. She said she would keep it private."

"Anyone else?" Josh's eyes bored into her.

"Nana," Jenn practically whispered. "I can't keep secrets from her. She loves you. She had no judgment at all. She's just worried for you, like us. Her prayers will work better because she knows what to pray for."

Without a word Josh stood up. He got his running shoes out of his closet and put them on in silence. Finally he said, "I'm going for a run."

"Josh, don't you have anything you want to say to me?" Jenn asked cautiously.

"No," he barked. "Get out of my way."

"It's late to be out alone."

"Mom, I'm going to explode if I don't go for a run." With contained fury he said, "Please move."

Resigned, Jenn stepped aside. She listened as he clomped down the stairs and then slammed the door.

"Where's Josh going?" Steve asked.

"For a run. He's furious at me. For good reason. Oh, Steve, I don't think I can do this." She started sobbing.

Steve wrapped his arms around her, and she rested against his chest. Then she felt another pair of arms around her. It was Rachel, which made Jenn cry even more. She wanted to be strong for her kids. To show them deep faith. But she was scared. What if Josh couldn't be cured? What would happen to his salvation then? What if this drove a irreparable wedge between them?

Jenn stepped back so Rachel could be in the middle. She held her daughter while her husband held her.

"The Lord will see us through this. We have great faith in Him," she said to her daughter. "It's just not going to be easy."

11

Friday morning, after Josh went to school, a group of eight women gathered in his room with Jenn. Only Lindsay knew the full reason why they were there; the others had been given only a more general sense of the reason for the gathering. As promised, Lindsay had set this up as one stop on a prayer circuit. They would take turns praying in one another's houses once a week that spring. Each woman held a Bible in one hand and the cross on her neck in the other.

Lindsay began the prayers: "God, guide Your son Josh in fending off the lust of the flesh and release him from the bondage of that lust. We invite the Holy Spirit to flood this place with the light of Jesus Christ. God, lead Josh in refraining from the lust of the eyes, lust in the body, and lust in the soul. Guide him in keeping the counsel of others. Forgive him for his lusts and release him from bondage. God, make Josh repent for submitting to pride and exchanging godly wisdom for the wisdom of the world. Lord Jesus Christ, bring him back to godly wisdom and to Your love. Amen."

When she finished, the group chimed in with "Amen." Then the woman on Lindsay's left spoke out loud. Her prayer was affirmed with an amen. The group went around the circle one by one, praying for Josh. Jenn felt the presence of the Holy Spirit build in the room. Gratitude surged through her body as these women spoke their prayers entreating God, the Holy Spirit, and Jesus to save her Josh. When it came her time to pray, she couldn't speak. Instead, she raised her hand and swayed her body in a wordless prayer, knowing these women and God would feel all that was in her spirit.

After the prayer circle, Jenn served food downstairs. They agreed that the Holy Spirit was present today and surely Josh would be cured soon. Jenn was grateful, so grateful, to have all this support. This was why she was in a church: to bolster her spirit and give her faith during hard times.

After eating, most people left, but Lindsay stayed behind to clean up.

"Jenn, can I make an observation?" Lindsay said carefully. "I don't want to hurt your feelings. I only say this to be helpful. Feel free to ignore my advice."

Jenn looked over at her friend. Her stomach twisted at the tone of Lindsay's voice, but she kept a calm face. "What? Please just tell me."

"Josh's room could be more masculine."

Jenn jerked her head back in surprise. That was not what she was expecting to hear. She imagined something much more critical of her. She thought about Josh's room. His wall had scenic pictures from national parks. Yosemite was his favorite place on Earth. He had posters of Half Dome and the valley. And on their trip to Zion and Bryce two summers ago, he'd gotten posters and postcards with beautiful images of rock formations and canyons. His bed was still covered with a blanket, since they hadn't had the time to get him a new comforter. His rug was the same color as the rest of the upstairs: sage green, with dark speckles.

"What do you mean?" Jenn's face contorted, and she asked, "Like girly photos?"

"Oh no, nothing that would conflict with his Christian values," Lindsay said. "I may be wrong—I'm no expert, of course—but I've been doing some reading. He needs to be surrounded by masculine images, like...NASCAR races or sports teams. That's what Michael has on his walls. Doesn't Josh love the Warriors and the A's?"

"Yes."

"Posters of things like that would support him in being manlier. That's part of the treatment, right?"

"Yes," Jenn said, thinking for a moment. It was painful to hear this, but she needed to face their failings. "Thank you. I know it's hard to bring up something like this. I appreciate it. You're right. I've been blind...to so many things. I'll take those down and send him to the store with Steve to look for more suitable, more masculine images."

After Lindsay left, Jenn found the pamphlet that Pastor James had given them. She typed up the prayers and Bible passages in it and then printed them out. She walked through the house taping them up in each room. It looked ugly, all these unframed words scattered around, but it was worth it.

Then she carried the wooden step stool into Josh's room. She carefully peeled up the corners of the posters from the national parks. She laid them gently on the bed, rolled them up, and slipped rubber bands around the ends. She'd go to the store to buy a storage tube for them before pick up. Jenn couldn't bear to just throw away Josh's posters. She studied the blank walls. It looked like someone was moving out…or in. Her heart twisted. She knew the old Josh had to move out to make room for the new one. But it was sad at the same time. It felt like she was packing away her child.

◆ ◆ ◆

Jenn drove Josh's car pool that afternoon. He climbed into the front, while his friends piled into the back. He acted like typical Josh, chatting and laughing with Phil and Grant in the middle seat. It was hard to imagine he was struggling with so much. Fifteen minutes later she dropped off Phil. She and Josh were alone in the SUV. She hated to sully his good mood, but she had to warn him about his room.

"Josh, I had a prayer circle for you today," Jenn told him.

"What? With who?" Josh asked.

Wanting to downplay it, she said, "Just a few women from church. Lindsay organized it. They're all good people. And we weren't specific about why we were having it."

"OK." Josh sighed and stared out the window. "Thanks, I guess."

"That's the right attitude, hon. I'm proud of you."

"I'm trying, Mom. Really, I am."

"I posted a lot of prayers around the house. I didn't have time to frame them, but we just need them up. We'll surround ourselves in prayer, just like Pastor James suggested."

Josh nodded.

"One other thing…" Jenn said carefully. She could feel Josh looking at her and went on. "I took down your posters."

"What? Why? What's wrong with them?" Josh sounded hurt.

"We, well, you need something more masculine on your walls. You and Dad can pick something out."

"Half Dome isn't masculine?" Josh asked.

Jenn told him, "We need external changes to represent the internal changes you want to make. This is an easy and small way to do that."

Josh was silent.

Jenn prodded him. "Josh?"

"It's not small to me," he mumbled. "I feel the Holy Spirit in those places."

Jenn's stomach dropped.

"Did you throw them away?" he challenged.

"Of course not. They're safe," Jenn rushed out. "I bought a tube for them. It doesn't have to be forever, Josh. Just while you're getting cured." She reached out to squeeze Josh's arm. "This is sad for all of us, you know."

"I know, Mom. I'm sorry to cause you so much work," he backed down, looking miserable.

"Josh, there's no need to feel bad. Just keep working hard like you are. You'll be cured soon, and our life can return to normal."

◆ ◆ ◆

Sunday was Jenn's favorite day of the week. She got to celebrate God and her Lord Jesus Christ in the company of others of faith. Usually, she loved getting ready for church. She took care to buy outfits for herself that were just right: attractive but not ostentatious. During the week she wore T-shirts and jeans, but on Sunday she wore a skirt or dress with coordinated jewelry, purse, and flats.

This morning, however, she felt a mild dread. Josh didn't ask directly if he could skip church, but he mentioned that it would be awkward to be there. She reassured him it wouldn't be, but she shared his concern. Word had spread. People knew something was amiss in their family. Like him, she feared being judged. But the only judgment that mattered was God's, and God knew Josh's heart. The family was going to worship together proudly. They had nothing to be ashamed of.

They picked up Sara at the BART station on their way to church. When the five of them walked into the sanctuary, there was a ripple of energy. It was subtle but noticeable that people were watching as they made their way to their usual pew. Before they sat down, Pastor James caught them in the aisle and warmly shook Josh's hand; then he gave a hug to each of the girls. He shook Steve's hand. After he hugged Jenn, he whispered in her ear, "I've got some great news. Find me after the service." Then he moved on to welcome another family.

They started to sit as they usually did, with Steve going in first, followed by Jenn and then the kids, but she stopped Steve before he stepped in. She directed Josh to go in first, followed by Steve, and then she filled in the pew, with Rachel and Sara sliding in after her. She felt bad having Josh sit by a stranger, but he should be next to Steve and not by his sisters or mother.

Jenn felt people looking at them. She closed her eyes and called on the Holy Spirit to dwell in her. She prayed, *Dear God, give me strength to be an example of righteous faith. Guide me in ignoring petty gossip and accepting judgment from anyone but You.* She put the people around her out of her mind and focused on the energy and rhythm of the praise band. She stood up to better be filled by the Holy Spirit. Steve and the girls joined her. They raised their arms and moved to the rhythm. She glanced at Josh. He leaned over with his eyes closed in prayer. She saw his lips moving. He was doing what he needed to do to get ready for worship. She smiled to herself and focused on opening her own soul.

By the time the worship leaders started speaking, she felt at peace and filled with grace. The sermon, on accepting what God put in your path, felt especially meaningful to her today. God was giving her an opportunity to deepen her faith and trust in Him. It was a sign of spiritual maturity to trust God even when it didn't make sense to you.

She was caught by surprise when their family was held up in the pastoral prayer. In the past she had felt touched deeply whenever they were included in this prayer. Today she had to remind herself to be grateful, not embarrassed at being mentioned so publicly. She glanced over at Josh to see how he was receiving this blessing. He was leaning over, elbows on knees and head in his hands. Jenn nudged Steve, who put his hand on Josh's shoulder. Josh turned his head to look up at his dad. He looked so pained. Steve patted his shoulder, and Josh sighed and slouched back in his pew. If all the attention was a challenge for her, she could only imagine how hard it was for Josh.

"Can we leave now?" their son asked as soon as the service ended.

"Sure," Steve said.

Jenn shook her head. "Pastor James wants to see us. He told me to find him in the back of the sanctuary."

"Can I just stay here until everyone clears out?" Josh asked.

Steve looked at Jenn. She gave a small nod. Jenn chatted with any congregants that approached them, while the rest of her family sat protectively around Josh. She monitored the greeting line, watching it get shorter and shorter as the pastors shook hands with folks on their way out. When the sanctuary was almost empty, she signaled to her family. They walked to the back and waited until they were alone with their pastor.

"Great news!" he exclaimed. "I spoke to some of my favorite colleagues and got some resources for you, including a wonderful opportunity for Josh—a conference in April."

"Oh," Jenn said. She had forgotten about the gatherings that Pastor James had suggested. "Where?"

"It's in Tracy, only thirty miles away, *and* it's during Dublin High's spring break, just before Easter. The Lord is taking care of you, Josh. This will be good for your family. The teens are there for eight days, and parents join in on both Saturdays. Here's a flyer about it. You can sign him up right away. Praise Jesus!"

"Praise Jesus," Jenn echoed. "Josh, isn't this great?"

"What?" he asked. It was obvious he hadn't been listening.

"Pastor found a program for us, for you," Jenn told him. She gave him the say-thank-you look with her eyebrows.

"Thanks," Josh said.

"Absolutely!" the pastor replied. "I know you're going to be one of the success stories, Josh. Our Lord Jesus has a plan for you."

Josh gave a small smile and nod.

Pastor James exclaimed, "And here's a great book to give you guidance as a parent. It's my gift to you."

Jenn took the flyer and the book. *Prevent Homosexuality* was in bold black letters on the cover. Underneath, in smaller letters, it said *A Guidebook for Christian Parents*.

"Thanks so much," Jenn said. It was mortifying to be going through this but uplifting to be supported by their pastor. She could feel the Lord showing up in their lives. She'd always heard that the cracks in your life allowed the Lord into your heart, and now she was experiencing that for herself.

◆ ◆ ◆

Jenn didn't try to draw the family out during the quiet drive to brunch at Mimi's. She hoped they were floating in the spirit of the Lord, too. She read the flyer from Pastor James:

Join us for
Resurrection Ministries Freedom Brigade
April 3–10, 2004
Freedom from Homosexuality through the Power of Jesus Christ
Do you struggle with Same-Sex Attraction (SSA)? Are you between the ages of fifteen and twenty-five? You are not alone. You have Christian allies in this battle for your soul. You can be transformed by God's amazing grace. Learn the root causes of your SSA and the treatment that can set you free.

If you submit your whole life to the Lord, you will find freedom to live in sexual and relational wholeness according to God's design. We will discipline and inspire you for the path ahead.

Sudden, radical, complete change is possible.

Jenn zeroed in on those words: *Sudden, radical, complete change is possible.* This was something powerful to cure Josh. She passed the flyer back to her son.

She said, "This is exciting, Josh! It's just what you need. God is watching out for you."

Josh read the flyer and then handed it over to Sara. "If I do this, do I still have to go to that other doctor on Monday?"

Jenn replied, "Yes. If he confirms he's Christian, we want you to meet with him. This retreat is weeks away. You need help right now."

Sara asked, "Are you sure this is a good idea, Mom? I've heard some of these things are really mean."

"From whom?" Jenn asked with a bit of heat in her voice.

"My roommate has a friend who's pretty down on Christians because her family stopped talking to her when she came out. We've had dinner a few times. I explained to her that not all Christians are bigoted against gays—that we hold up the possibility of healing because of God's love, not hate."

Steve said, "You know we'd never stop talking to you guys. No matter what, right?" He looked into the rearview mirror.

The girls nodded.

"Right, Josh?" Steve pressed.

"I guess," Josh finally replied.

"No. Not 'I guess.' You understand what I'm saying? I don't want you to worry about that. We're not kicking you out of the house. We're not cutting you off. We're getting you the help you need. We're all on the same team here."

Josh bit his lip and nodded. "Got it."

Jenn was surprised at the intensity in Steve's voice. She didn't know where that came from. No one was advocating abandoning Josh.

Out loud she explained to Sara, hoping Josh was listening, "I trust Pastor James's judgment. If he says it's a good organization, then I'm confident this is right for Josh and our family. I'm sure there are some people who hide their bigotry behind their Christianity, but that's not us. Our passion comes from our desire to live biblically and our desire to bring others to the salvation that our Lord Jesus Christ offers. I'm sure this conference will be in line with our family values."

"We all have to go?" Rachel asked. She sounded upset.

"I don't know, Rachel. We'll do whatever they say is best," Jenn scolded. "Josh's well-being is the most important thing right now."

"I didn't mean that, Mom. Of course...whatever Josh needs. It's just..." Rachel paused. She sounded like she might cry. "We aren't going to go to Monterey, are we?"

Jenn's face softened. She looked at the flyer. The conference was the week they'd planned their trip.

"Oh. I'm sorry, hon. We have to postpone. Maybe in the summer?"

Josh sighed. "I'm sorry, Rach. I know how much you wanted to see the otters and the penguins. You guys should just go without me."

"It's OK, Josh. Really," Rachel soothed her brother. "Summer's soon enough."

"I'm ruining everything. For all of you," Josh said. Then he leaned his head back and closed his eyes.

Sara replied, "Joshy…of course not. You aren't ruining anything."

"Josh," Steve said, "don't be dramatic. It's fine. You'll meet with these people and take care of the problem. Got it?"

"Yes, sir," Josh said slowly.

Jenn couldn't tell if Josh was being sarcastic or actually compliant. She hoped it was the latter and that he truly believed this camp would take care of his problems. Faith was the ultimate solution, but she couldn't give that to her son. He had to find it for himself.

12

Monday morning Jenn called the therapist after her prayers. His voice mail picked up, so she left a message: "Good morning, Kyle. This is Jenn Henderson. My son, Josh, has an appointment tonight at seven o'clock. I need to confirm that you're a Christian and will provide counseling in line with Christian values. I hope you understand our need to know the answer to that question before he meets with you. Thank you."

Kyle called while she was grocery shopping. She picked up the phone in the cereal aisle. "Hello?"

"Hello, Jenn? This is Kyle Goss, returning your call."

"Thanks for getting back to me."

"Of course," Kyle replied. "To answer your question, yes, I'm Christian. I attend church on Sundays."

"So your treatment with Josh will be in line with Christian values?"

"Not all my clients are religious. However, my work is deeply grounded in Jesus's teachings."

Jenn was relieved. "That makes me feel so much better."

"Good," Kyle said. "So I'll meet you and Josh tonight?"

"You'll see Josh but not me," she explained. "Steve will bring him. We're having them do more things together at the suggestion of our pastor."

"All right, then. I look forward to meeting Steve and Josh tonight and perhaps you on a different date."

Jenn hung up. Tears pressed against the back of her eyes. She leaned on the cart, exhausted and overwhelmed. She had just gotten off the phone with a therapist for Josh. How did she get here? She felt like a child, naive and unprepared. Up until a week ago she had known, without a doubt, that she was raising her kids right.

But that feeling was gone. Good parents didn't raise a child with same-sex attractions. Jenn thought about Josh from the moment she woke up until she went to sleep. Her head was filled with what she should or shouldn't say and what she should or shouldn't do. She questioned her natural reactions constantly. She'd start to hug Josh or ask about his day and then stop herself because it was damaging to him.

Jenn obsessively reviewed his childhood, thinking back on every mistake she made. They had let him be on cross-country instead of football. He helped with the dishes just like his sisters. The whole family went camping together rather than it being father-son bonding time. Their poor choices had hurt their son.

She was tired and insecure, but she didn't want to show or tell anyone. She'd never felt so supported, yet so alone at the same time.

"Excuse me," a woman said.

Jenn was blocking the oatmeal. She pushed forward despite her misery. She grabbed some Frosted Mini-Wheats and continued down the aisle.

◆ ◆ ◆

That night Jenn lay in bed reading the book that Pastor James gave her. It was hard to take in the information. She realized now that she and Steve had made so many errors. The reasoning was outlined clearly. With each page her spirit sank lower and lower until she felt sick to her stomach.

"We shouldn't have given him a name that started with the same letter as mine," Jenn told Steve as he climbed into bed.

Steve looked confused. "What are you talking about?"

"It made him identify with me. It's even worse since he looks like me. And now I'm scared for Sara. She looks like you, and you share a first letter." Jenn's voice cracked. "Why didn't anyone tell us these things before they were born? All I cared about was giving them biblical names."

"Are you sure that's what the book says?" Steve said, sounding incredulous. "I've never heard anything like that before."

Anger flashed up in Jenn. "I'm not stupid, Steve. I can read a book. It says it's best to name sons after their fathers so they'll have strong masculine identities, especially if they favor the mother. We can't take his name back now."

Steve took a deep breath. He looked like he wanted to say something, but he kept it in.

"What?" Jenn barked.

"I think we need to focus on the future and not the possible mistakes we made in the past. He has his name; he looks like you. What does it say we need to do now?"

"All the stuff Pastor James told us: He needs to spend more time with you and less time with me. He must only do masculine activities—I guess he doesn't set the table anymore. And we have to find the root cause, the sexual abuse that traumatized him." Jenn's eyes welled up. "I think about that one over and over and over. If he can't remember it, he had to have been so young. I just can't believe it was my dad or your dad or…How could it be anyone we know that we trusted with him? It makes me think about awful things—with our Josh." Jenn started sobbing. It was horrifying to know that Josh had been sexually abused and she didn't stop it.

Steve took the book from her lap and wrapped his arms around her.

"Jenn," Steve spoke quietly when she was done crying. "It's good you're doing a lot of reading and that we're doing everything we can to help Josh. But…this book may not be one hundred percent true."

Jenn pulled away from her husband and looked at him incredulously. "You don't believe Pastor James is guiding us well?"

"I didn't say that. I just know you can't believe absolutely everything you read. People have strong opinions. I find it hard to believe that Josh's name would make him a homosexual."

Every time Jenn heard that word her stomach churned. She picked up the book and waved it at Steve. "This is the Christian way. We are Christians. We must have faith or we'll jeopardize Josh's recovery. I need to know that we're in this together, Steve."

"Jenn, you know part of being a Christian is listening for God's truth for yourself. That's why we pray. I've been praying a lot, just like you, and listening for God's guidance," Steve reassured her. "We're together on this. We both know Josh can be cured through faith. I just don't want you beating yourself up and beating our family up. Kyle told me we have to be gentle with each other and trust in God's love. I think he's right."

Jenn leaned back against the headboard with her eyes closed. The words echoed in her head: *gentle...trust*. She felt very far from either of those things. She was full of blame and fear. She wanted to take action, do something, fix this problem, not be gentle and trust that it would work out.

"What else did he say?" They hadn't had a private moment to talk about Josh's first appointment earlier that evening.

"I didn't have much time with him—maybe ten minutes in the beginning before he asked me to leave so he and Josh could speak alone. Next time I need to bring something to read. The waiting room only had old *Newsweek*, *People*, and *Better Homes* magazines. He walked Josh out to me after they were done and said that thing about being gentle and trusting God."

"Well, what did you talk about in your ten minutes?"

"He asked about who was in our family and what brought us there. He wondered whether any of our friends or family were homosexual. He asked about our church and how we're feeling as a family."

"What did Josh talk about with him?" Jenn probed.

Steve shrugged. "I didn't ask, and he didn't tell."

"You didn't ask about it?" Jenn was shocked.

"No. It's private. Josh and I don't talk about things like that," Steve said. "I'm sure your book thinks that's just fine."

Jenn smiled with a snort. "You're right. I just hate not knowing."

"Guess it's a guy thing. I don't need to know. I don't want to know."

◆ ◆ ◆

They made the changes that the book and Pastor James suggested. No more movies as a family on Fridays, so that the kids could watch gender-appropriate films. That meant Josh and Steve watched thrillers, adventures, or science fiction and the girls watched romantic comedies. Jenn discouraged Josh from doing anything in the kitchen other than taking out the garbage. He and Steve spent time in the garage building something or another. Jenn and the girls got mani-pedis on Saturdays while Josh and Steve watched sports with Mark and Michael.

Jenn avoided interacting with her son as much as possible, though they did have family dinners together. She drove him places only if they couldn't make another arrangement. She didn't go to his games, ask him about friends or school, or watch TV with him. She missed Josh. It was a huge loss for both of them, but they accepted the need for it.

Jenn fluctuated between hope and despair multiple times a day. She wished she could see some outward sign of healing, but Josh looked the same as always. He went to school, to practice, and then came home. He did his homework, ate dinner, did more homework, and went to bed. Jenn checked the history on the computer every morning to monitor his web surfing, always on the alert for anything that would undermine his recovery. But she never found anything to raise concern. In fact, he hardly went to any websites at all.

Jenn kept asking Steve to register Josh for the SAT, but day after day that didn't happen. She didn't want to risk her son's entire future to Steve's busy schedule, so one night, after dinner, she broke her self-imposed rule of separation and knocked on Josh's door.

"Come in," Josh called from inside.

He was studying at his desk. Jenn stood in the doorway and looked around. The room felt foreign because of the changes. Steve and Josh had bought all this stuff during a single trip to Target. The new bedspread had a bold plaid on it. The walls were covered in posters of cars and sports teams. A few baseball players stared intently from the walls. It didn't seem like Josh at all. She supposed that was a good thing. Here was an outer manifestation of the inner change they were working for.

"Can we register you for the SAT right now?" she asked. "We can do it online. The deadline is in two days. You don't want to miss it."

"Sure, Mom," Josh said as he closed up a book. They walked together down to the computer. Jenn waved him to the chair in front of the keyboard. She pulled up a chair next to it.

"You do it," Jenn instructed him. "I'll sit here if you have any questions and give you my credit-card number."

Josh filled in his demographic information. On the next screen, he chose the location of the test: Dublin High. Before paying, he had the option to fill out information about himself, including what type of school he wanted to attend. He checked off business and accounting as potential majors. Then he marked schools on the East Coast, some of which Jenn had never even heard of. She was shocked. After all they had been through, she expected him to list only nearby schools.

"Josh, you think you might go to college in New York City?" Jenn asked when he checked NYU, trying to keep the outrage from her voice.

"Yeah. Or Boston or Washington, D.C. I've lived in California my whole life. I'd like to be in a big city."

"With what's happening with you?" Jenn snapped. "We are not working this hard for your recovery to have you throw it away by going to school far away. If you aren't completely cured, you'll be living at home while you go to college."

"But, Mom," Josh argued, "everyone is looking at schools all over the country. The counselors talk about them all the time."

"You are not everybody. Of course you'll go to college. I hope you'll be accepted to Cal like your sister. Maybe Cal State Hayward or even Saint Mary's. If all goes really well at camp, maybe UC Davis. But New York? No, Josh." Jenn shook her head. "That is not happening."

"But—"

"Does your father know you were considering out-of-state schools?" Jenn asked.

"I guess so. Yeah."

Jenn was suddenly furious. Her son's life was unraveling entirely, and she seemed to be the only person who realized it.

Josh argued, "Sara applied to Williams and Vassar. They're out of state. Why isn't it an option for me, too?"

"You're not Sara. Don't you understand? Do you know that I worry about you—day and night?" Heat rose in her voice. "All I think about is your future. Your future is not in New York City. Or Boston or D.C. If you want to put Christian colleges on your list—BIOLA, Chapman—I'll think about you going to Southern California, near Nana and Poppy and Grandma and Grandpa. But New York City? Come on, Josh. I don't think you understand the gravity of your situation. I'm not having you all the way across the country. Or even halfway across the country. Do you know what kind of influences there will be?"

Josh tentatively suggested an alternative: "How about Vassar or other schools that aren't in a big city?"

"Josh! Stop arguing with me. You're going to college in California. Erase those schools. Put in my credit-card information, and let's be done with this."

13

The next day Jenn had an appointment with Kyle Goss. It was her first time meeting with him in person. He'd requested this interview, saying he wanted to know about her goals for Josh.

Kyle welcomed her warmly into his office. She had imagined him as white, but he wasn't. Maybe he was mixed black and white. Maybe Middle Eastern or Hispanic. He had dark-brown hair, brown eyes, and light-brown skin.

"It's nice to meet you, Jenn," he said as they shook hands. "Sit wherever you like." He pointed to a dark-green love seat and coordinated chair. She looked between the two pieces of furniture and finally chose the love seat. He settled into the chair across from her. She noticed a box of tissues on the small table between them.

"Whenever I'm working with a teen, I ask to have some time alone with each parent. It's best to know one another and for me to learn your goals. So please—tell me how you are doing. What are your concerns and hopes for Josh?"

"I want him to live his life in conformity with God's will as expressed in the Bible. He cannot be homosexual, so he needs to eliminate any unhealthy attractions. He's getting pastoral counseling on occasion from the youth minister at our church. And he'll be going to a camp to treat same-sex attractions. But that's not until

April—during Easter break. We want him to be cured as soon as possible, so he's seeing you."

Kyle nodded slowly and pursed his lips. "Do you have any other concerns? School pressure, grades, attitude?"

"He's a very good student. I worry that he works too hard, but he seems fine with it. I'm concerned that he doesn't understand the gravity of his situation. Last night, when he registered for the SAT, he indicated an interest in colleges on the East Coast—including New York City. He argued with me when I pointed out that it would be dangerous for him. I was stunned."

"Why is that?" Kyle sounded curious.

"You think it's appropriate for him to live in New York City? I don't let our children visit San Francisco without me. He doesn't need those kinds of influences. He would be exposed to people who would encourage him to be homosexual."

Kyle asked, "Do you mind if I play devil's advocate here?"

"Go ahead," Jenn replied, though she didn't like the sound of it.

"What if Josh is gay and he can't change that?"

She flinched at the words *Josh is gay*. She took a breath and asked as calmly as she could manage, "You can't cure him?"

"I'm not saying that," Kyle replied. "I'm asking, what if he can't be changed?"

"The flyer promises that complete recovery is possible through God's grace. I believe in God's grace, and I know He'll offer it to Josh."

"The flyer for the conference he'll be going to?"

Jenn nodded.

"Some of those programs can be very harsh, bordering on abusive." Kyle looked concerned. "Kids can be locked in closets, given shocks, and pressured to reveal very personal information publicly."

"I'm sure this program is not like that. Pastor James loves Josh. He would never recommend something to hurt him. Do you believe Josh can be cured?"

Kyle's voice was calm. "Some treatments will make Josh more depressed. He's responding very well to therapy with me. Do you agree that he is doing much better than a few weeks ago?"

"Josh is depressed because he's afraid he's homosexual. He feels hopeful that he will be cured; that's why he is doing well right now," Jenn explained. "When he's cured of his same-sex attractions, he won't have anything to be depressed about."

"I just want to make sure you and Steve know this camp might make Josh's depression worse. I've seen it happen. For some kids the pressure is too much, too fast."

Jenn shook her head. She couldn't believe she had to explain this to Josh's therapist. He was supposed to be the expert, not her.

Jenn said, "If Josh had cancer, would you tell me not to give him chemo because it will make him feel bad? No, you would understand that the chemo was ultimately for his own good. This camp is the chemo to get the cancer of homosexuality out of my child."

Then Jenn started to cry. Not just pressure pushing at the back of her eyes. Not just a few tears rolling down her cheeks. For the first time since this all began, she sobbed. She buried her face in her hands as moisture poured from her nose and her eyes. Kyle sat patiently, not saying a word, until she stopped.

Eventually Jenn stammered, "I...I'm so scared for him. All the time. It's a constant anxiety eating at me. I've never, ever had to deal with anything like this in my life. Suddenly I question everything. I used to believe I was a good parent. I knew we were living right. And now I've discovered we made so many mistakes. My poor judgment is putting Josh's soul in danger. It's all my fault."

"Josh is a wonderful person," Kyle reassured her. "Every parent makes mistakes. You've given him an amazing base. He has a strong relationship with God and Jesus. We talk about that a lot."

"That will help him, right?" Jenn grasped at this straw of hope.

Kyle nodded. "Enormously. It can be the difference between life and death in these situations."

Jenn started crying again. "He's not going to try to kill himself again, is he?"

"I can't know for certain, but I don't think so. He's showing strong signs of moving past the desire to hide from himself...and from you."

"I'm so tired." Jenn sighed.

"So is he," Kyle said. "Please be gentle—with yourself and with him. These things take time. Don't expect an instantaneous change in either of you. Pray for strength, guidance, and compassion."

"Do you have prayers you can give me?"

"I like the Serenity Prayer."

"From AA?" Jenn was surprised.

"It's good for many situations. Asking God to give you courage, serenity, and wisdom can help all of you."

Jenn left Kyle's office with a little hope. She was still demoralized, but she wasn't as mad at herself for being confused. When she got home, she Googled the Serenity Prayer and pasted it into a Word document. Then she changed the font to make it nicer, printed two copies, and glued them on two cards with flowered borders. She went to her room, sat at the edge of her bed, and read the prayer out loud: "God, grant me the serenity to accept the things I cannot change, the courage to change the things I can, and the wisdom to know the difference."

She placed one card by her bed and the other one on the cupboard by the kitchen sink. She'd add this to her daily prayers. Maybe courage, serenity, and wisdom would reduce her constant anxiety.

◆ ◆ ◆

A few weeks later, Jenn had a pastoral-care meeting with Pastor James. Jenn was grateful that he'd made time for her throughout this ordeal to offer support and guidance. After they prayed, he asked if Josh was ready for camp, which started on Saturday.

"Do you have any questions?" he asked Jenn.

"No, I think we're all set. Steve and I are looking forward to being there with him. I'm nervous, but I keep saying the Serenity Prayer. It helps a lot."

"Excuse me? The Serenity Prayer!?" Pastor James scowled.

"The one from AA. Josh's therapist suggested it to me. He thinks we need to be gentler, give Josh time, and not be so anxious."

"Josh doesn't have time," Pastor James replied passionately. "He hasn't yet acted on his same-sex attractions, but if we aren't careful, he will. That would be his doom. We need to cure him before he does."

的

"Oh," Jenn replied. Confusion rushed back in. She'd been so comforted by Kyle's words and the prayer, but maybe it was just a distraction.

"Jennifer, it's very easy to be misguided by good intention. I think we should look up this therapist."

"Why?"

"I question whether his practice is in line with biblical teachings."

"I asked him if he was Christian, like you suggested."

"Did you ask this therapist if his work is biblically based?"

Jenn shook her head. Her throat closed up in fear that she had made yet another mistake.

"I'm sorry. I should have been more specific. Many so-called Christians aren't really. I mean, they think they are, but they're not born again. I'm afraid this person may be sending Josh signals that he should accept being homosexual. It's very common, you know. We're working against a huge anti-Christian swell."

The minister turned to his computer and asked her the name of the therapist. Jenn watched him type and read and then type some more. He pursed his lips and then exclaimed, "Ah...thought so! Jenn, he sings in the choir at the UCC church. That confirms my suspicions. He can't be trusted with Josh's salvation."

Jenn was shocked. "Are you certain? He's been helpful to me and Steve. And Josh looks forward to his time with Kyle."

"Jenn, you want Josh one hundred percent cured. Right?"

"Yes."

"Then he needs to be surrounded by people who have faith in the treatment. If his therapist doesn't believe in the cure, Josh won't believe in it. This is a time that calls for the deepest faith. There is no room for any doubt."

Those words penetrated to the core of Jenn's body. Complete faith. No doubt. She didn't have the luxury of time or doubt.

"You're right. Josh should stop seeing Kyle."

◆ ◆ ◆

Steve looked incredulous when Jenn told him about the conversation with Pastor James. "We insisted that Josh see a therapist. He looks forward to talking with Kyle, and you want us to make him stop?"

"I think Pastor James is right," Jenn replied. "All the adults in Josh's life need to be on the same page. He fears Kyle might be encouraging Josh to accept his same-sex attractions."

"I've gone along with everything you asked. We redecorated his room. I don't call Sara anymore. I drive Josh whenever I can. He and I watch sports and 'masculine' movies. But this?" Steve shook his head. "I'm not sure it's a good idea."

Heat moved through Jenn's body. She was so mad that she didn't care if she hurt Steve's feelings. She practically yelled, "What I asked? This is not about what *I* want. This is about what *our* son needs. It's not my fault. It's our fault. You're the one who's been a poor role model. You always favored Sara, and he could tell. We all could tell."

Steve looked outraged. He practically shouted, "That's ridiculous! I don't love Sara more than I love Josh or Rachel. You're not making any sense."

She shot back, "Are you going to be supportive of his recovery or not?"

"Of course I am," he countered. "You're just so hard on him right now. You're angry all the time."

"I'm not angry with Josh. I'm angry with myself. And you." All the heat went out of her voice. She softened. "I'm sorry. But it's true."

"Jenn, this is just one part of Josh." Steve's voice got quiet. "You have to see all of him. He's a good kid. We can be proud of him for working so hard."

"He needs to be focused on his recovery, not distracted by college in New York or a therapist who doesn't believe in his transformation. This is the most important thing in his life, in our lives. Don't you see?"

"He needs to know we're on his side. He's done everything we asked him to do. Give him a break. I'll agree to stop taking him to see Kyle, but you have to stop being so hard on him."

Jenn sighed. "I'm terrified for him."

"Me too. But we have to show him that we have faith if we want him to have faith. We need to surrender our lives to God if we expect him to."

The words were like a blow to Jenn's stomach. Steve was right. She *was* trying to control everything, not giving control to God and Jesus.

"Will you say a prayer over me?" she asked. "For surrender."

Jenn knelt in front of Steve. Her husband prayed, "Lord, we ask You to guide Your servant Jenn to live in accordance with Your will. Help her to let go of the sin of control. Let her surrender to Your will in all things. Guide her in being the best mother she can be to Sara, Josh, and Rachel. Help our family to avoid immoral practices and help us to refrain from judging those who engage in them. In Jesus's name we pray. Amen."

"Amen," Jenn echoed. Surrender to His will. *I will surrender to His will.*

14

Jenn was excited and nervous when she woke up on Saturday, April 3rd. Camp started today. She and Steve would stay for special family programming, and Josh would stay for the week, where he would get the tools and support he needed to overcome the sin of same-sex attraction. Jenn was confident that when they picked him up in a week, Josh would be transformed and healed.

Jenn cooked Grandma's pancakes before they left. Sara was home to keep Rachel company for the day. Before they left, the family prayed in a circle, taking turns asking God for Josh's full recovery through the love of Christ.

They were a jumble of feelings as they drove an easy thirty minutes east up the 580 to Tracy. Josh was quiet, but he had been packed and ready to go early in the morning, so Jenn thought he was ready. It made sense that he'd be nervous. They were going to uncover some hard truths. It wouldn't be easy, but it would be life changing in the right direction. She was scared, too, and yet hopeful that Josh would be cured.

The large cinder-block building looked like a Home Depot or Costco. The parking lot was already filled with cars and SUVs. Jenn hadn't realized that so many people would be here. It was nice to know they weren't alone in their struggle.

"You ready for this, Josh?" Steve asked after he pulled into a spot.

"I am!" Josh pumped his fist as if he were getting ready for a game. Jenn thought he probably wasn't really that excited to be here but wanted to psych himself up. She didn't blame him. So much rode on the success of this week that it was nerve-racking.

A woman with long brown hair greeted them with a wide smile as they walked into the building.

"Welcome! I'm Donna, one of the local hosts. We're so glad you're here, ready to receive the transformative blessing of our Lord. This is going to be an amazing, Jesus-filled week of healing and release. Find your name tags right here. The symbol on the corner tells you which spirit circle you're in." She looked at Josh. "They will be your family this week, but also for the rest of your life."

"Thank you. We're glad to be here," Steve said.

Jenn searched the name tags. All three had the same symbol on the upper right of the badge: an Easter lily. Donna looked at the tags in Jenn's hand.

"Oh, goody! My husband is one of the leaders of Josh's spirit circle. His name is John."

Jenn gave her a questioning look.

"Our daughter struggled with SSA," Donna explained. "With the guidance and support of Exodus Ministries, she's cured. She's getting married in June. I can't tell you what an incredible journey it's been. At first I was devastated, but now I know it was part of God's plan to call us more deeply to His work. Before Kathy's troubles I was a Sunday-morning Christian. Now I'm a twenty-four-seven

Christian. What a blessing it's been. Oh, listen to me going on. You'll find out for yourselves."

Donna's enthusiasm was contagious. Jenn liked hearing that this whole experience was a plan to bring their family closer to God. Donna was living proof that it could. She was excited.

Pointing, Donna said, "Josh, you can put your things in Faith Hall and then go into the sanctuary for the opening program. Welcome to your home for the week. Welcome to your people for always."

The sanctuary was enormous. Jenn guessed it seated at least a thousand people. The front was already full. She was taken aback by the sheer size of the space and the crowd. They slid into a pew and looked around. She thought everyone would be sad and serious, but it felt more like a celebration. A band was playing, and people walked up and down the aisles hugging, shaking hands, and chatting. A huge banner filled the back of the chancel. The first line said *Resurrection Ministries: Freedom Brigade*. Underneath that it said *Change Is Possible*. Flowers and balloons covered the chancel, adding to the feeling of festivity.

Jenn gazed at the crowd. The kids looked normal. A few girls had short, spiky hair, but most of them looked like regular teens. Upon closer inspection, she realized the kids' moods didn't quite match the energy in the room. Josh would be in good company. He was committed to being here, he didn't argue about coming, but Josh looked like he was getting ready for something necessary but unpleasant, like a root canal. Hopefully the celebratory mood of the leaders would rub off on him.

Most people were standing up, moving to the beat of the music. A praise band played loudly. The lyrics filled Jenn's soul. Eventually a man with blond hair held in place with hair gel stepped up to the mic. He waved at people in the crowd, pointed at others, and mouthed *welcome* over and over again. The music faded away. The congregation sat.

"Welcome, everyone!" the man practically screamed into the microphone.

"Thanks, Doug!" a few people yelled back.

"We are so excited to have you with us for this Jesus-filled week of healing and release with Resurrection Ministries. Are you ready?"

A few people in the crowd spoke back *yes*.

"I can't hear you." Then he said even louder, "Are you ready?"

"Yes!" the crowd shouted. Jenn joined in.

"I still can't hear you! *Are you ready?*"

"*Yes!*" the crowd answered. Jenn heard Steve joining in right next to her. This was not what she was expecting.

"That's more like it!" Doug said from the chancel. "Let's start with a song, my favorite."

The band began to play, and the words flashed on the screen. Jenn, Steve, and Josh stood up and joined in with the crowd. Even Josh was singing out. It felt so good to be part of something, to be with people who knew what she was going through. Pastor James was right: this was going to be great for their family.

When the song ended, Doug began his speech. "I'm just going to come right out and say it. We're all here today because our lives are affected by the sin of same-sex attraction. You or someone you love is struggling with homosexuality. Look around this room. Go ahead. Right now, look around. Look at these wonderful people and know…you're not alone. Everyone here knows what you're going through. Raise your hand if you're here for the first time."

Most of the crowd raised their hands, but a lot of them didn't— probably a quarter of the room. Jenn was surprised there were so many repeats.

"I want to praise you for being here, for making a commitment to living a biblically based life. You know that Jesus is the only answer, and here is where you'll find Him.

"All homosexual relationships are sinful. That's just a fact. It's also a fact that everyone can go from having homosexual attractions to having heterosexual attractions. Change is possible."

Someone yelled out, "Change is possible."

Jenn's heart swelled. In her head she repeated, *Change is possible.*

Doug smiled. "It sure is. Amen. I'm living proof of that. I have been set free from homosexuality. It wasn't easy giving up the homosexual lifestyle. I wrestled with the devil for my soul…and I won!" The crowd cheered. He went on. "I count my blessings each day that I live my life in conformity with God's will as expressed in the Bible. I know what you're going through. And I know your suffering can end. Jesus died on the cross for our sins. He died for you so that you may be saved. Are you going to throw that gift away?"

Jenn looked over at Josh. He mouthed *no.*

"No," came a few voices.

"Are you going to throw the resurrection away?"

"No!" shouted even more voices.

"No. You are not. We're here to guide you on that path. We will equip your children to walk in freedom away from same-sex desires. But our emphasis is not to simply change one's attraction. No! We are calling all of you—parents and children—into a deeper walk with Christ to allow Him to do transformational work in the world through you. We are especially blessed to be on this sacred path during Holy Week. We are going to live the crucifixion and the resurrection." Then he shouted at the top of his lungs, "We are Resurrection Ministries!"

The band started up with a loud guitar. The congregation rose up, cheering. Energy filled the room. Everyone sang. People swayed and clapped; many were crying and singing. Jenn was surrounded by people dealing with the same issues, some of whom had come through to the other side. These people were living examples of God's grace and mercy.

She looked past Steve to Josh. His handsome face and strong hands were turned up to the Lord. His eyes were closed, and he swayed to the music. It looked like the Holy Spirit was in his body. Jenn felt a chill move up her spine. The Holy Spirit was filling her up, too—filling her with hope.

◆ ◆ ◆

The rest of the morning and afternoon was spent in their spirit circle. Jenn listened intently as each family told their story. Some of them had been dealing with this for years. Others were new to it, just like her family. She realized it was a blessing to have Steve here.

Several of the parents did not have their spouses with them, because they doubted the treatment.

The leaders assured them that there would be lots of prayer and lots of good Christian fun during the week. It wouldn't be all work. In fact, building Christian community among the teens was essential.

They outlined the causes of same-sex attraction. It was a form of arrested psychosexual development, resulting from an incomplete bond with the same-sex parent. Fortunately this could be repaired in therapy. It was nearly as hard to hear now as it had been in Pastor James's office. Jenn took Steve's hand. She wanted him to know that she still loved him and that she had faith that he and Josh could form a healthy attachment. His hand was stiff and clammy. Jenn suspected he was more nervous than he was showing with his calm expression.

Pamphlets were handed out describing the therapeutic process. Nothing was new to Jenn because she had been doing her homework. The leaders were optimistic that all of these young people could change with deep commitment and hard work. However, they warned that it might not be instantaneous. Many kids needed only one week of intensive treatment, but others required ongoing therapy. They cautioned the parents not to be attached to immediate and complete transformation. God was in charge here, not them. Surrendering their child to God's will was their spiritual task.

Surrender, Jenn reminded herself. *Surrender*. But in her heart of hearts, she desperately hoped Josh would be in the category of those who experienced a total transformation this week.

In the afternoon, the three of them had private time with Andrew, Josh's counselor for the week. He wanted to know all about their family. He was particularly interested in what kinds of activities they liked to do together. He was delighted that they attended church regularly and that Steve had been one of Josh's soccer coaches.

"Now, for the difficult conversation." Andrew switched to a somber and empathetic tone. "Abuse. We know there was a root trauma. Have you uncovered it?"

There was silence, and then Jenn shook her head. "I've been thinking and thinking. So has Josh, right?"

Josh gave a small, noncommittal nod.

"A teacher, a grandparent, a scoutmaster—it could be anyone," Andrew said. "Josh, really, you have no recollection?"

Josh shook his head and said quietly, "I don't think there was anything."

"Denial is the enemy of healing. It must have happened when you were very young, under four years old, or it must have been extremely traumatic. It's one of those two things. We'll do good work together to help you uncover it."

Josh slouched in his chair with his shoulders hunched. It looked like he was trying to disappear. Jenn didn't blame him. It was a tragedy she couldn't fully accept. She blamed herself for being neglectful, though she didn't know how, exactly. It was her job to keep him safe, she had failed, and he was dealing with the consequences.

"Are there any practicing homosexuals in your lives? Friends, family, coworkers?"

"Absolutely not," Jenn said.

At the same time, to Jenn's surprise, Steve nodded.

"At work. We have a lot of employees." Steve shrugged. Then he explained, "Safeway is an openly tolerant workplace. A lot of homosexuals work there. And I have a cousin who I'm pretty sure is gay."

Jenn felt betrayed that Steve was telling her this now. "Who?"

"Justin," Steve said quietly.

"But he's married."

"Was married," Steve corrected her. "Remember they got divorced two years ago? I'm pretty sure this is why."

"Those poor children. Why didn't you tell me?" Jenn asked.

"I'm sorry, Jenn. No one said anything to me outright. I'm not absolutely certain, but my mom alluded to never hosting Thanksgiving again, since he's not welcome in her home. She didn't say why, and I didn't ask, but I think that's the reason."

Her mind started to spin. There had been a strange undercurrent she didn't understand when Thanksgiving was moved from Steve's parents' home to his aunt's house. At the time she chalked it up to sisterly dynamics.

"Well, there's your root cause." Andrew sounded excited. "Did Josh spend time with this Justin when he was young?"

"Justin is the nicest guy ever," Steve protested. "He wouldn't hurt Josh."

"He wouldn't see it as hurting. They think differently—people who choose to live the homosexual lifestyle."

"Josh, don't listen to him," Steve countered. "You don't need to be afraid of Justin."

Jenn slapped at Steve's arm. He looked at her, and she gave him the look—the big-eyed look that said, *Be quiet*. Steve raised his hands in surrender. Josh looked confused.

"I know this is hard to hear," the counselor said. "I was resistant to my root cause for a long time."

Jenn asked, "You struggled with SSA?"

"Yes, of course. That's why I'm so committed to this ministry." Andrew beamed at them.

"And you're cured?" Jenn asked. "Are you married?"

"I'm still on my journey. God hasn't put a wife in my path, but I know He will when the time is right. Just like He will for Josh, praise Jesus."

"Well, our time is up. We've already made a lot of progress," Andrew went on. "I know this will be a fruitful week for Josh. He's going to deepen his relationship with Jesus, strengthen his masculinity, heal from his root trauma, and weed out his same-sex attractions. I'm excited and hopeful for our time together."

◆ ◆ ◆

"I can't believe you didn't tell me about Justin," Jenn chastised Steve over dinner. They were eating spaghetti, bread, and salad in the large social hall, sitting in folding metal chairs at a long plastic table surrounded by other parents. Josh wasn't with them. He stayed with his spirit circle for bonding time while they ate.

"The poor guy is being shunned by half his family. I don't see how it helps to have more people speculating about him."

Jenn was hurt. "Do you think I would be rude to Justin? Shun him?"

"No," Steve said. "It's just none of our business. His life is his life."

"It's our business where our children are concerned," Jenn challenged.

"They see him once a year for three hours over dinner. It's not going to hurt them. I don't care what that guy said. Justin's a good person. Jenn, he was an usher at our wedding. Do you really think he would hurt Josh?"

Jenn took a breath and exhaled. "No. I guess not."

"You know I work with people who are practicing homosexuals. It's not like it's contagious."

"I never said it was," Jenn said. "You're treating me as if I'm in the wrong here. Who's a homosexual at work?"

"Bethany," Steve said with a shrug.

"Your secretary?" Jenn's head dropped forward, and her mouth opened in surprise. "But she's beautiful."

"Remember how I told you that you didn't need to be jealous of her?"

Jenn nodded.

"Now you know why." Steve winked.

Jenn's eyes got big; she shook her head. "She's really a homosexual?"

Steve nodded. "The world is changing. It's complicated, Jenn. I'm not going to compromise my values, but sometimes being Christian means being respectful of people who don't share my beliefs. I don't have that luxury of choosing who I'm around all day. I work with all kinds of people. I'm responsible for creating a good working environment for each of them."

Jenn patted Steve's arm. "I love that you're a great boss. But we have to be in this all the way for Josh. We have to believe. We have to be a team."

"We are a team. And like all teams, we each have a position. You play the mom part, and I'll play the dad part. You have to trust me, OK?"

Jenn nodded. *Surrender*, she told herself. *I'm surrendering.* Steve squeezed her hand, and then they turned to the people at the table next to them and introduced themselves.

◆ ◆ ◆

After dinner Doug welcomed them back to the sanctuary. Josh sat with the other teens. Jenn held Steve's hand as they sang hymns and listened to speakers tell their stories. Toward the end the parents were invited to do a laying-on of hands on the children. The kids bunched up in the front of the sanctuary, and the parents closest to them circled around them. The rest of the parents made concentric circles, touching the backs of people who were touching the backs of people who were touching the backs of people who were touching the kids. Jenn could not see Josh in the midst, but she felt him in there.

Doug prayed out loud from the inner circle, "Lord, thank You in the name of Jesus. God, thank You for the power of the Holy Spirit. We ask that Your presence fill us with wisdom and revelation so that we may follow You, love You, and serve You entirely. Bind up all distractions and show us Your will.

"Lord, we ask for Your blessing on these children. They are ready to live surrendered lives. Jesus Christ, our Lord and Savior, we know You have not given them more temptation than they can bear. They are ready to reject homosexual desires and turn their minds to wholesome thoughts.

"Lord God, these babies have been wounded by their pasts. We know they can only be healed through Your mercy. I call on You and Lord Jesus to save these children. We know You want to protect them from homosexual behavior. They are ready to work with You, Lord, so that they may be agents—no, warriors—for Your will on earth. In Jesus's name we pray. Amen."

Everyone in the room echoed, "Amen."

After that powerful worship service Jenn was filled with hope when they found Josh to say good-bye. She couldn't quite read how he was feeling. Even though people were watching she gave him a huge hug, squeezing her love and hope into him as he started his heroic journey.

"I am so proud of you, honey. I want you to walk this week surrounded by the Holy Spirit. You're a special person, Josh, touched by God. There's a reason for this struggle that will be revealed to us in time. I love you."

"Bye, Mom. I love you, too," Josh said. "But not too much!"

Jenn laughed. Josh was making a joke! This was working already.

"I love you," Steve said. Then he hugged Josh, and Jenn heard him whisper into their son's ear, "No matter what they tell you, I have always loved you. From the moment you were born."

When Steve released Josh, they both wiped their eyes. It wasn't very masculine, but it was bonding.

"Come on, Josh," Andrew called. "We'll take good care of him. I promise."

Jenn watched him walk away with his "family" for the week. His golden-brown hair poked above the others; he was even taller than Andrew. Her chest ached with love. Steve put his arm around her, and she leaned into his support. They watched until Josh disappeared into a room and the door closed tight. Then she pulled away from Steve and looked around. She was surrounded by parents watching their sons and daughters walk away. All of them were entrusting their children's precious souls to the care of Resurrection Ministries.

15

" I 'm thinking about taking Rachel to Monterey this week. What do you think?" Jenn asked Steve as they drove home.

"Sure. She'd love it."

"We need more mother-daughter time. You'll be at work. Josh is in great hands. Why not?" Jenn was excited. Things were really looking up. She felt like she was finally getting back to being herself.

It took some doing to find a hotel at the last minute, but Jenn found something suitable within walking distance of the aquarium. When she told her daughter on Sunday as they were driving home from dinner at the Bishops', Rachel literally squealed with delight. They packed up and left by ten in the morning. Jenn bought day passes to give them plenty of time with the penguins, the otters, and the jellyfish. Whenever Jenn worried about Josh, she reminded herself that he was in God's hands and she needed to let go. This was Rachel's time, so she focused on her youngest child, which meant they went to each scheduled penguin feeding while they were there.

During one of the feedings, Jenn slipped away for a few minutes, supposedly to go to the bathroom. Really she went to the gift shop to buy stuff for Easter. She chose a small stuffed animal for each kid: a penguin for Rachel, an otter for Josh, and a jellyfish for Sara. They'd roll their eyes, but Jenn knew they loved that she still hid baskets for them.

In the jellyfish exhibit, the Holy Spirit filled her body, sending a chill through her spine. She felt utterly connected to God's creation. All at once she felt both small and big, like she was a tiny atom in God's heart. For the first time in two months she was truly at peace.

When it was time to leave, Jenn felt ready to return to her life. She and Josh would both be transformed this week, more certain of their faith and their relationship with their Savior.

On the drive home, Jenn's cell rang. She passed it to Rachel.

Jenn heard Rachel say, "Hey, Josh; it's Rachel. Mom's driving, so she can't talk now. Want me to give her a message? How's your camp?"

Rachel listened for a bit.

"Oh," she said into the phone. "That's too bad. I'll ask her."

To Jenn, Rachel said, "Josh wants to come home. Can we go get him?"

"How is he calling me? He doesn't have a cell phone." Jenn was incredulous. Josh was supposed to be on his way to a cure, not quitting his treatment.

"Mom wants to know how you're calling her." Rachel listened to Josh's reply. "He's at a pay phone in the church. Can we get him?"

"No!" Jenn declared. "Tell him no. He needs to stick this out."

"You heard, huh? Sorry, Joshy. We'll see you on Saturday. I miss you. The house is too quiet when you're gone."

"I love you, Josh," Jenn yelled, hoping he heard her.

"He says he loves you, too," Rachel said to Jenn. Then into the phone she said, "Bye, Josh. Cheer up. It's almost over...two more days until you can come home."

After Rachel hung up, Jenn asked, "How did he sound?"

"Not good," Rachel said matter-of-factly.

"What did he say?"

"He said, 'Ask Mom if I can come home,'" Rachel said in a low voice, mimicking Josh.

"What else?"

"Nothing." Jenn felt, more than saw, Rachel shrug.

Once again Jenn was plummeted back into a pit of anxiety. The calm mood brought on by two blissful days surrounded by sea life had completely evaporated. She started fixating on Josh again. Hopefully he was just homesick, not resisting treatment. She wondered if she had made a rash decision in telling him to stick it out and decided to speak with him.

After she parked in the garage she hit redial, but nobody answered the pay phone. She went to the family room, dug through the papers on her desk to find the emergency contact number at Resurrection Ministries, and dialed.

A woman answered the phone.

"Hello. May I please speak to Josh Henderson? He's attending camp this week."

"May I ask who's calling?"

"This is his mother, Jennifer."

"Hello, Jennifer, this is Donna! Remember me from the first day? My husband is John, one of Josh's spirit-circle leaders."

Jennifer was relieved to hear a familiar voice. "Yes, Donna. Of course I remember you. How are you? How's camp?"

"Blessed and wonderful, praise God!"

"Josh called while I was driving; may I speak to him, please?"

"Oh dear," Donna said in an ominous voice. "Talking with parents is counter to the program. I'm sorry to hear he called you. You know I'll have to report him."

"Excuse me?" Jenn asked.

"For his own good. Andrew, John, and Elaine will need to know so they can adjust treatment as needed. Josh knew that calling outside was forbidden without express permission from Andrew."

Jenn's stomach sank, and she got a metallic taste in her mouth. She sighed. Tentatively she asked, "Do you know how Josh is doing?"

"Well...because my John is with him, I *have* heard a few stories. I don't want to alarm you," Donna said slowly, "but apparently Josh is having difficulty with complete surrender. It's common, so don't be too concerned. Andrew knows how to handle this type of oppositional behavior. He's a very experienced leader."

Jenn bit her lip. "I'm so sorry. He's never been oppositional before."

"For some reason SSA can open the door to all kinds of unwanted behaviors and attitudes. That's why you were wise to just nip this in the bud. We'll have him shaped up by the time you get him on Saturday...or at least further on his way to recovery. I'll be holding you, and him, in my prayers tonight. Good-bye," she said cheerfully.

"Thanks," Jenn squeaked out. She was on the edge of tears once again. This roller coaster of emotions was exhausting.

She dialed Steve at work. He agreed Josh needed to see this thing through. That gave her the strength to do the right thing and stay home.

But it didn't stop her from worrying about her son.

16

On Saturday, Jenn and Steve got up early to make the drive back to Tracy. Jenn told Steve she was too excited to eat, but she was actually scared. She was afraid Josh was mad at her. She was afraid he wasn't cured. She was afraid to hear what they were going to tell her about Josh. She wasn't hopeful at all.

Donna was at the door again to greet people as they arrived.

"Welcome back," she said. All traces of enthusiasm and excitement were gone. Jenn felt like she had done something wrong.

"Hello," Steve said.

"How's Josh?" Jenn asked, worry tinging her voice.

"You'll be reunited with him soon enough," Donna explained in a formal voice. Her eyebrows arched up. "You'll get a full report from his counselor after worship. Just go right into the sanctuary."

Jenn felt thoroughly dismissed. The energy in the sanctuary was a stark contrast to her mood. The band was playing raucous music, and there was a lot of excitement in the room. None of the kids were there, but there were seats roped off in the front, presumably for them. Jenn walked as close as she could to the teen area. At 9:00 a.m. sharp, Doug stepped out onto the stage.

"Blessings, parents and family!" he yelled into the microphone.

"Blessings, Doug," the well-trained crowd yelled back. Jenn didn't join in.

"Parents, family members, you should be so proud of your children! They did the work of the Lord this week. The Holy Spirit has been in the house! Please stand up and give them a big round of applause as they come in."

The congregation stood and cheered. Jenn and Steve rose with them. At the front of the sanctuary, the doors on both sides swung open. The kids filed in one at a time led by their spirit-circle leaders into the saved rows. They were singing a song. Jenn could barely make it out, but as more kids filed in, she recognized the comforting and powerful words: *Our God is a loving God. Through Him we are saved.* Her pulse raced in anticipation. She turned her head from side to side, looking for Josh. She recognized a few of the leaders but not all of them. Then, on the right, Andrew was coming through the door. She grabbed Steve's hand and pointed. Kids filed in behind him. Josh would be coming through soon. Jenn focused on each face. Josh was the last person from his group. He looked straight ahead. He wasn't smiling or singing like the others. She held her hand up, ready to wave, but he didn't look for them.

"I know you want to see your kids, but we have a special ceremony first," Doug said over the singing. "Your reunions will be well worth the wait."

The kids stood in the reserved rows. Jenn could make out the top of Josh's crown above the crowd. *He needs a haircut*, she thought automatically. She stared at the back of his head, willing him to look for her, but unlike most of the other kids, he didn't turn around and wave to his family. The words to the song flashed on the screen. Everyone joined in the singing until it was over. When they sat down, Josh slouched in the pew so low Jenn couldn't see his head. The pit in her stomach got bigger.

"This week has been filled with the work of the Lord! The spirit is in the house!" Doug yelled.

The congregation cheered.

Then people came forward and started giving testimonials. Middle-aged people, young adults, and teens spoke about the transformative love of Jesus Christ and the power of complete surrender to God's will. Person after person reminded the crowd that change was possible. They told stories about their own journeys away from the temptations of the homosexual lifestyle and to the transformative love of Jesus.

After the testimonials, Doug invited the teens and spirit-circle leaders to come to the left side of the chancel. In neat rows they stood facing their families. Josh was so far to the back that Jenn could not see him very well, but she tracked where he was standing.

Doug spoke to the parents. "Families, you have entrusted your children's souls to us. We have honored that trust with hard work and dedication to bring your children in line with biblical living.

"Parents, do you promise to keep faithful to God and our Lord Jesus Christ regardless of the secular and ecumenical pressures that may tempt you away from a holy life for you and your children? If you agree, please say, 'We will.'"

Jenn took Steve's hand, and together they said, "We will," along with the crowd.

"Spiritual warriors," Doug said to the spirit-circle leaders, "you are doing God's holiest work. We thank you for what you have given to these young souls. What you have done here this week will ripple out into the world, bringing our earth a little closer to God's kingdom.

"Let us pray. Lord, thank You in the name of Jesus. God, thank You for the power of the Holy Spirit. Watch over these beautiful children, dear God. Lead them away from same-sex attraction and guide them toward healthy, biblically based living. Transform them with the power of Your love. Do not let their faith falter, for without You they are doomed forever. Amen."

Jenn was focused on the area where Josh stood. She searched for any indication of how he was doing. She desperately wanted to know that he was OK, but he was too far away for her to see his facial expressions.

"Teens, though you walk away from the members of your spirit circle, they will remain within you always. Take the lessons you have learned here and live out the teachings of Jesus in the world. Promise to renounce the devil and any temptations that will lead you from God's path. Commit to living biblically, so that you may know the transformative and healing love of our Lord Jesus Christ on earth and so you may live with our Lord and His Son in the life to come. Do you commit to a full and complete transformation through our Lord Jesus Christ? Do you promise to avoid temptations both physical and spiritual?"

One of the teens walked to the center of the stage. She spoke into the mic in a shaky voice. "I renounce homosexuality and commit to my faith in God and our Lord Jesus Christ."

"Amen!" cried Doug as the young woman crossed to the right side of the stage.

Another teen stepped to the middle. His voice was strong as he said, "I renounce homosexuality and commit to my faith in God and our Lord Jesus Christ."

"Amen!" Doug shouted, and this time he was joined by other voices from the crowd.

That teen was followed by another, and another, and another speaking into the mic and then being affirmed by the congregation with a loud amen. Some cried when they spoke. Others cheered. Some were serious, but most spoke quickly and got it over with. Clearly many of them did not like public speaking. Josh was comfortable with a microphone, so that wouldn't be a problem for him. The group of teens on the right grew as the group on the left dwindled. Soon there were just a few teens surrounded by the spirit-circle leaders, including Josh. Jenn saw Andrew whisper something to him.

Josh walked slowly to the microphone. He stood there, looking out at the crowd, his face stony. He was waiting so long it felt like a challenge. Jenn started to sweat.

He stooped over. Very slowly and with no emotion in his voice, Josh said, "I renounce homosexuality and commit to my faith in God and our Lord Jesus Christ."

Jenn's stomach dropped. She didn't believe a word her son had just said.

◆ ◆ ◆

After worship the families were going to be reunited in private meetings with the spirit-circle leaders. Steve and Jenn joined other parents in a waiting room. Jenn was much too distressed to make conversation with these strangers, so she pulled out her phone, opened solitaire and pretended to be absorbed in the game. But really she was listening intently to the conversation around her.

"This is our third camp," came a low male voice. "We did one through Exodus, and the other was also through Resurrection."

"Your child isn't cured?" a mom asked, sounding confused and disappointed.

The dad replied, "I used to pray for a full recovery. Now I pray for celibacy. She's committed. We know she is, but she refuses to date any boys. She says she doesn't want to be a liar."

Another parent nodded and said, "This is our second camp. Our son Mark needed a strong tune-up. We hope this will get him back on track. Too many people were encouraging him to accept the homosexual lifestyle. We took him out of the public high school and have been homeschooling him."

The first mom asked, "Is that going to be a problem for college? How old is he?"

"He's a senior. He'll be going to Chapman next year—living at home and surrounded by people who share our Christian values."

"You came from Southern California for this?" Steve asked, his leg shaking up and down. He looked as nervous and jumpy as Jenn felt.

"This was an easy drive. One camp was in Texas."

Steve whispered to Jenn, "Guess we were lucky this was so close."

Jenn nodded. She was shaken by the conversation. When she signed Josh up, she believed this would be a one-time thing.

Complete transformation was promised. She'd thought this would be the end of their journey, but from the sounds of the other parents, that was unlikely.

Jenn's phone vibrated. She looked at the screen.

When will you be home? Sara texted.

Jenn texted back, *Not 4 a while. I'll let u know when we leave.*

The couples were called in one by one. As they left, the parents wished the others well and offered to pray for them. Eventually Jenn and Steve were alone, nervous and lost in their own ruminations.

"Do you think this is a bad sign?" she asked Steve. Her eyes started to well up.

Steve sighed. "I don't know. Someone had to be last."

The door opened, startling Jenn.

"Here we go," Steve sighed.

Andrew beckoned them into the room. Josh was standing in the middle of the large space. A black Naugahyde couch and a metal folding chair were next to him. Jenn started toward Josh, opening her arms to give him a hug.

"Stop!" Andrew said. "A verbal greeting is called for."

Jenn felt like she had been slapped. Her face flushed. It had been a long time since she was embarrassed enough to turn red.

"Hi, Josh. I missed you," Jenn said.

Josh nodded. Then he put his hand out to Steve.

"Yes, a handshake is a good masculine greeting for your father. Nice work, Josh," Andrew said. "Have a seat."

They settled into the couch, with Steve sitting between Josh and Jenn. They were sandwiched in so close to one another that Jenn couldn't see Steve's or Josh's face.

"I'm here to give you a report on Josh's progress this week. As you know, it has not been easy for him. He was surprisingly resistant to treatment at first, but I think we had a very powerful breakthrough just yesterday. Wouldn't you agree, Josh?"

Jenn's mood lifted a little when she heard the word *breakthrough*. Maybe Josh was transformed.

"Yes, sir." Josh stared at the ground.

Steve asked, "What do you mean by 'resistant'?"

"For the first few days, he was unable to face the truth of the treatment. We spend time on all parts each day: parental relationships, root trauma, same-sex attraction, and prayer. His strength is in prayer. He was able to pray for himself and others and accept prayers on his behalf. However, he insisted that his relationship with each of you is fine. I trust you will not encourage that thinking. And he is in denial about a root trauma, even though we uncovered it when you dropped him off. We encouraged him to speak about the abuse from your cousin Justin, but he refused. As I said, he is in denial."

Jenn had mixed feelings about the counselor's report. It was a nice consolation to hear that Josh said his relationship with each of them was good, and she also didn't believe that Justin abused Josh, but she wanted him to be cured. For that he needed to surrender to treatment. That was why he was here. He had to surrender his life to God.

Andrew kept going. "As for the same-sex attraction, it's unclear whether we made progress on that front. Josh says that we have, but to be honest I believe he may be withholding information from us."

Jenn blinked. "So he's not cured?"

"It's usually a long process. I'm sorry if you misunderstood. Not many are entirely changed in one week. There are more camps, and we have a list of wonderful counselors who can work with him on an ongoing basis." Andrew handed them a piece of paper.

"'Change is possible,'" Jenn declared. "That's what you said. 'Change is possible.'"

"Of course it's possible. That's true. Just not in the case of Josh right now. But I haven't given up hope on him. Not in the slightest. As I said, his prayer life is beautiful. That's not true for many of the other teens. The journey back to a right relationship with God is not short, but it is so rich and meaningful. I wish you all the best."

He stood up, clearly finished with them, and opened the other door. They stood up too. He shook each of their hands as they walked out. Josh's stuff was waiting in the entry, and he picked up his belongings. Steve took the suitcase from Josh's hand. Her eyes burning, Jenn still wanted to touch her son, but she resisted the impulse. The entryway was vacant, with all the signs and balloons gone. They were the last ones to go.

After she buckled the seat belt, she faced forward so Josh could not see how upset she was. *Resistant to treatment*, *oppositional*, *homosexual*: those were not the words she wanted to hear about Josh. *Cured*. That was the word she was longing to hear today. *Cured*.

Jenn had no words for her son. Apparently neither did Steve. They drove along in silence all the way home. She looked over at her husband. Steve's jaw was clenched and his hands twisted on the steering wheel. He looked as upset as Jenn. This journey felt too much like the ride from the hospital.

Two months had passed, and Jenn feared they were no closer to a cure.

17

As they pulled into the driveway, Jenn searched for something to say. She pushed out weakly, "It's not hopeless, Josh. We have to hold on to faith. I know you can do this."

"Well, I don't," he said, slamming the car door.

Steve took her hand as they walked inside. The living room was filled with balloons and a big sign that said, *Welcome Home, Joshy. We Missed You!* Rachel and Sara walked in from the family room.

"Surprise," they said weakly, and then rushed to embrace Josh.

"You said you would text when you were on your way!" Rachel chastised Jenn. "We were gonna be waiting! Josh, we made you a mocha cake; come see."

"Thanks, guys," Josh said without enthusiasm. "I'm not hungry. Maybe after dinner. I'm going to rest."

Sara looked at Steve with a quizzical face. Steve shook his head. He waited until Josh was gone and then explained quietly, "It's been a long day. Camp wasn't so good for Josh. We're all disappointed."

"Baking a cake was a very sweet thing to do for your brother," Jenn assured them. "Thank you." She hugged her daughters tightly.

"I'm going to talk to Josh," Steve said, and went upstairs.

Rachel returned to the family room to finish her TV show.

"Was it really bad?" Sara asked Jenn, her eyes filled with concern.

Jenn nodded. "Could you please go for a walk with him after he's done talking to Dad—before dinner?" she suggested. "It might help. I'm scared for him, Sara."

"What happened?"

Jenn sighed. "I don't really know. They didn't say that much, and Josh didn't tell us anything on the way home. But basically, he didn't surrender and…" Jenn's voice cracked. "Well, he's not cured."

Sara rubbed Jenn's arm and said. "I know this is hard for you, but I'm not worried about Josh. He's an awesome person. He's going to be fine. I'm certain of it."

"Thanks, Sara." Jenn hugged her daughter. "That means a lot to me."

◆ ◆ ◆

The talk with Steve and the walk with Sara transformed Josh. He almost seemed like his old self when he came to dinner. Jenn was dying to know what they talked about, but she let them have their privacy. She'd be satisfied just seeing him looking hopeful and happy. They all reached around the table to hold hands for prayer.

Steve spoke up. "You'll be glad to know your brother got an A in prayer at camp. I think he should show off his skills by leading our prayer."

"Hear, hear," said Rachel.

Jenn winked at Steve and then bowed her head.

Josh spoke clearly and emphatically. "Merciful God, we thank You for this glorious bounty. May the spirit of Your love and Your

Son fill our souls that we may be guided to do Your will for us on this day and in all the days to come. Amen."

Josh's words felt strong and true. He really did love God. Jenn's mood was lifted even higher by his words.

When she looked up, Jenn asked her children, "Are you too old for Easter baskets?"

"No. I want my basket," Rachel said, "until I'm eighteen! And I don't want to hunt for it alone." The others laughed. Jenn had asked this same question last year; she knew the answer and was ready for the morning. Many mothers in their church didn't hide Easter baskets because they considered it too pagan, but Jenn thought it was harmless fun and was glad Rachel had pushed for the tradition to continue. Jenn was in no rush to put the fun of hiding baskets behind them.

◆ ◆ ◆

Easter was usually one of Jenn's favorite days of the year. She loved being in church and hearing about the physical resurrection that brought her spiritual salvation. But this year it was hard to be in the building.

Most of the church service washed past Jenn. But the sermon grabbed her attention. Pastor James said, "Jesus was killed on the cross, died, and rose again for *you*. You do not have to do anything for the gift of His sacrifice besides believe. It was a gift freely given by God for you, because you are sinful. And by your faith you shall be saved. Isn't God glorious? Didn't He make a beautiful design? And He did it for you. For each of you, because He loves you so much."

God's love filled Jenn in that moment. She felt Him holding her, telling her that she was saved. Then she thought of Josh, throwing away the gift of the resurrection. It was unfathomable to imagine being in heaven without her whole family. It wouldn't be paradise without Josh. The grace she felt from God's love slipped away again.

After the service Pastor James gave the whole family warm greetings, hearty handshakes, and big hugs.

He looked intently at Josh and solemnly asked, "How are you?"

Josh tilted his head noncommittally.

Pastor pushed, "Wasn't camp inspiring? Did you feel the Holy Spirit?"

Steve replied, "Josh was praised for the depth of his prayer life. Jenn and I are very proud."

"Praise Jesus!" Pastor James replied. "May the blessing of the resurrection fill your lives today. I'm sure you feel it more strongly than ever. A tested faith is a stronger faith." And then he moved on to greet the next family.

◆ ◆ ◆

Steve had put a great spin on it with Pastor James, but Jenn knew she'd tell him the rest of the story soon. She spent the afternoon obsessing over their next steps while she made shortcake for Easter dinner at the Bishops'. Her mind kept returning to the conversation with Andrew and the pledge she had made to commit to Josh's soul. She looked over the list of camps and counselors that they had handed out yesterday. She decided that a monthlong camp over the summer, along with weekly counseling with Pastor James, was the best strategy to keep the momentum going.

That evening at the Bishops' Jenn and Lindsay were alone in the kitchen putting the finishing touches on the meal. Everyone else was in the family room playing Celebrity. From their behavior, no one could tell her family was in crisis.

"So? How did it go for Josh? He looks great," Lindsay said.

"Oh, Lindsay." Jenn choked up.

Lindsay put her arm around Jenn and gave her a squeeze. "Take your time. What's happened?"

"He's not cured. Not at all. They said it might take a long time. I thought it was going to be over by now, but he needs more treatment."

"I'm so sorry, Jenn. I know you were so hopeful." Lindsay made an empathetic face. "You must be so disappointed."

Jenn nodded.

"But you have to keep faith in the Lord," her friend reminded her firmly, sounding like a schoolmarm.

"I have faith. Sometimes that feels like all I have."

"No! Don't say that; you have us. We're with you every step of the way," Lindsay said. "You know that, don't you? Every night you're in our prayers."

"That means so much to us. Some of the parents at camp said the whole experience brought their family closer to God. I'm fighting for that for us." Jenn sighed. "But to tell you the truth, I'm exhausted. I just want a rest."

"You're the mom," Lindsay replied. "You don't get that luxury. Do you?"

Jenn shook her head. She didn't get to wallow in self-pity. She had to push on through and show faith.

The meal was delicious: salmon with lemon dill sauce, fresh asparagus, homemade rolls, and strawberry shortcake with whipped cream. Jenn hardly tasted the food. She went through the motions but didn't feel the spirit. They were there to celebrate Easter, but her soul wasn't light with the good news of their Savior's resurrection. It was heavy with the knowledge that Josh needed more treatment—and the sinking suspicion that he didn't want it.

◆ ◆ ◆

After dinner, as Jenn drove her to BART, Sara asked, "You OK, Mom?"

"Well, as you know, Josh didn't make the progress we hoped for," Jenn said. "It's hard for me. I worry about him constantly."

"He thinks you don't love him anymore," Sara told her, "and that he's a total disappointment to you."

"Oh, Sara. That's simply not true. Not at all. I love him so much," Jenn explained to her daughter. "I just need to show it less. That's part of the remedy."

"Don't you think that's messed up?" Sara asked, charged with emotion.

Jenn asked, "What do you mean?"

"What kind of treatment tells a mom to ignore her sons and a dad to ignore his daughters?" Sara asked with heat in her voice.

Shocked at Sara's attitude, Jenn replied, "Daddy's not ignoring you."

"Practically." Sara's voice cracked. "He won't talk to me on the phone. He tells me to ask you if I want advice. We hardly ever spend time as a family anymore. I didn't do anything. Why am I being punished?"

"You aren't being punished," Jenn said. "We just don't want to make the same mistake with you that we made with Josh." Carefully, she said, "We don't want you to start having same-sex attractions."

Sara laughed. "I assure you, Mom, that you don't have to be worried about that."

"Really?"

"Yes, really. I'm as straight as they get. I promise. I'm like a zero on the Kinsey scale."

"The what?" Jenn had no idea what her daughter was talking about.

"You know, the human-sexuality scale that goes from zero to six. Zero is all the way straight, and six is all the way gay," Sara explained.

Straight? Gay? Jenn hated that Sara was using those words so casually. "No. I don't know. Where did you learn about such a thing?"

"Intro to Psych," Sara explained. "It's been around for a really long time, like since the fifties. I'm surprised you haven't heard of it."

"We never learned about it at BIOLA—that's for sure." Jenn said. Then she was hit by an awful thought. "Have you ever...? With a boy?"

"No." Sara laughed. "I'm not even dating anyone. I just know who's attractive to me, and it's not girls."

Relief flooded Jenn's body. She didn't even realize she'd been anxious about Sara. Until recently, she'd thought her kids told her everything, but now she knew better. Sara and Rachel might be keeping big secrets from her, too.

"What about Rachel?" she dared to ask.

"She can't stop talking about the cute boys in her classes, so I think you're safe there," Sara said. Then she spoke cautiously. "Is it really so bad that Josh is gay?"

Those words were still like a slap to Jenn. "Excuse me?"

"I've met a lot of really great kids who are gay. Some are even Christian."

"Being homosexual is incompatible with scripture," Jenn insisted. "You know that!"

"I know God loves Josh," Sara said.

Jenn was struck speechless. She had the painful realization that Sara had given up on Josh's transformation, which meant Josh had given up on it too—he just hadn't told her. That was why he was happier last night; he was done fighting for his soul. Her throat closed up like a vise; it was hard to breathe.

Sara broke the intense silence. "Are you allowed to tell Josh that you love him? Or give him anything?"

"Yes," Jenn squeaked out with a nod. "I'll talk to him. I promise."

◆ ◆ ◆

Jenn calmed down as she drove home. It wasn't really a surprise that she had to hold on to the faith for Josh and Sara. Parents were often moral role models. Her faith was strong enough to do that for them. As she had promised Sara, Jenn went to speak with Josh as soon as she got home. He was sitting on his bed in his room, with textbooks spread out in front of him.

"Shouldn't you be working at your desk?"

He looked up at her, chewing his lip, and sighed. "If you want." He started to stand.

"No, Josh. Sorry. You can do your schoolwork however you like," Jenn said from the doorway. "You're a good student. You don't need me telling you how to study."

Josh sank back onto his comforter. He put his math textbook on his lap and grabbed a notebook, ignoring her. Jenn watched as he started working. He was handsome, her seemingly perfect son. It hurt to know he was so flawed.

"Josh, will you tell me what happened at camp?"

He slowly looked up at her. His face was stony, hard to read. "Do you really want to know? Do you really want to talk to me, your shameful son?"

"Don't be like that. I do want to know. Of course I want to know. I'm not ashamed of you," Jenn explained. Quietly she said, "I'm scared for you."

Josh closed his eyes and blinked them a few times. She could tell he was trying not to cry.

Without looking at her, he mumbled, "They kept asking me about all the ways Dad disappointed me or ignored me or made me feel like I wasn't a man. I couldn't think of any. Other kids lied. They made up stories just so they could earn food and free time."

"What do you mean 'earn food'?"

"I never went hungry," Josh explained, still mumbling. "But kids who 'made more progress' got good food. At first I lost dessert and then fruit. Eventually all I got to eat was PB and J." His eyes welled up. He shrugged.

"Oh, Josh. I'm sorry. I had no idea."

"They screamed at me, Mom," Josh said, energy building in his voice. Looking Jenn straight in the eyes, he said, "They yelled in my face, telling me I had to love Jesus or I would go to hell. It didn't matter to them that I do love Jesus. They kept doing it, especially when I didn't make up some story about Dad's cousin Justin." He looked back down at his bed. "That was the day I called you. Then I was put in isolation—for two days. They wanted me to have time to 'talk to God.' It was better than being yelled at. I still like talking to God." He had a sweet smile on his face as he wiped his eyes.

It hurt Jenn to see him in such pain. She resisted the urge to hug him; instead, she took a deep breath. She spoke in a steady voice, wanting to explain to him the need for this treatment in a way that he could understand. "I'm glad you like talking to God. It will save your life. I'm sorry camp was hard. It's for your own long-term good, though it may not seem like that right now. I know it seems like I don't love you, but that's absolutely not true. It's the farthest thing from the truth. I love you so much. Do you understand? It's like chemo for cancer. It hurts all of you, but it's only meant to destroy the cancer."

Josh's face went blank. "OK."

Jenn had failed to communicate. She could see that Josh didn't understand. Like most teenagers, he couldn't always see the big picture.

He asked, "Can I get back to my work? I have a lot to do before school tomorrow."

"Yeah." Jenn nodded. "Good night. Thanks for talking with me."

He looked up at her. His face was intent and sad. "I miss you, Mom."

"Me too, Josh." She looked at him with longing in her heart, hoping he could feel the love she couldn't outwardly express.

18

The next morning, when Jenn went out to the front yard to get the newspaper, her gaze was caught by something unusual at the end of the driveway. She walked toward it. In bright-pink chalk the word *faggot* was written on the concrete.

A hot wave passed through her body, leaving her feeling nauseous. Her lungs clamped tight as a vise. Josh mustn't see this. She ran into the house, determined to talk to Steve before her son came out of his room. She found her husband getting dressed in his closet.

"What's wrong?" he asked as soon as he saw her.

In a jerky voice, she managed to say, "Out front... You have to fix this. Please clean it up before he leaves for school."

"What are you talking about?"

"Someone wrote something horrible...about Josh...on our driveway. I can't even say the word. Please. Wash it away." She started crying. "How can anyone be so mean? I don't understand. Our Josh is a good person. He's good and kind and beautiful..." Steve started to give her a hug, but she cut him off. "Now, please. I don't want Josh to see. He's so fragile."

Jenn was still shaky as she served breakfast to the kids. They were partway through eating when Steve walked back in, damp from the hose spray.

"What're you doing, Dad?" Josh asked, looking puzzled.

Jenn shot Steve a look, but he was prepared. "A dog made a mess in the driveway," Steve said. "I was cleaning it up. But now I need to change. Jenn, can you take the kids to school so they won't be late?"

"Sure."

When Josh and Rachel finished breakfast, they piled into the Land Cruiser for the three-and-a-half-mile drive to Dublin High. Jenn pulled into the drop-off lane to let them out.

"I love you, Josh," Jenn cried after him as he slammed the passenger door.

"What about me?" Rachel asked.

"You, too." Jenn smiled at her daughter. "It's not a competition."

"It sure feels like it…these days." Rachel scowled before slamming the back door.

Jenn shook her head and sighed. There was no way to win. She watched Josh yell out a greeting to his teammates Scott, Joe, Grant, and Phil. They let him into their circle and did that handshake thing she didn't understand with a fist bump at the end. He sure looked like he fit in with those boys. Did they know? Had one of them written on their driveway even though they'd been friends for years? She studied the scene, looking for any sign of hostility toward Josh but didn't detect any. She considered parking the SUV and reporting the incident to the principal but decided drawing more attention to Josh would not help the situation.

◆ ◆ ◆

That night, Jenn walked into her bedroom to get a sweater. She was startled to see Steve sitting on the flowered comforter, the phone on the bed next to him. His skin was blanched, and his eyes were red rimmed. Jenn's body went on high alert.

"That was my mom," Steve said. He leaned over and started sobbing—not quietly but actual sobs. *James must be dead*, Jenn thought. She'd feared, but expected, this phone call saying one of their fathers had simply passed.

She sank down onto the bed next to Steve and wrapped her arms around him. He leaned his head into her. She stroked his hair. Her eyes burned.

Jenn asked gently, "Your dad...He's passed?"

Steve shook his head. He pulled back and looked at Jenn. "She... doesn't want to see Josh again," he stammered out. He cleared his throat. "My mom."

"What?" Jenn didn't understand.

"She heard that he's gay...from someone at church who knows Lindsay's mom."

"Oh." A knot tied in Jenn's stomach.

Steve said, "She...I knew she would disapprove, but I didn't think she'd just cut him off. She called to tell me that the rest of us are welcome. But not...not Josh." His eyes bored into Jenn. "I'm never, ever doing that to him. No matter what happens. It's not an option."

"No, of course not."

Jenn leaned against her husband, once again at a loss for words. Her stomach churned. This wasn't going away; it was getting worse. She'd been so foolish and naive. It hadn't occurred to her that people who loved Josh would ostracize him.

"She'll change her mind when he's cured," Jenn said, sounding more confident than she felt.

Steve shook his head slowly. "I don't know that I can ever forgive her, even if she changes her mind. How can she do this to our son? To me? To all of us?"

"I don't know."

"I told her that I won't go anywhere Josh isn't welcome...but she didn't care." Steve looked incredulous. "She said that was my choice but she isn't going to compromise her Christian values."

"Oh, Steve, I'm so sorry." Jenn wept, too. "Did you talk to your dad?"

"Mom said she spoke for both of them." Steve punched the bed. "I just want to hit something," he said through clenched teeth. "You know what I thought about after she hung up?"

Jenn shook her head.

"Justin. And Aunt Michelle. I didn't do or say anything when my mom banished him from her home. Do you know what that makes me?"

Jenn shook her head.

"A coward."

"No, Steve."

"Yes," Steve insisted, "I'm a coward. I didn't stand up to my mom; I didn't call Justin. I just let it be. Not out of any principle— only because it was easy. I didn't say anything to you because I didn't want to talk or think about it. That doesn't make me righteous. It makes me lazy. And disloyal."

"You're a good cousin to Justin."

"Not when he needed me. Not when it was hard." Steve blew out his breath. "I don't know if he'll forgive me, but I'm going to apologize."

Jenn couldn't think of anything to say that would be helpful to her husband. She studied his face as he stared at the wall in silence; it was clear that he was thinking by the way his eyes darted around.

"I'm not going to tell Josh about my mom," Steve said. "He doesn't need this right now. It's not like he sees her much anyway. He might not even notice. Agreed?"

Jenn nodded. "Absolutely."

"Jenn, promise me. No matter what happens to Josh, or any of our kids, we won't cut them off."

"Of course not."

"Even if Josh stays homosexual?" Steve pushed.

Jenn took a breath to calm herself. "I can't imagine a scenario where I would give up on Josh's salvation. But that doesn't mean I would cut him off." She added carefully, "But if he were a heroin addict, would you want me to come around to supporting that?"

"If one of our kids was a heroin addict, they would be welcome in my home; would they be welcome in yours?"

Jenn heard the challenge in Steve's voice. *His* home and *her* home, as though they would be two different houses. Jenn's pulse picked up. Josh's condition was driving a wedge between them. Her head was light, and she felt dizzy.

Deliberately, she chose her words. "I want him cured. All the way cured. I will never give up on that goal. If he were a drug addict, I would never stop fighting for his recovery. If he had cancer, I would fight for his physical life."

"But would he be welcome in your house?" Steve demanded.

"Yes, Josh will always be welcome in my, in *our*, home," Jenn agreed. "But I won't stop praying for his recovery. Will you? Are you just giving up because it's a hard fight? I am never, ever giving up on Josh...or Sara...or Rachel."

Steve nodded. He looked satisfied with her reply.

"Do you know something?" Jenn asked, terrified of the answer, but she had to find out. "Has Josh told you he's given up on his recovery?"

"Josh hasn't said anything directly, but it just seems that his spirit is not in this fight anymore," Steve replied, searching Jenn's face.

A wave of emotion passed through her body. She had just stopped crying, and now tears were streaming down her face again. She closed her eyes and exhaled.

"I can't pretend that doesn't tear at my heart." She appealed to her husband. "How can it not break yours? Our Josh living the homosexual lifestyle? I want him to have a normal life: respect, church, children. I can't just give up on him. Have you? Can you imagine heaven without him? All of us with God, but without Josh?"

"Jenn, I haven't given up on him," Steve replied. "It's just..."

"What?" Jenn's heart hammered hard.

Steve sighed and stared into Jenn's eyes. He was thinking about his words.

"What, Steve? Just say it, please."

"I haven't given up on his salvation, but we can't push so hard that we shove him away from us altogether. I've seen that in some families. So have you."

"I don't want him to think we've given up on him," she pleaded.

"Me either, Jenn."

She took in a deep breath. Steve had said the words she wanted to hear, but she wasn't so certain that they meant what she wanted them to mean.

◆ ◆ ◆

On Thursday morning Jenn walked with Lindsay in the neighborhood. Their walks had become increasingly awkward recently. Jenn had a feeling Lindsay wanted to say something, but she was holding back. She wasn't surprised. She found herself avoiding talking about Josh with Lindsay. Not so long ago she would have told Lindsay all about Marilyn's behavior, but today she wasn't interested in hearing her friend's thoughts about her mother-in-law.

After walking, Jenn gathered Josh's laundry. As always, she checked the pockets of his clothes before she dropped them in the wash. Mostly they were empty, but in the back of a pair of jeans she found a folded piece of paper. She opened it up and read:

<u>Welcoming and Affirming Church</u>
Wherever you are on your personal journey, we will love you and embrace you just as God does. We seek to live out Jesus's love on earth.

Jenn's breath caught, and her stomach dropped. Josh was learning about another church? Her mind flew to Kyle Goss. He was encouraging Josh to embrace the homosexual lifestyle. No wonder Josh was giving up hope. She was furious—with Kyle, with Steve, and with herself. Pastor James had warned them about secular dangers, but she hadn't taken his concern seriously enough, and now Josh was paying the price. She dropped the jeans into the washer but didn't take the time to start the load.

Jenn drove to Kyle's office without calling. She knew it was a ridiculous thing to do even in the midst of doing it. He might not be there, or he might be with someone, but she was so mad she couldn't just leave him a message. When she found him, she was going to yell right in his face.

She wanted to pound on his office door but restrained herself and sat in the waiting room. It was ten thirty, and though she was furious with Kyle, that was no reason to interrupt someone's time with him. So she sat on a couch, thumbing through the old magazines, looking at the posters on the wall, and rereading the note from the so-called church.

At ten to eleven, the door swung open. Understandably, Kyle looked surprised to see her. He said good-bye to the woman leaving his office and motioned Jenn to come in with a tilt of his head.

"Hello, Jenn," Kyle said. "How's Josh?"

"Have you been seeing him against my wishes?"

Kyle shook his head. "No. Steve told me you were going to focus on his other treatment."

Jenn held up the paper in her hand and waved it in front of Kyle's face. "How could you give this to him?" she yelled. "You know it goes against everything we value."

"Would you like to have a seat? I see you're upset about something," he said very calmly.

Rejecting the offer to sit, she challenged, "I'm upset that I trusted my son to you and you betrayed us."

Kyle sat down. "I don't know anything about that piece of paper."

"You didn't give this to Josh? Encouraging him to find another church?" She handed the paper to him.

Jenn finally sat down. Slowly Kyle read the flyer. When he finished, he looked up and said, "This isn't from me. It's the church I attend, but I didn't give this to Josh. It would be unethical for me to encourage Josh to attend any religious community besides the one you have chosen for him, most especially my own."

Jenn glared at Kyle. "You lied to me. You told me you're Christian. You knew exactly what I meant when I asked that question."

"I answered honestly. My work is deeply grounded in Jesus's teachings," he replied calmly.

Jenn challenged, "You don't live a biblically based life."

"On the contrary, I turn to the Bible on a daily basis. It's rich, complicated, and contradictory scripture. I wrestle with it every day to try to understand what enduring truth is in there and what is human bias."

Jenn shot back, "It's all enduring truth."

"Slavery, polygamy, stoning?" Kyle questioned. "Those are enduring truths?"

"You know what I mean!" Jenn retorted.

"With respect, I don't know what you mean." Kyle changed the subject. "I'm sorry, but I have another client arriving very soon. I need to be ready to meet with him. I'd be happy to schedule time with you, if you like. And with Josh, if you decide you want that.

Josh is a lovely human being. He has a deep well of faith, and he loves you very much."

Jenn stood up. She stammered, "B...But what about..." She waved the flyer.

"I don't know." Kyle shook his head. "You'll need to ask your son."

Jenn felt deflated as she left. She'd been so full of righteous indignation as she drove over, and now she was just confused. Slowly she walked to her car. Sitting in the Land Cruiser, she prayed to God, asking Him to take away her confusion and guide her on a righteous path. *Surrender*, she reminded herself. *Surrender to God's will.*

◆ ◆ ◆

She was waiting to speak with Josh when he got home. He walked into the family room and blanched when he saw the flyer in her hand.

"Mom, let me explain—" he started.

"Where did you get this?" she asked calmly.

"At school. From a teacher."

Jenn was stunned. "A teacher is handing out religious flyers to kids? Dublin High is a public school. Separation of church and state. I'm going to get him fired."

"No, Mom!" Josh pleaded. "She wanted to help me."

"Help you? What kind of help involves luring a child away from his religion? It's wrong, Josh. She needs to know that."

Josh dropped onto the couch. He buried his head in his arms, obviously very upset. Jenn was being too hard on him again. She sat next to him and put her arm around him. He leaned into her. Even though she knew she was going against his treatment, it was sweet to have him close.

She said gently, "Josh, you didn't do anything wrong. She knows better. Don't beat yourself up about this."

"I shouldn't have gone to her with my doubts."

"I wish you had come to me or Dad."

Josh popped his head up and stared at Jenn. "Really, Mom? Come to you? With my doubts? Like you want to hear about it."

"I do, Josh," Jenn said. But if she were being honest with herself and him, she didn't want her son to have any doubts.

"Complete and immediate transformation. That's what you want, Mom. I've tried—for years. You have no idea." Josh shook his head, looking pained. "I've thought about this and prayed about this so much. I'm left with either God not loving me at all or loving me just as He made me."

Jenn didn't like either of those choices. The best option was that Josh surrender his life to God. He had to refocus.

"Why did you talk to that particular teacher?" she asked.

"She's the GSA adviser, so she understands what I'm going through."

"The what?" Jenn quizzed him.

"The Gay-Straight Alliance," Josh mumbled.

"What?" Jenn yelled. "You've been going to that group? After all Dad and I have been through to help you? Are you so willing to throw your salvation away?"

"No. I don't want to throw my salvation away. Or my relationship with my Savior. That's why Ms. Hodder gave me that flyer. She says I don't have to pick between being honest about who I really am and loving God. She told me there are some churches that think being gay is part of God's plan."

Jenn was speechless. She wanted to scream at Josh and shake him. They were working so hard for his complete transformation through faith, but she was losing him. She had pledged to protect him from secular influences at Resurrection Ministries, but clearly she was failing.

"She's enticing you to come to her church?" Jenn was incredulous.

"It's not her church."

Jenn stared at him.

Josh said, "Really, it's not her church. She's a Unitarian."

"That's supposed to make me feel better?" Jenn retorted. "You're getting spiritual advice from a Unitarian. It is absolutely unethical for her to encourage you to leave your own church."

"Promise you won't get her fired," Josh begged. "I'd hate myself even more if that happened."

"Josh, no...there's no reason to hate yourself."

"Come on, Mom!" Josh stood up. His face was red and contorted. "You're crazy! Do you even listen to yourself? You can't have it both ways. Either I'm an abomination or I'm not!"

He stormed away, and she heard a door slam upstairs.

Jenn was shaking. Josh had never, ever screamed at her like that before. Her first impulse was to call the principal of Dublin High to report that teacher, but she didn't trust her own instincts. She considered Lindsay, but rejected the idea. Her platitudes about the simplicity of surrender were more frustrating than supportive. She really had no idea what Jenn and Josh were going through. It just wasn't that simple. Jenn knew Steve would tell her to leave it alone, so she called her mom, looking for sympathy and advice.

Jenn finished telling the story and asked, "Do you think I should call the principal?"

"Well, dear, I think it would cause Josh to trust you less. Do you want that?"

"No, of course not. I just want him healed. He's given up on his own transformation. It's devastating. His salvation is at stake!"

Her mom said, "To be honest, I'm not so certain about that."

"What?"

"It just seems like this issue became so important to our pastors out of the blue. I blame that Anita Bryant."

"What are you talking about?" Jenn asked her mother.

"She got all worked up about it, and then everyone followed. No one used to care about such things."

Jenn was confused to be hearing her mother talk like this. "Are you sure?"

Her mom insisted, "I absolutely never heard a word about homosexuality in church until you were a teenager."

"Because everyone agreed it was wrong."

"I don't know that that's true," her mom said. "Remember Uncle Bob?"

"Grandma's brother? Barely. I was twelve when he died."

"Remember his friend Joe? The one he lived with? We included him in all the family gatherings; we just didn't talk about it."

"They were homosexual?" Jenn's mind reeled as she took in this information. "But they sang in the church choir."

"Everyone knew they were special to each other. We just didn't make a show of it. They never hurt anyone. Uncle Bob sure loved Jesus."

She thought back to Uncle Bob and Joe. Suddenly she saw them in a whole new light.

"That's why Joe came to family events even after Uncle Bob died?"

"We weren't going to just abandon him. We were the only family he had. Even if we never said so. What is it they call it? You know President Clinton's words?"

Jenn replied, "Don't ask, don't tell."

"Yes, that's it. I guess we were ahead of our time. We didn't ask, they didn't tell, and we all got along just fine."

"Are you telling me you don't care if Josh has a..." Jenn paused for the right words. "A special friend when he grows up?" It was hard to believe she was having this conversation with her mother.

"Well, dear, of course I want him to change. He's my precious grandson. I want him to have a good life. But I've been doing a lot of thinking and praying ever since you told me, and if Josh decides to lead a homosexual lifestyle, I don't think God will be bothered. And if our Lord isn't bothered, why should I be?" her mom said.

Jenn's throat got tight. "Does Daddy feel the same way?"

"Oh, goodness, dear. Your father and I don't talk about things like that. But I'm sure he'd go along, like he usually does."

"You really don't think Josh will go to hell?" Jenn asked.

"I'm not a theologian, dear, but I know God has forgiven much worse."

19

The next morning Jenn got a text from Lindsay: *Can we have coffee? Starbucks at ten?*

Her stomach clenched when she saw the request.

Sure, Jenn replied, but she didn't bother with the pleasantry of *c u soon*.

At ten o'clock, Jenn spotted Lindsay through the glass window. Her friend looked anxious. Jenn got herself a tall decaf, added cream and sugar, and then joined her friend.

Getting right to the point, Lindsay said, "Jenn, you know we love you all, as much as we love our families."

Jenn stared without saying a word, not wanting to make this easy for Lindsay.

"Please don't hate me…It's just that…well, Mark and I have decided we can't keep exposing our kids to Josh right now. Michael looks up to him; he wants to be like Josh. You have to understand. When Josh was open to treatment, he was a fine influence. But now…" Lindsay shook her head.

Jenn was hurt but not surprised.

"Say something," Lindsay begged.

Jenn started to speak. She stopped. She took a deep breath. "What makes you believe that Josh has given up on treatment?"

"He told Michael. Well, he said he would never do another camp again. And he says he's quit youth group."

Jenn felt nauseated. She stared at the table, blinking back tears, keeping her exterior under control. Though she'd suspected Josh had given up, having her fear confirmed out loud felt like a blow, physically and emotionally.

Lindsay took Jenn's hand. "I'm sorry, honey. My heart is breaking…for all of you. You're so important to us. But we just can't risk our kids' salvation. You understand, don't you?" Lindsay asked as she wiped her eyes.

Jenn bit her lip. She did understand. Before all this, if the tables were turned, she might very well have drawn the same line. She gave a slight nod.

"We're still praying for you," Lindsay said, her eyes red. "I hope it's just for a little while…until he gets back on track."

Jenn just stared wordlessly at Lindsay. Her head buzzed, but she had nothing to say. Lindsay had made up her mind.

Very gently, as if she were soothing a child, Lindsay said, "You may not want to hear any advice from me…but if he were my son, I'd move him to Valley Christian, now. We're moving Michael and Mel there in the fall. The secular influence is just too overpowering at DHS."

Lindsay squeezed her hand, stood up, and gave Jenn a tender kiss on her cheek. Then she walked out of Jenn's life. As far as Jenn was concerned, eighteen years of friendship had just ended.

Jenn put her head in her hands and cried silently, even though she was embarrassing herself in public. She prayed in her head: *Lord, guide me to do Your will. Please, God, help me to understand. I'm doing my best to carry out Your work on earth. I know I'm being tested, but why? Why would You put these feelings in Josh and not take them away, when all He wants to do is follow Your path...?*

Jenn couldn't go on. She was filled with shame. It wasn't her place to question God's path. She shouldn't be asking God why she was being tested. First they'd lost Steve's parents and now the Bishops. It scared her to admit it, but her faith was wavering. She desperately needed to feel God's love more than ever, but instead she felt abandoned and alone. After her tears ran out, she drove home.

◆ ◆ ◆

Lindsay was right about one thing: Valley Christian would get Josh back on track. Jenn waited to approach Steve with the idea when they were alone in their bedroom after dinner.

"For the last quarter of his junior year?" Steve looked doubtful. "What about his AP classes?"

"They have AP classes at Valley. Those will be the easiest ones to transfer into, because it's a set curriculum."

Steve shook his head, "I don't know that Josh needs such a big change. He's very fragile. I think this will tip him over to a bad place."

"He is suffering, *right now*. Can't you see that? He told me he feels like a loser! He's going to keep hating himself until he roots out the same-sex attraction. We have to do everything we can for him."

"I don't know that Valley will help him, Jenn." Steve shook his head.

Jenn's neck tensed, and she eyed her husband. "You don't condone him going to the GSA thing, do you? Did you know about it?"

"I've been doing some reading," Steve explained tentatively, "on the PFLAG website."

"The what?" Jenn questioned.

"Parents and Friends of Lesbians and Gays. Bethany thought it might be helpful to me...to us. I'm not certain anymore that complete change is possible. Most psychologists say you can modify behavior but not attraction."

Jenn's pulse raced. Steve was giving up too. "They aren't spiritual leaders, are they? We're talking about a spiritual transformation, not a psychological change. Andrew said there was no reason to give up on Josh. Doug said there would be secular pressures. With God all things are possible. You know that! He needs to have faith, or there's no hope for transformation at all."

"I need to think about this, Jenn...and talk to Josh," Steve said. It felt as if he were placating her, but he wasn't saying no. "Why now?"

Jenn let out a big sigh. "Lindsay had a 'talk' with me at Starbucks today. The Bishops don't want their kids to be around Josh until he's cured."

"Shit!" Steve exclaimed, his eyes big. Emphasizing each word, he asked, "Are you serious? When were you going to tell me this?"

"I didn't want to say anything in front of the kids," Jenn defended herself.

Steve closed his eyes and took a deep breath. "You were right to wait till we were alone. I guess you learn who your real friends are at a time like this."

"She said it wasn't forever. Just until Josh is committed to a cure. Can you blame them?" Jenn asked. "We might make the same choice, if the tables were turned."

Steve stared at her, fury burning in his eyes. "No, Jenn, I would never make that choice. And I'm sorry to hear that you would."

Jenn's stomach dropped. She felt sick, and her eyes welled up. She'd never felt this separate from Steve before, never seen him so angry. She struggled for the right thing to say to him, to assure them both that they shared the same values, but her mind was blank. She was afraid that anything she said would just make him angrier and the rift between them even larger.

Steve stood up. He started to leave but turned at the doorway. "I think we really need time as a family. Can we please do something fun together tomorrow—the five of us together?"

"Of course," she agreed quietly, grateful he wanted to do something to bring the family closer. "What do you want to do?"

"How about hiking Mount Diablo? Then dinner and a movie out? Nice family time where Josh isn't the focus or the problem."

She nodded slowly. Steve was right. It had been too long since they had family time. "That's a great idea. I'll talk to Sara and Rachel. You ask Josh. How about we plan to leave around two?"

Steve nodded and left. Jenn said a prayer in her head.

Dear God, help me find the words I need to hold up Your will for my family. In Jesus's name I pray. Amen.

◆ ◆ ◆

April weather could be all over the place in the East Bay, but it was a perfect day for a hike. Though Jenn put on a happy face, she was acutely aware of the tension between her and Steve. She'd packed a backpack full of snacks and water bottles.

They let Rachel pick the movie they'd see afterward, ignoring the rules about feminine and masculine films. She was excited to see one of her favorite childhood books come to life: *Ella Enchanted*. They'd eat at Applebee's and then go to the 7:20 p.m. show.

During the hike from Mount Diablo to Rock City, everything felt normal again. At Rock City, Steve and the kids climbed over the amazing formations while Jenn watched from a distance, sitting on a flat red stone. They were the center of her world. She wished she could be like Steve and just trust that everything would be OK for Josh. But she was constantly consumed by the need to stop their life from being entirely unraveled. She didn't know if her concern was too extreme or Steve's care was too minimal. Yes, she was on edge all the time, but that seemed like an appropriate reaction to the kind of crisis they were dealing with.

Steve walked over to Jenn and sat down next to her. He looked at her watching the kids. Finally, he broke the tense silence. "Josh is a great person. They all are. You can be proud."

"I don't feel so proud these days."

"I have faith he'll be fine."

She looked at her husband. "But maybe not fine in the way that matters most to me."

"You might need to redefine what matters most."

Jenn's heart skipped a beat. "What if I can't, Steve? I'm afraid I can't and I'm going to lose him altogether." *And you, too,* Jenn thought, but she didn't want to make this conversation any tenser.

"I have faith that you can."

"What?" Jenn asked.

"Every day I pray for you, Jenn," Steve said tenderly. "That you can accept Josh."

Fury exploded in Jenn's chest. She hissed at Steve, "You pray for me to accept him being homosexual rather than for Josh to be cured! How is it that we're not on the same page about this? We're a team. You and me. One team. When did you get traded?"

Jenn could not bear to look at Steve for another second after that betrayal. She was so mad she wanted to slap him, but instead she stormed away, not caring what her kids noticed or thought. She rushed back down the trail toward their car.

As she walked, Jenn replayed the conversation in her mind, becoming less certain of what she'd heard with every step. Did Steve really say he wanted Josh to be homosexual? That was unlikely. But he did say that Jenn was the problem in their family. Well, maybe not exactly that. The more she thought about it, the less she was hurt and the more she was embarrassed. By the time she got to the SUV, she felt sheepish. She didn't have a key to the car, so she sat down on the hot wooden railing in the shade. She watched a dragonfly with a bright-blue head and striped body land gently on a nearby rock and then lift into the air and fly away. She watched it become a small speck in the sky and finally disappear altogether.

Watching it brought her toward peace. By the time her family came down the path a half-hour later, Jenn was acting perfectly calm.

"Sorry to rush off; I had to go to the bathroom," she lied to her kids. "Are you ready for dinner and *Ella*?" Really she just wanted to go home and crawl under her covers, but she pushed aside her desires. They were going to have cheerful family time, no matter how she felt.

◆ ◆ ◆

"No way, Mom. No way!" Josh declared when Jenn casually suggested that he transfer to Valley Christian.

"We're just thinking about it," Steve reassured Josh. "We wanted to know your preference."

"I don't want to be some new freak at Valley Christian—that's what I think," Josh said.

"There will be fewer distractions there, Josh," Jenn said. "You can focus on your recovery."

"We aren't forcing you. Just think about it," Steve said.

"I don't need to think about it." Josh was adamant. "Valley Christian is not for me. What about track? You want me to just stop my life?" He stood up. "I can't take this anymore," he said and stomped out of the family room.

"You didn't even encourage him to do it, Steve," Jenn said.

"I agreed to ask his opinion," Steve countered. "I didn't agree to move him to Valley. We asked. He answered. As far as I'm concerned, he's staying at Dublin High." He walked out of the room, leaving her alone.

"God, my Lord and Savior, guide my words and my actions," Jenn prayed aloud. "Lord, please, I beg of You, keep my family together. I have never wanted anything but to love my family and love You and Your only Son. I surrender my life to You. Amen."

The home phone rang. It was Sara.

"Mom! What are you doing to Josh?" Sara asked.

"Sara, don't be dramatic. We're only thinking of switching schools."

"He's furious, Mom," Sara explained. "Please don't keep pushing him so hard."

"Pastor James said this is when the transformation happens, when he's really tested. He has to choose."

"You're asking too much. Give him a break. How many times do Dad and I have to tell you that?"

"I don't understand why you and your father are ganging up against me!" Jenn yelled into the phone. "Am I the only one who cares about Josh?" And then she hung up on her daughter.

What kind of mother was she? She was losing her mind.

Jenn went to bed. It was only seven thirty, but she needed to be away from everyone and in the sanctuary of her room. She didn't say good night to anyone, not even Rachel.

By the time Steve came to bed, once again she felt foolish rather than angry. She sat up to talk to him.

"Sorry, Steve," she said. "God, how many times am I going to say that? I can't seem to do anything right these days."

"This is hard on all of us," Steve said kindly. "None of us know the exact right way to be."

Jenn started sobbing. "I miss my certainty. I miss us being a team. I miss my son."

"Me too," he said. But he didn't give her a hug or sit close. He left to brush his teeth.

She texted Sara: *Sorry*.

20

The next morning Josh didn't come down for breakfast at the usual time.

Jenn called up, "Josh, your food's ready."

A few minutes later, he still hadn't come out of his room. She walked upstairs, but he ignored her knock on his door. Finally she turned the knob, daring to make him angrier. The room was empty. Josh must be furious to have left without eating. She'd hoped to apologize over breakfast. Instead, she texted him, *Sorry. We'll work this out.*

She slipped her phone into her pocket, anticipating his reply. Throughout the day she checked her phone, but there was nothing from Josh. She fluctuated between being annoyed with him for ignoring her and scared that he might hurt himself again. When he didn't come home at his usual time, Jenn called his car-pool driver after track. Carmen said that Josh had said he had to stay late. Jenn lied, chalking up the confusion to her faulty memory.

As soon as she hung up, she called Steve. "Josh didn't come home."

"Maybe the car pool is running late."

"I called Carmen. Josh told her he was staying late. What's he up to? I'm scared."

Steve sighed. "It's still daylight. If he's not there by the time I get home, I'll worry. But for now, I think he just needs some space from you."

"Me! Why am I the problem?" Jenn hung up on Steve. As soon as she did it, she felt bad. She was completely out of control. She texted him an apology. All this texting was going to cost them a small fortune.

◆ ◆ ◆

Josh wasn't home by dinner. Jenn was frantic.

"Do you think he ran away?" Rachel asked.

"Why would he do that?" Jenn challenged.

"It's not like he's feeling the love here."

Jenn wanted to slap her. "You're not helping, Rachel. Daddy and I are taking care of the situation. I'll let you know when we know more." When had her children become so utterly disrespectful?

Steve looked at his phone. Flipping it open, he read a text. He sighed and then passed the phone to Jenn.

It was from Sara: *Josh is with me. He's safe. Don't come.*

Jenn blinked at the screen. Intense and contradictory emotion flooded her. She was relieved Josh was safe but furious that he had gone to Berkeley without permission. Rachel was right. He couldn't stand to be home.

"Let's go get him," she said to Steve.

"Jenn." Steve shook his head. "We have to trust Sara. He went to her for a reason."

Jenn ignored him and went to get her keys.

Calmly, Steve took the keys from her hand. "Stop. Call her first. She said not to come."

Jenn glared at him but dialed Sara's dorm room. The phone rang and rang, so she tried Sara's cell. No answer. How could Sara leave her hanging like this? They had gotten her a cell phone so they could be in touch when necessary. She paced around the house, fury building. She just wanted to get Josh home where he belonged, but Sara and Steve were thwarting her plan. Any sense of peace she felt knowing where Josh was had vanished.

"I'm going for a walk. You two eat without me." Rachel looked scared, but Jenn needed to cool off before she could be any comfort to her youngest daughter. She grabbed the leash and called for the dog.

While she was walking with Wynnie, Sara texted, *I'll call when I can.*

Jenn resisted the urge to smash her phone into the street. She strode fast to release the tension in her body, moving from block to block, pounding her frustration into the pavement. By the time she finished her loop, she wasn't burning with anger any longer. She was ready to go back home. Rachel and Steve greeted her as she walked into the dining room.

"I'm sorry, Mom," Rachel said. "I was being snotty."

"I'm sorry, too, hon," Jenn replied. "I'm not as patient and loving as I'd like to be. I'm working on it. I promise."

Rachel got up and wrapped her arms around her mother, and Jenn returned the embrace, rocking her daughter. Steve came and wrapped his arms around both of them, and Jenn rested her head against his chest. At moments like these, she had faith they could still make it through this as a strong family.

"Eat," Steve said after a while. "It'll be good for your body and your soul."

Jenn sighed, and a small smile tugged up her lips. She'd made Josh fettuccine Alfredo as a peace offering. She could eat it in honor of him instead of with him.

Sara called on the home phone just as Jenn was finishing her food. Steve answered and brought the handset to Jenn.

"Here's your mom," Steve said into the receiver. "I'll get on the extension upstairs."

"Thanks for calling, Sara. How's Josh?" Jenn asked.

"He's upset and feeling desperate. I think it's good he came here, don't you?"

"I suppose. I'm glad he's safe. How's his spirit?"

"Not good, Mom. That's what I just told you," Sara lectured.

"I'm here," Steve broke in.

"Can we come get him?" Jenn asked.

"He doesn't want to go home. I'm afraid he'll just run away again if you drag him back. Or maybe not get in the car. There are tons of street kids living on Telegraph Ave. I don't want to see Josh living like that, do you?"

"No, of course not," Jenn said. "I want him home."

"I really think it would be best for him to stay here for a while," Sara replied.

"What's he going to do? Drop out of school? That's crazy!"

"It's a long commute, but he can get to Dublin. BART's walkable from here. Dad can pick him up on that end."

Steve said, "Absolutely."

"Dad. Just Dad?" Jenn was furious. She made a fist and hit it against the wooden farm table, glad that no one was in the room with her.

"For now," Steve said gently, "maybe that would be best."

A hot wave ran through Jenn's body. "How long are we going to let him do this?"

Steve said, "Don't get ahead of yourself. Let's take it one day at a time, Jenn. He's safe right now. Thank God for that. And thank you, Sara."

"Of course. He's my brother." Sara's voice cracked. "I love him."

"We all do," Jenn said. "Sara, tell him that, OK?" she begged her daughter. "Please. Tell him that I love him."

"I will, Mom. I promise."

Rachel was staring at her when she got off the phone, a question in her eyes.

"Josh is going to stay with Sara for a few days. Just until he cools off."

"Can I send him a text?" Rachel asked.

"Sure." Jenn started to slide her phone to Rachel, and then she stopped. "Use Dad's." It was sad but true: Josh would most likely ignore a text from her phone.

"Can I use your phone?" Rachel asked Steve as he came into the room. He handed his phone to his youngest child, and she walked out of the kitchen with it.

Steve said, "I'm going to take Josh to see Kyle on Wednesday."

Jenn wanted to scream and yell and cry. Everything was heading in the wrong direction.

"He needs all the support he can get," Steve explained. "It was a mistake to cut him off from Kyle. I want him to have that."

Jenn felt thoroughly defeated. She nodded without saying a word.

"Are you OK?" Steve asked. He was being kind, but it felt patronizing.

In a sharp, angry whisper, so Rachel couldn't hear her, Jenn hissed, "How can you ask me that? Of course I'm not all right. I'm devastated. Josh has given up…" She took a shaky breath, trying not to cry. "My son, *our* son, has lost faith. And I have no idea what to do. No, I'm not all right, and *you* shouldn't be all right either!"

Steve offered a hug, but Jenn didn't want comfort. She deflected her husband and said, "I'm taking Wynnie for a walk."

"Again?"

"It's better than exploding," she snapped.

"Do you want company?"

"No," she replied harshly. She paused. "Thank you," she said more kindly.

Jenn sobbed as she walked with Wynnie. Grateful none of the neighbors could see her too clearly in the dark, she stormed through the neighborhood. She replayed the week in her head, imagining how it could have gone differently. She took some comfort in the thought that things could be much worse. They could be back at the hospital. By the time she got home, she was sad but not angry.

She sent Josh a text: *I love you. Please come home.* There was no reply by the time she went to sleep.

The next morning Jenn woke up at six, as usual. She checked her phone from bed. Nothing from Josh. She didn't get up. Instead, she rolled over and went back to sleep. At seven thirty Steve brought her some coffee and toast.

"Are you sick?" he asked, sitting on the edge of the bed.

"I don't know," she said. "I guess so."

Steve patted her shoulder. "You rest. Rachel and I have the morning covered. Josh just texted. He's almost at the Dublin station."

"OK." Jenn felt like she should say more, but she didn't have the energy.

"I'll see you for dinner."

"Hmm," Jenn replied before Steve walked out the door. She doubted he even heard her. Jenn reached for the cell phone by her bed. Nothing from Josh. She rolled over and went back to sleep.

By ten o'clock she forced herself to sit up. Every movement was hard, but sleeping the day away was only going to make it worse. After drinking her cold coffee and eating her hard toast, she went to her prayer chair. She needed that big hug from God more than anything. She started her prayer: *Lord, thank You in the name of Jesus. God, thank You for the power of the Holy Spirit. I ask that Your presence fill me with wisdom and revelation so that I may follow You, love You, and serve You entirely. Bind up all distractions and show me Your will for me.*

"God." Jenn's voice cracked as she spoke aloud. "I need You more today than ever. I know I keep saying that, but it's still true. Help me know what to do to rebuild my family."

She waited for the comfort and clarity from God to fill her up. She wanted to pray, but her mind raced in circles. She imagined finding Josh after school and him falling into her arms in gratitude and sorrow. She pictured herself holding him and saying just the right prayer to transform him. She envisioned her faith alone being strong enough to heal him.

Then her thoughts raced to the opposite spectrum. She imagined the look of anger and disgust on his face if he saw her. In her mind he snarled at her, "You don't understand, and you never will. Kyle understands. God made me like this. He's not going to change me, whatever you want. He's not."

Jenn felt impotent, so she turned to prayer. "God, please transform Josh. Open him to Your wisdom and guidance. Help him to know the divine path You have for him. Amen."

◆ ◆ ◆

Jenn left early to pick up Rachel from school so she could get a parking space as close as possible to the campus. Perhaps she would get a glimpse of Josh. She searched the crowd of kids after the bell rang, but there was no sign of him. Steve would be taking him directly to the BART station after practice today, so this was her only chance to see him.

After Rachel climbed into the front seat, Jenn asked, "How's your brother?"

"My day was fine. Thanks for asking."

"Rachel, don't be smart."

Rachel sighed. "He's fine, Mom. He seemed the same as always, just tired from getting up early to take BART."

"How did he sleep? Did he get breakfast?"

"I don't know." Rachel shrugged. "Dad didn't ask him about any of that. They talked about track and chemistry."

Jenn sighed. *Track and chemistry.* She shook her head. Jenn asked, "Did you pray together before you went to school?"

Rachel gave Jenn an incredulous look. "No."

"Would you please, from now on, say a quick prayer for your brother before school? Right in his presence. It can be in your heart; it doesn't have to be out loud. But try to touch him for part of it. OK?"

"Sure, Mom. If you want," Rachel said, but Jenn suspected she was placating her.

All of her children were slipping away. She'd ask Steve to pray for Josh.

◆ ◆ ◆

Jenn made two lunches in the morning and poured extra prayers into the one for Josh. On Wednesday, Jenn offered to drive the kids, but Steve rejected her idea. He assured her he was fine doing it and explained that it was too soon for Josh. She acted like she accepted the *no* graciously, but she was hurt. She felt so alone. In the past she would have talked this all through with Lindsay. But now she didn't have anyone. No one understood what she was going through.

Thursday she called Sara to plan. "Are you coming for the weekend or at least for church on Sunday?"

"I'll check with Josh again, but I think the answer is still no."

"You already asked him?" Jenn asked.

"Yeah. He wants to go to church," Sara said carefully, "...just not our church."

"Did you tell him that was OK?" Jenn challenged. "Are you encouraging him to give up on his transformation? Sara, he looks up to you! You can save your brother's soul with the right words. Do you understand the gravity of his situation?"

"Yes, Mom. I do, more than you know. I just don't think the same as you anymore—at least when it comes to gay rights."

Jenn wanted to scream at her daughter but instead asked, "When did you have this change of heart?"

"I've been praying, thinking, and talking about this since Josh came out to us."

"You make it sound like it's a fact that he is homosexual," Jenn countered, "but there are treatments!"

"Mom, they aren't real," Sara said, as if she were talking to a child. "I know you want them to be. We all wanted them to be, including Josh. But they're a lie. Those Resurrection people make a lot of money off of fear and hatred."

"Hating a sin is not wrong. This is about faith."

"I'm not going to argue with you," Sara said calmly. "I feel the way I feel. Josh is who he is."

"What about his salvation?"

"'Our God is a loving God'—that's what you always told me. How could God not love Josh?"

Jenn felt ill. Her own words were being used against her. "Well, I'm disappointed in your decision."

"I'm sorry, Mom. I know this is hard for you to hear," Sara said, her voice shaky. "In time I think you'll agree with me or at least understand."

"I will never give up on Josh's salvation, Sara."

"Me neither, Mom. 'Bye."

First Josh. Now Sara. There was a huge breach between Jenn and her children. Suddenly she needed to know where Steve stood, too. She walked around the block to calm herself, and then she called her husband.

"Do you know that Josh doesn't want to attend church anymore?"

Steve let out a big breath. "He has a different church in mind."

"You knew this and didn't tell me!" Jenn yelled into the phone. "Unbelievable!"

"He wants to start attending First Congregational."

"No! Absolutely not."

Steve replied, "I'm glad that he wants church in his life at all. He still loves God and Jesus. He just doesn't want the judgment."

"Like you get to pick and choose what God wants for you," Jenn rebutted. "How naive and self-centered can he be? You support this?"

"I want him to have church, Jenn."

She squeezed her hand in anger and hissed into the phone, "I don't know you. I don't know you at all anymore. Who are you? You certainly are not the man I married. We were united in this. Raising our children in the one true faith. Instilling a sense of obligation to God and Jesus. What happened to you?"

Jenn hung up before Steve spoke. Because she knew the answer: she was alone, all alone, in her desire to save Josh. Somehow Steve and Sara and Josh had lost faith in Josh's transformation. She wanted to run away, too.

◆ ◆ ◆

Steve was patient and kind over the weekend. Jenn didn't fight with him, because there was nothing she could do or say to get Josh or Sara to come to church. But inside she was angry and grief stricken, and her family knew it.

Jenn could hardly bear to be in the sanctuary Sunday morning. People noticed it was just the three of them. They kindly asked about Josh and Sara. She didn't want to tell anyone that Josh was staying in Berkeley, so she lied and told them Josh was sick and Sara was studying. This was what her life had come to: lying in church. Instead of church being a comfort and a sanctuary, it was a glaring reminder of all that was wrong in her life.

She took in a long, steady breath. These words started to run through her mind: *God, grant me the serenity to accept the things I cannot change, the courage to change the things I can, and the wisdom to know the difference.*

She didn't know what she could and couldn't change. She didn't feel serene, courageous, or wise. But if she asked often enough, she might start to.

21

Over the next days and weeks, the Serenity Prayer ran through Jenn's mind constantly. She returned to it again and again as she went through her days, and in the middle of the night when she woke up in a panic. Every time anxiety started to rise in her at the thought of losing Josh, she said it. It was a small comfort that kept her from having a mental breakdown. She knew Pastor James didn't approve of this prayer, but its simple directions were just what she needed to keep her sane.

Midway through the second week of his absence, Jenn felt like she would die if Josh didn't come home. Each day he was away, he walked farther and farther away from her. In desperation, she turned to the only person who could persuade Josh to return: Kyle Goss. Though she'd been thoroughly disrespectful the last time she saw him, he graciously let her make an appointment. He greeted her kindly, and they settled in chairs in his office. He started by asking how she was doing.

Jenn had hoped to be calm and reasonable, but instead she spewed out, "I've lost my son—in this life, and I'm afraid for the next. I can hardly breathe I'm so overwhelmed with it. I don't know what to do. I've done everything I can to help him. But he doesn't want my help anymore. He doesn't want me. He won't talk to me or text me or see me. I'm desperate. I need your help. Please? Convince him to come home."

"I understand it's very hard for you that he's staying with Sara. And…I hope you can be grateful that he has a safe place to be."

"Gratitude is not high on my list right now," Jenn snapped. After she heard the words she had spoken, she said, "That sounded awful. I'm sorry."

"From what I can tell, he's going to school, too. That's absolutely remarkable for a teen who has left home," Kyle explained.

"It sounds like you think I should be proud of my son. Proud of him for running away?"

"He's making safe choices for himself."

"I want him back. I want him home. I want him in my life. What do I do?" Jenn begged.

"I can't tell you what to do. I can tell you that Josh is a lovely young man and, yes, you can be very proud of him."

"I feel like I have to choose between my son and my Lord. I can't do it."

Kyle sat there quietly. After a few moments, he said, "I know someone who was in a similar situation. She's also an evangelical Christian. When her child came out to her, she was devastated. It took years, but she eventually came to peace with it."

"How?" Jenn was doubtful. "The two things are irreconcilable."

Kyle shrugged. "It's her story to tell. Ask her. I know she'd be willing to speak with you."

"How do you know that?" Jenn wondered.

"It's her ministry. She believes God put her on earth for that very purpose."

Jenn stared at him, uncertainty struggling in her.

Kyle said gently, "She knows what you're going through, Jenn. More than anyone else I know."

A tingle of the Holy Ghost passed through her. Someone who would understand her felt like a gift from God. Jenn nodded. "All right. I'll call her."

◆ ◆ ◆

Jenn's hands were shaking as she pulled up to Maya's house. The woman lived in Pleasanton, just across the freeway, in a 1990s development similar to theirs. Jenn didn't know what to expect from this conversation, and that made her very nervous. She was afraid of being judged and getting into a fight with a woman who knew nothing about her or her faith, but she was desperate. And Kyle had sounded convinced that Maya would be understanding, so Jenn decided to go through with it. Steve told her it couldn't hurt and it might even help.

The woman who opened the door didn't look as Jenn had pictured in her mind. Maya was shorter than Jenn, with brown hair and hazel-green eyes. She wore makeup and jewelry even though it was a Thursday morning. She was a little older than Jenn but not much—maybe in her early fifties. She exuded simple elegance that caused Jenn to feel dowdy in her jeans.

Maya smiled warmly and said, "I'm a hugger. Can I give you a hug?"

Jenn laughed despite her nervousness. "Sure." It was surprisingly nice to be embraced by this stranger.

"Come on in," Maya said as she led Jenn through the beautifully decorated house. "I'm so glad you reached out to me. I know how hard this is for you."

Jenn teared up.

"I've been there. He's your child. There is nothing you wouldn't do for him. And your heart is breaking."

Jenn nodded even though Maya's back was to her. She didn't trust herself to speak. Kyle was right: this woman did understand.

"Sit." Maya pointed to the couch in the family room. Jenn admired the mission-style couch, noting that it worked in this contemporary house.

Maya asked, "Can we start with a prayer?"

Jenn was surprised, and happy, at the request. She nodded. Maya took her hands and spoke out loud, "Lord, thank You in the name of Jesus. God, thank You for the power of the Holy Spirit. We ask that Your presence fill us with wisdom and revelation so that we may follow You, love You, and serve You entirely. Bind up all distractions and show us Your will."

Chills ran up Jenn's spine. These comforting, familiar words meant so much to her. This woman knew her heart and spoke her language.

Maya went on, "Lord, guide us in being agents of Your love for Your child Joshua Henderson. May our words and our deeds glorify You on this earth and be worthy of the sacrifice of Your Son. May the Holy Spirit fill us with the power to do Your will. Amen."

"Amen," Jenn echoed. "Wow. I was not expecting that. Thank you."

"For me, prayer comes in the beginning, in the middle, and at the end."

"Kyle told me you're Christian. He also said you've accepted your son's homosexuality. I guess I was expecting something different."

"I'm happy to tell you my story. But first, tell me about your Josh."

Jenn thought for a moment. "He's taller than me now. I'm still not used to it. I have to look up at that little boy I used to carry around. He looks like a man, but sometimes he's a boy inside. He's in between. I guess that's normal at this age. He loves his teams: cross-country, basketball, and track. He's a great student. He has the crazy notion of going to school in New York City." Maya was listening intently. Jenn smiled and went on. "He loves God. He's the most devout of my three kids. I'm sorry. I'm rambling."

"I asked because I want to know about him. He sounds like a lovely human being."

"He is."

"And he's gay?" Maya asked gently.

That word again. It was a slap to her soul every time she heard it. "Well, not exactly. He says he has same-sex attractions, but he's never acted on them. So no, not really."

"But that's why you came to talk to me. Right? To hear how I came to understand that homosexuality is not incompatible with living biblically."

Jenn bit her lip and nodded. Her mouth was dry, and it was hard to swallow. It felt like sacrilege to listen to this woman.

"You don't need to agree with anything I say. Hear me out and then decide for yourself. You can ask me questions. You can argue with me. It's all OK."

Jenn felt scared again.

"As you can tell, I love God and our Savior Jesus Christ. As a teen I knew without a doubt that God put me on earth to spread the good news of salvation through Christ."

"Me, too," Jenn said.

"You understand how devastated I was to learn David was gay. It was ten years ago. He was eighteen—just starting college. My whole world fell apart."

Jenn nodded. She did understand.

Maya went on. "After a few years of immense struggle, I immersed myself in prayer and Bible study. I won't go into every thought I had, but I'll share with you the insight that allowed me to accept that God loves David. It was a very profound experience—like being born again." Maya asked, "The Ten Commandments are the most important rules in the Old Testament. Right?"

Jenn nodded.

"Don't you think keeping them would be the most important teaching at church?"

Jenn nodded again, feeling wary inside.

"I realized I was breaking one of them over and over again, but no one talked about it in church."

Jenn was puzzled by Maya's assertion. It seemed unlikely she was sitting next to an adulterer or a murderer.

"I break the Sabbath," Maya explained. "And I cause others to break the Sabbath."

Suddenly Jenn realized it was true for her, as well. "Us, too!" she blurted. "It never occurred to me we were breaking one of the Ten Commandments." They ate out almost every Sunday. People worked on the Sabbath so she could eat brunch after church.

"Crazy, huh? One of the big ten, but we don't follow it. We watch sports, eat out, go shopping. All on Sundays. Many Christians work on the Sabbath for various reasons, but I have never heard a sermon, not one, about the abomination of football after church."

Jenn's mind was reeling, but before she could form a response, Maya went on. "I also realized that, more than anything else, Jesus asks us to love one another. He tells us to throw away so many rules that are in the Old Testament because they don't serve to create love in the world. Why did I feel compelled to follow one rule of Leviticus about a man lying with another man but not so many of the others, like eating shellfish or wearing mixed fabrics? It seems laughable that someone would go to hell for eating shellfish. I asked myself, why are we elevating one law so far above the others? Does caring about that law create more love or less? When it came to my judgment of my own son, it was less."

Jenn had heard secularists make that argument about shellfish and other laws in Leviticus before. She'd dismissed it long ago because her religious leaders knew better than secularists.

"It's more important," Jenn said, "because our ministers say it is. How could you reject your minister's wisdom?"

"I didn't discard it lightly," Maya replied. "I prayed on it. I asked God. I'm not saying you'll come to the same answer. But after a lot of prayer—hours and hours—it finally came down to this: I could love the child God gave me right now, or I could love an ancient law written so many years ago. As much as I wanted to believe that the Bible was the literal truth, I couldn't. I love the Bible. I still read it every day. But I came to understand it couldn't be all true or we Christians would advocate for slavery, polygamy, and many other things we don't support. I don't believe our God intends for us to have those institutions. Once I realized we were choosing which parts to follow and which parts to leave behind, I listened to God more than to the minister of my church."

Maya continued, "It was scary at first. I felt like I was unfaithful to God. It's ironic that listening the most carefully to God felt like I was betraying Him. But that was how it felt at first."

Jenn nodded. She felt like she was being disloyal by listening to this woman. She sat with Maya's words. This argument was similar to what her mom had said about Anita Bryant just making up this issue. Could it really be that her church was just wrong?

Maya went on. "In my prayers, God told me to love David. To just love him as a holy gift. Once I came to that, everything else melted away. I knew that God loved David, and I didn't have to pray for him to change. I never felt closer to God in my life." Maya's eyes glistened.

"Really?" Jenn felt hope. "You felt the Holy Spirit? Telling you it was OK?"

Maya nodded. "Absolutely. It was the most beautiful moment of my life. I came to utter peace with David. It was then that I truly surrendered my life to God."

Jenn gasped. She felt goose bumps rise on her arms. Maya gave a knowing nod and a smile.

"For years I told David he needed to surrender to God's will. And all along it was me who needed to surrender. I found what God was calling me to do. I knew without a doubt that I had to tell others. God put me on this earth to spread the good word…of His love."

Jenn took in these words. They challenged so much of what she believed but mirrored so much of it too, and they offered her a promise of reconciliation with her son *and* her faith. "Now you and David are close?"

"He isn't with us on earth anymore," Maya said softly. "David's with the Lord in heaven."

"Oh, I'm sorry." Jenn's eyes welled up. "Kyle didn't tell me. I had no idea. He got sick? Cancer?"

"He died of suicide," Maya replied.

Jenn's chest clenched, and a wave of fear and sorrow passed through her. "Oh, dear God. I'm so…" She could hardly breathe. That could have been Josh.

"I entered this journey after his death," Maya explained. "I was so mad at God, I can't even describe it. For a while I felt like I lost David and our Lord. Why didn't He listen to our prayers and change David? David wanted it as much as I did. We would pray together for hours for his transformation. But it never came. David was distraught, beyond reach.

"After David was gone," Maya continued, "I realized that God made David just as he was. David was a gift from God. My imperfect, beautiful son was a gift I was rejecting. David didn't need to be transformed."

Transformed. The word cut through Jenn. She'd been praying for Josh's complete transformation for months.

She asked, "What if you're wrong? Am I supposed to give up on Josh's soul because of what you felt?"

Maya looked at Jenn with compassion. "God has His own path for you. I can't tell you what to do. What I know for certain is that God loves Josh even though he's gay. And He loves David even though he was gay and he died by suicide. They are saved through their devotion to Christ. That's all that's asked of us. That's my faith."

Jenn was stunned. She also believed in salvation through devotion to Christ. Josh was as devoted to Christ as anyone and more than most. Could it really be that simple? She sat there quietly in her confusion. Maya gave her time.

Jenn finally said, "Thank you...for taking the time to speak with me. You've given me a lot to think about. And I'm sorry...so sorry about David." Her eyes welled up again. She was so tired of being on the edge of tears all the time.

"Thank you for listening to me. I honor David and feel close to him each time I tell our story," Maya said. "Feel free to be in touch if you have any questions or if you just want to talk. I know it's a lonely place."

Jenn nodded and bit her lip. She did have another question. "Have you...? What church do you go to?"

Maya scrunched her face and shook her head. "That hasn't been easy. I still feel evangelical, but my congregation had a hard time with my new message. My husband and I joined First Congregational, but every few months I attend my old church in Livermore. I stay in the back and feel the power of the Holy Spirit in the room. Sometimes

I just need to be there to feel God and Jesus best. I miss it, that energy. There's nothing else like it."

After closing with a prayer, Jenn drove home. God had put Maya in her path for a reason. Was she a challenge to Jenn's faith or a guide to a deeper faith? Her mind spun in circles.

At home she went right to her prayer chair. She opened herself up to God, the Holy Spirit, and her Savior. She surrendered more fully than she ever had before, and then she listened.

Love your son was all that came to her. She desperately wanted *Love your son just as he is* or *Love your son enough to fight for his soul* or *Love your son but not his sin*. But she didn't get the end of the sentence. All she got was the direction to love her son.

Her stomach rumbled, letting her know it was lunchtime, but she didn't move. She sat in her prayer chair, waiting to hear more, but no more words came. She wanted certainty, but she'd have to act without it. She would have to decide how to finish the sentence for herself.

22

Jenn was at Dublin High when the final bell rang, waiting by the door to Josh's last class of the day. A swirl of teens passed by, some noticing the stranger in the hallway, most walking by without a glance. Josh looked surprised, and a little scared, when he saw her. How had it come to this, her own son afraid of her?

Jenn said gently, "Josh, I'd like to speak with you in private. Please? Come to the car."

He shook his head slowly and spoke quietly, "I don't know, Mom. Maybe we should wait for Dad. Or meet with Kyle? Kyle wants me to invite you to a session."

"Please just hear what I have to say," she pleaded. "I'm not going to fight with you. We can meet with Kyle later if you want. This won't take long."

Josh thought about it and finally nodded. She led him to the car, caught up in the crowd of teens rushing toward their afternoons.

Once they were settled in the Land Cruiser, Jenn took a deep breath and then spoke. "I want you to come home."

Josh started to reply, "No, I'm n—"

Jenn held up a hand. "Please hear me out, and then I'll listen to you. I want you to come home. That's the most important thing. You can stay at Dublin High; you can go to whatever church you want; you can have whatever you want on your walls."

"Really?" Josh sounded surprised.

"Really."

Josh cautiously asked, "You're OK with me being gay?"

That disturbing word again. She took a breath before she spoke. "I...It's not that simple, Josh. But the bottom line is I love you. And I want you at home."

Josh instantly deflated. "I don't know, Mom. It was so tense there between us. All the time."

"You're taking the SAT on Saturday morning, right?"

"Yes," he confirmed.

"It will be easier to get there so early from home. Try it for the weekend. You can always go back to Berkeley after that."

Josh didn't reply. Jenn waited, projecting patience, but in her head she chanted, *Say yes. Say yes. Say yes.* Biting her lip like a desperate teenager, she forced herself to settle back into her seat and wait.

"I'll think about it," Josh finally said.

That would have to do. "OK."

"I gotta go to practice."

"I love you, Josh. That was never in question."

"I love you too, Mom. Really, I do." Josh teared up. "I never meant to cause you such trouble. I'm sorry. I didn't ask for this, you know."

"Oh, baby." Jenn opened her arms. Josh hesitated and then leaned across the emergency brake into an awkward hug. "I know you didn't."

Josh wiped his face before he left the car. Hope and sorrow had a tug-of-war in Jenn's spirit as she watched him walk away.

◆ ◆ ◆

The phone rang as Jenn was arriving home. *Steve at work* showed on the screen.

"Josh just called," Steve said. "I wish you'd talked to me first."

Jenn was annoyed. "I can't ask my son to come home without your permission?"

"You don't need my permission. I just want us to be on the same page."

"*Now* you want us to be on the same page?" Jenn retorted, starting to get angry.

"That's not fair, Jenn."

Humbled once again, she sighed, "I'm sorry. You're right. I should have called you first, but after my talk with Maya, I felt completely desperate...and totally clear. The only things that matter are that Josh knows I love him and that he belongs with us."

Jenn told Steve about her conversation with Maya and about David's suicide.

When she finished, Steve said, "Wow. That's sobering."

"We can't risk Josh's physical life."

Steve probed gently, "Can you let him be? Just as he is?"

"It'll be hard," Jenn admitted, "but I'll keep my hopes to myself. I'll pray for his transformation, but I won't ask him to do anything. I know I can do that. I even told him he can go to any church he likes."

"Really?" Steve sounded pleased but skeptical.

"Yes. I'm serious. We need him home whatever the circumstances. Did he sound like he wanted to come home?"

"I couldn't tell for certain. He asked me if I could drive him to Berkeley to get his stuff either tonight or tomorrow night. It's a good sign that he's making a plan."

"Why didn't you tell me that?" Jenn got excited. "We can all go. Maybe eat dinner out there."

"Don't jump the gun, Jenn. But yes, that's a good plan, if he agrees."

Jenn replied, "Call me if he gets in touch."

"You, too."

◆ ◆ ◆

The minutes crept by. Jenn was desperate to hear from Josh, but she knew she had to wait for him to make the next contact. It took all her self-control not to reach out to him. Just before five her phone vibrated.

It was a text from Josh: *OK. I'll give it a try.*

Jenn squealed before she texted back: *great :)*

Just after she hit Send, the phone rang.

Steve's voice came through her cell. "He wants to get his stuff tonight."

"He called you?" Jenn asked, knowing she sounded jealous and immature. She regretted her tone as the words came out of her mouth.

"Yes. Sorry, Jenn."

"Well, he texted me," she reassured herself. "That's something. And he's coming home. That's all that really matters. Right? Did you make a plan?"

"I'll pick him up after track and then swing by for you and Rach. We'll go to Sara's, grab his stuff, and then eat out. He wants to go to the Smoked Cows or something like that."

"Anywhere is fine with me, so long as we're there as a family. Thank you, Lord Jesus." Jenn squealed.

"God is good," Steve agreed.

As soon as they hung up, Jenn went to the garage. She retrieved the cardboard tube from the corner and brought it up to Josh's room. Carefully she pulled out his posters and unrolled them. Her breath caught when she saw the image of Half Dome on the top. Jenn had missed it, too.

She left the posters rolled out on the bed, giving Josh the chance to make his own decisions about what to have on his walls.

She ran outside the moment she heard Steve pull up. When Josh climbed out of the driver's seat, her heart leaped at the sight of him. Without holding anything back, she rushed to give him a huge hug. After their embrace ended, she reached up to cup his face with both of her hands, and studied his face, looking for changes. But there weren't any on the outside. She patted his cheek and then covered it with kisses, like when he was young. He scrunched his face and squirmed away, but she saw the smile on his face.

"I'm *so* glad you're home!" she exclaimed.

"Me too, Mom." Josh smiled at her.

◆ ◆ ◆

Usually, Jenn hated driving in Berkeley. The rules of the road were different here, incomprehensible as far as she was concerned. The streets had too many bicyclists, were too narrow, and seemed to come and go randomly. The city planning was haphazard. But today she was thrilled to be in Berkeley, like a child on Christmas morning, ready to get the best gift ever.

Steve was behind the wheel as they drove up Telegraph Ave. They passed clumps of grungy people sitting on the sidewalk, leaning against buildings. It was nearly as bad as San Francisco. Sara was right: a lot of these homeless people were Josh's age. It was sad to imagine what circumstances brought them to this place in life. In the past she'd assumed they were from bad homes, but now she realized that some of them might be in Josh's situation or something similar. Jenn said a quick prayer for God to watch over them and keep them safe, and she thanked Lord Jesus that Josh wasn't one of them.

When Steve turned right on Durant, it suddenly looked like a college town. A swarm of young adults carrying backpacks and messenger bags hurried along the sidewalk like busy ants. As usual there wasn't any parking in front of Sara's dorm. Steve turned the corner onto College Ave and double-parked.

"I'll circle around while you get the stuff, OK?" he suggested to the kids.

"Sure," Josh said. He and Rachel opened their doors. "Are you coming, Mom?"

Jenn had imagined staying in the car, but if Josh wanted her, she would go with them. She smiled at Steve and squeezed his arm in affection.

They stood in front of Freeborn Hall, waiting for Sara to come down to let them in. Before she arrived, a student held the door open for them. Jenn had mixed feelings about that. It was polite but dangerous to let strangers into the building. She held back, but Josh didn't hesitate to enter and went straight to the elevator, knowing exactly where to go. Everything had seemed normal in the car. Now Jenn was reminded Josh had been living here for ten days.

He texted Sara while they rode up in the elevator. It was dirty, but thankfully it didn't smell like beer. Freeborn was Cal's substance-free residence hall. Jenn was grateful that Sara had chosen a "clean" environment, if not an entirely sanitary one.

Getting off the elevator, Josh turned right and led them through Sara's door. The room was empty. Sara must be looking for them. A minute later she popped in through the entryway.

"Mom! You haven't been here since you dropped me off in August," she said when she saw Jenn.

"That's not true. I've picked you up once or twice since then."

"You've never come up. Normally you just wait in the car."

Jenn thought about it. Her daughter was right. She hadn't realized Sara would track something like that. "Well, I'm glad to see your room now."

She looked around at the pictures and sayings on the wall. There were some she'd never seen before.

"I love this one," Jenn told her daughter, pointing to a sign that said, "Promise me you'll always remember: 'You're braver than you believe, and stronger than you seem, and smarter than you think.'—A. A. Milne."

"Kaitlin gave it to me," Sara explained. "It's from *Winnie-the-Pooh*."

It hit Jenn that she'd only met Kaitlin on the day she dropped Sara off at Cal. "You two are pretty close, huh?"

Sara nodded. "She's a great roommate. She was so chill with Josh staying with us. You know we put in to room together next year."

Jenn realized she owed a debt to Kaitlin too. "You got lucky."

"I like to think God was watching out for both of us."

Jenn smiled at her daughter.

"Let's go," Josh said.

"Smokehouse, here we come!" Sara said.

"Does Kaitlin want to join us?" Jenn offered.

"Nah. She left for dinner already. Besides, we need some family time. In fact, group hug before we leave."

Sara spread her arms wide and beckoned with her hands. Rachel fell into place under Sara's right arm. Josh got a look on his face that said, "I'll humor you, Sister," and put his arm over Sara's left shoulder. He lifted his left arm, and Jenn slipped under it, wrapping her arms around Josh and Rachel. She hugged her three kids close.

Sara spoke. "Lord, we thank You for this time together. Thank You for opening our hearts that we may receive Your love, Your truth, and Your will. Amen."

"Amen," echoed from Josh and Rachel. Jenn's throat was too full to speak, so she mouthed the word.

The Smokehouse was so old it didn't have a bathroom, but being in Berkeley, it did have veggie burgers. It was like something out of a 1950s movie. It couldn't even be called a restaurant—more like a hamburger stand with pseudo tin walls and a cement floor. It felt like you were outside even when you were under the metal roof. Half the tables were in the open air next to a patch of grass. It was sort of like the old McDonald's restaurants that were still around when Jenn was a child.

"Can we sit outside?" Sara asked.

The rest of the family nodded and pushed their way through the glass door. They settled on a picnic table with benches. Josh and Sara sat on one side, and Rachel squeezed in between Jenn and Steve. The table was shiny with new brown paint, but Jenn saw carvings in the wood. She ran her finger across some of the letters.

"Penny from heaven!" Josh said, pointing to the ground.

Jenn saw a shiny coin under the next table.

Rachel said, "Pick it up, Josh."

Josh shook his head. "Nah, God left that one for Mom."

Jenn smiled and picked up the penny. It was from 1988—the year Josh was born. She showed it to him.

"Best year ever!" Josh said.

"Uh-uh," Rachel and Sara disagreed in unison when they saw the date. Steve and Jenn laughed.

Three kids were running around on the grass. One of them ran up to the nearby adults and said something too quietly for Jenn to hear. The man nodded. The child said, "Hooray!" and jumped up and down in delight. She ran back to the grass and told the other kids the good news.

The adults lined up on the grass with two of the kids. The "mother" stood on the other side of the lawn.

She said, "Nico, you may take three jumps forward."

"Mother, may I?"

"No, you may not!" The girl laughed.

Nico growled at her.

"Just kidding. Yes, you may."

The boy named Nico bent his knees and took one big jump. Then he steadied himself and took another big jump. He was making the most of his three jumps. On the third jump, he lost his balance and put his right foot out so he wouldn't fall down. The "mother" gave him a scolding look. He brought his legs back together and stood at attention. She scrunched her face, giving something careful thought, and then looked away from him and back to the line of waiters.

The "mother" said, "Julia, you may take two giant leaps forward."

Rachel leaned against Jenn. "I used to love Mother, May I!"

"That was a lifetime ago, huh?" Jenn said. She looked at Josh watching the kids. "You were more of a Red Light, Green Light guy, weren't you?"

"I was awesome. Best on the block, if I do say so myself." He grinned at her.

Jenn realized how right this felt. After weeks, really months, of struggle, it felt normal to be together. She took Steve's hand, kissed the top of Rachel's head, and smiled over at Josh.

Sara got up and walked inside. Jenn saw her head over to a tall counter but couldn't tell what she was doing. She returned in a minute with napkins, straws, and ketchup.

"Food's up," Sara told Steve. They went inside to get it.

Jenn was struck by her oldest child's maturity. It made her proud and sad all at once. She enjoyed sitting here and letting her daughter take care of things, but it felt bittersweet. It was trite but true: her kids were growing up too fast.

At her core Jenn was still desperately afraid for Josh, but she was going to keep her worries to herself. Maya hadn't convinced

Jenn that homosexuality and salvation were compatible, but she had convinced Jenn that she needed to be much more patient and loving. Taking a hard line with Josh would only drive him away. Jenn held the penny tight and vowed to privately keep praying for his salvation and transformation. She hadn't given up faith but was going to be gracious and indirect. That was the most righteous path to walk in this complex, heartbreaking situation.

23

Josh let Jenn drive him to the SAT on Saturday morning. He came home in a good mood, believing he'd done well. Rachel was feeling neglected, so Jenn made her favorite for dinner: tacos. She sang as she cooked. Everything felt better now that her family was together again.

Over dinner they made plans for Sunday. Jenn was jerked back to reality when Josh said, "My friend Dash will pick me up for church and give me a ride home after youth group. We have it right after church, so I'll be home by lunch."

Her whole family looked at her. Jenn took a deep breath to steady her nerves. She felt as if this were a test. Not trusting herself to speak, she gave a little smile and nodded. Josh said *we* like he belonged there. He had a friend that she had never met. He was still slipping away from her.

"I want to go, too," Sara said. "I can drive us if I can use a car."

"You don't mind waiting for me while I'm at youth group?" Josh asked.

"No. I'll study," she said.

Jenn literally bit her tongue. She glanced at Steve. He gave a small nod.

"That's fine," Jenn squeaked out, though in her heart it was anything but. *Josh is home. That's what matters most.*

Rachel looked excited. "Can I go with them too, Mom? I've never been to any other church. I want to see what it's like. Please?"

Once again all eyes were on her. Jenn closed her eyes and nodded slowly. She slid her chair back and quietly said, "I'll be right back."

She walked into the bathroom, and as soon as the door closed she burst into tears. She bit her hand so she wouldn't make any noise, the tears coming hard and fast. Somehow these last few days had lulled her into thinking she had her life back. The idea of walking into church on Sunday with none of her children was humiliating. It would be one of the biggest disappointments of her life. And she had to pretend with her family that she didn't care at all.

When she stopped crying, she washed her face, wiped the mascara from under her eyes, and went back out. She appreciated that her family pretended she was just fine, though they all knew the truth.

◆ ◆ ◆

Jenn felt ill as she got ready on Sunday morning, but she hid it. She prepared breakfast for everyone and made appropriate small talk over the meal. They agreed to meet at noon at the Copper Skillet for lunch. She hugged each of her kids good-bye before they left for church without her.

Steve gave her a wordless embrace. He kissed the top of her head and said, "You're doing good. I know it's hard. But you're doing it. Ready?"

She grabbed her purse and let him drive her to church. She dreaded walking into the sanctuary and hoped they could avoid the people they knew best, but right as they pulled up, Lindsay and family were getting out of their car.

"Just you two this morning?" Lindsay inquired.

Jenn's mind raced to find a response that was a slanted truth. When she found it, she replied as casually as she could muster, "The kids decided to worship elsewhere today. They're taking an interest in broadening their understanding of Christ."

"Oh, I'm sorry, honey," Lindsay said, taking in the news. She looked visibly shaken and full of empathy. "We would never allow that."

Jenn forced a tight smile and walked away. She thought to herself, *Yeah. That's what I used to think, too. Well, sometimes your kids stop letting you decide everything. I can't wait until it happens to you.*

Jenn knew she was being immature, but it felt good. She held her head high as she and Steve entered the sanctuary.

◆ ◆ ◆

Sunday night Sara took BART back to Berkeley. Jenn must have passed the test, because Josh didn't go with her. She opened a bottle of white wine to celebrate, but she kept her joy to herself, acting as if it were perfectly normal to have Josh in the house. And she knew much better than to bring up treatment, but internally she vowed to continue praying for Josh's complete recovery.

"Mom, Pastor James is on the phone for you," Rachel yelled from the family room.

Jenn sighed as she picked up the extension. She really didn't want to have this conversation. Before she spoke, she took a deep breath to calm her nerves.

Pastor started talking as soon as she greeted him. "We've noticed that Josh is no longer attending church or youth group. We're so worried about him."

"Thank you for calling, Pastor. I've been meaning to make an appointment with you. I just—well, it's been so hard. As you know, Josh is struggling with a big issue." Jenn attempted to find the right words. "He, um, feels as if our congregation isn't right for him at this point in his life."

Jenn waited for a reply. The line was silent.

"Are you there?" she asked.

Pastor James cleared his throat and asked, "You and Steve support his decision?"

Jenn chose her words carefully. "*Support* is too strong of a word. We've prayed on this, a lot. *Accept* is more like it."

"You've given up on his salvation?" Pastor James questioned.

"No." Jenn shook her head. "Not at all. I pray for his full recovery every night and every morning. It's just, well, we've learned that many teens in his situation succeed in committing suicide. We don't want to put too much pressure on him."

"Do you understand that spiritual suicide is eternal?" he asked.

Jenn stammered, "I...We've decided that what's most important is that Josh feel loved and supported by his family."

"Don't you know that's how you got into this situation?"

"Excuse me?" Jenn asked, feeling attacked.

"You showered him with too much maternal affection," Pastor lectured. "That's why he has these homosexual feelings. You did read the materials I gave you?"

Jenn felt heat rise in her face. "Yes. I read everything," she said, in a voice that came out calmer than she felt. "We followed your recommendations. You know he went to camp. We appreciate your support—really, we do—and I pray Josh will return to treatment again. But for now...Well, I've come to accept that this is the best we can do for the time being. He's home, and he's safe. That's enough for me."

"It doesn't matter what's enough for you, Jennifer...It only matters what's enough for God."

Jenn was at a loss for words. She wanted to be respectful to her pastor, but he wasn't a parent, and he really couldn't understand the situation. If she'd learned nothing else from this, she had learned that she couldn't control her children anymore. But rather than argue with Pastor James or defend their decision, she replied, "I'll keep that in mind. Thank you for your concern and your support. I'll let Josh know you asked about him. I'm sure that will mean a lot to him. I'll see you at the welcome-team meeting on Thursday."

"I'm glad you brought that up," Pastor James replied. "We've decided to go in a different direction with the team and won't be needing your leadership any longer. Why don't you plan on this meeting being your last. OK?"

Jenn's stomach lurched. "What? You don't need me to be the chair?"

"We want to make room for new energy, so we won't need you on the team at all. But thank you for your service," Pastor informed her matter-of-factly.

"You're pushing me out…because of Josh?" Jenn asked, anger and indignation coming through in her voice.

"Jenn, there's no need to overreact," he admonished her. "It's just not the right ministry for you anymore. I hope you understand."

"No, I don't understand." Jenn had a sickening thought. "Are you asking our family to leave the church?"

"My goodness, Jenn, no!" Pastor James sounded shocked. "You are taking this too far. I am not asking you to resign your membership in the church—only your leadership on the welcome team. My deepest desire is that you and your whole family will be back in right relationship with our Lord and Savior before too long."

Somehow Jenn managed to get off the phone. She was so stunned by the end of the conversation that it all became a blur. She never imagined her pastor would reject her leadership, but then she wouldn't have believed before this that Lindsay would end their friendship, either.

Betrayals, from the people she trusted to love and support her through life, hurt deeply. She realized she was getting just a small taste of what Josh was experiencing. After the conversation with Pastor James, she was utterly certain she'd made the right choice to bring Josh home, to not be one of the people rejecting him. She would stay by his side, even if she didn't agree with his choice to give up on his salvation.

Jenn found Josh in the family room working at the computer. Tenderness filled her throat.

He turned around. "What?"

"Josh." Jenn cleared her throat. "I'm sorry that I did anything to make you feel that I didn't love you."

Casually, he replied, "It's OK, Mom."

"No, Josh, it wasn't. I was just so scared…am so scared. But that doesn't excuse my behavior. I really am sorry." Her eyeballs started to burn. She blinked to calm them. "And I promise I'll do better."

"Thanks." Josh offered a tender smile and turned back to the machine.

Jenn hoped her words were a small consolation for the past few months, but she knew she had a lot to make up for.

◆ ◆ ◆

Blessedly, the family fell back into a comfortable rhythm. Sara moved back home full-time after her last final on May 21. She found a babysitting job nearby to earn spending money for the year and registered for a class in the late-summer session so the family could go on their annual family trip to Southern California in July.

Over dinner they made plans. Excited, Jenn shared an idea: "I was thinking of getting two-day park-hopper tickets. There's just too much there now to do Disneyland in one day."

"Yes!" Rachel exclaimed. "California Adventure, here we come."

"And Manhattan Beach," Josh chimed in.

"Are we doing the split thing? Half at Nana and Poppy's and half at Grandpa and Grandma's?" Sara asked.

Jenn's chest squeezed tight. She looked at Steve. He took a big breath. "Well...we aren't going to stay at Grandma and Grandpa's on this trip."

"What?" Rachel asked.

Steve stuttered, "I haven't wanted...It's hard. I can't believe it, but they don't..." He looked at Jenn, obviously afraid to go on.

"They're old," Jenn said carefully. "They're set in their ways. It's harder for them to accept Josh..."

Jenn saw Josh's head drop to his chest, and he squeezed his eyes shut tight. Her heart ached for him.

"That is so messed up!" Rachel said.

"Well, I never liked staying there. Sorry, Dad. No offense," Sara declared.

Steve replied, "None taken."

"You can see them without me," Josh said quietly.

"No." Steve shook his head. "I'm not giving them that. All of us or none of us."

"They're being stupid, Josh," Rachel said.

"Rachel!" Jenn admonished. "They're still your grandparents."

"Well, they are," she insisted.

Sara chimed in. "It's their loss!"

"It sure is," Jenn agreed.

◆ ◆ ◆

Jenn went to track meets again since she no longer avoided time with Josh. Steve joined them for the last one of the year at Skyline High in Oakland. Sitting in the bleachers on a warm May day, Jenn studied her son on the field with his friends. He burst out laughing, and then threw an orange peel at Grant.

"He looks happy, doesn't he?" Jenn said to Steve. "Like before he was …."

It was still hard to say the word homosexual out loud. Then Jenn corrected herself, "I mean, before we…knew." Jenn shrugged and looked at her husband.

Steve rubbed her back and smiled, "He does look good."

"It's for the best that we know, isn't it?"

Steve agreed. "The secret was killing him. He was afraid he'd lose everything."

"I'm glad, really I am." Then she said tentatively, "*And* I still pray for his recovery."

"I know you do. Thank you for doing it, and for not letting Josh know."

Jenn asked, "Do you still pray for him?"

"Of course."

"That he's cured?"

The track coach walked up to them before Steve could reply.

"Hi Jenn," he greeted her. "Are you Josh's dad?" The slight man with brown hair reached his hand out. "I'm Coach Bell."

"Steve Henderson," her husband shook his hand.

"Josh is a great team member. He's very encouraging of the Freshmen, which I can't say about all the Juniors. I'm glad to have him for another year."

"Thanks," Jenn and Steve said in unison.

"I know he had a rough patch last month. I'm glad he's back at home."

Jenn's heart beat hard and fast. The coach knew Josh had run away? What else did he know? She dug her nails into her palm, but kept quiet until they stopped talking and the coach walked away.

"Does everyone know?!"

"Dublin High has been a great source of support to him. It's hard to hear, but we should be grateful."

"I know," Jenn sighed. "It's just so humiliating to know people are talking about us."

She leaned against her husband. Steve kissed the top of her head. Really, she *was* grateful. Grateful Josh was alive and enjoying himself on this beautiful day, and grateful that she and Steve seemed to have made it through this crisis. She just wanted to stop blundering into uncomfortable social situations that caused explosions in her stomach.

◆ ◆ ◆

The last few weeks of Dublin High were filled with papers, finals, and track for Josh and Rachel. Ordinary life was a blessing after those hard and divisive months. Jenn cautiously began to trust the new equilibrium in their family—until the morning Steve pulled her into their room to talk two days into Josh and Rachel's summer break.

"What?" Jenn asked suspiciously. She could tell something was up.

"Sit. You're not going to like this," he told her.

Jenn sat. "What now?"

"Josh asked me to march with him in the pride parade in SF."

Jenn stared hard at him. She wanted to scream. Instead of doing it out loud, she closed her eyes and yelled inside her own head. It actually helped.

Lord, give me patience, she prayed silently. Then out loud she calmly said, "What did you say?"

"I told him, 'Thanks for the invitation. I need to think about it.'"

"He didn't ask your permission, did he? He just told you he was doing it."

Steve nodded.

"Do you think he needs our permission to do this?" she challenged Steve.

"Jenn, I don't think that's what's really at issue here."

"What *is* at issue?" she demanded.

"He wants our love and support."

"He has my love. I don't support his homosexuality. It's all I can do to keep quiet about it. And now he wants us to literally march in a parade. He's asking for too much." Jenn looked at Steve. "You're going to say no, right?" she asked.

"I haven't decided."

Jenn bit her lip. She didn't want to say something she would later regret. Her brain pulsed with white noise. Finally she said, "I hope we can agree that marching in a parade is beyond what we're willing to do to accommodate him. Far beyond." She felt good about her calm demeanor.

"The girls are planning to march with him," Steve told her.

"What!" Jenn shrieked before she could stop herself. "He asked them too? And they said yes?"

Steve nodded. Jenn rubbed her eyes. "Aren't we going to forbid that? Rachel's just a child."

Steve replied, "I certainly don't want Rachel going without a parent."

Jenn was incredulous. "You are seriously considering going to that parade and taking your fourteen-year-old daughter? I don't know you."

"Do you want to know me? Or do you want to be so certain you're right that you lose all of us?" Steve shouted at Jenn, "He's my son! He's their brother! I would take a bullet for Josh. I'd cut off my arm for him. I'd do anything for him. So why not this?"

Steve stormed out. Jenn was left alone, stunned and hurt. She would take a bullet for Josh, too. Didn't Steve know that? That was why she was fighting this hard for his soul.

◆ ◆ ◆

The Monday before the parade, Jenn found an envelope with her name on it on the kitchen table.

> Mom,
> I guess you know about the pride parade on Sunday. We're gonna leave at nine and march with the PFLAG (Parents and Friends of Lesbians and Gays) and the church. You can come if you want, but no pressure, OK?
>
> Love,
> Josh

No pressure. What a joke. She flipped on Fox News. While she cooked, she stewed inside. Obviously, *we* meant her whole family. They were going to this parade without her. Jenn had already bent as far as she possibly could. She was being tolerant and respectful and giving Josh a lot of leeway, but she couldn't publicly celebrate.

She decided to write back without being harsh or rude. She considered *Have fun without me* or *Are you crazy?* or *I have other plans* or *Thanks, but no, thanks.* She finally settled on.

> Josh,
> Thanks for the invitation. It's not for me.
>> Love,
>> Mom

She crossed out her name on the envelope, wrote Josh's instead, and then slipped it under his bedroom door. Later that morning, she took the opportunity to have a good cry in the shower.

24

The day of the parade, Jenn forced herself to get up and make breakfast. She prepared everyone's favorites: eggs for Steve, smoothies for Sara and Josh, and white toast with jam for Rachel. She felt sick, so she didn't make anything for herself.

They came down dressed in shorts, T-shirts, and hoodies. The weather report said it would be a rare warm day in San Francisco, so she didn't send them back upstairs to put on long pants. They all sat down, and Josh reached out his hand for a prayer. Jenn's breath caught. She held Sara's hand on the right and Rachel's on the left.

"Dear God, in the name of Jesus, our Lord and Savior, we pray. Holy Spirit, fill us with love, light, and protection as we journey on this day. God, please watch over my mother"—Josh's voice caught—"and protect her heart. Amen."

Jenn felt small squeezes on her hands. "Amen" came in a chorus from her family. They released hands. Jenn gave Josh a small sad smile. She appreciated his care, but it also felt patronizing.

Rachel asked, "Is there any more smoothie?"

"You want some smoothie?" Jenn was surprised.

"It's going to be a long day. I need protein," Rachel explained.

"Protein gives you energy," Jenn agreed with a tight smile. "Smoothie coming right up."

They ate quickly and then rushed out the door. Jenn mustered the grace to hug them good-bye.

Steve whispered in her ear, "I know this is very hard on you. I love you."

"I love you, too," Jenn whispered back. "I keep telling myself it could be worse. He could be dead."

Steve hugged her tight and then left.

Jenn washed the dishes and walked out to the garage to go to church. She sat in the car surrounded by so many things: outgrown bicycles, scooters, helmets, sports equipment. They hadn't needed some of this stuff for years. She rested her head back and closed her eyes, imagining her family getting on the BART train, joining a sea of humanity without her.

She turned the ignition on and pressed the garage door opener. The bright light stung her eyes. Jenn couldn't face going out there. She pushed the button again and then turned off the ignition and reclined her seat. Overcome by exhaustion, she didn't even have the energy to go back into the house. She'd just rest right here in the dark garage.

She dozed for a while. When she woke up in the hot car, she was disoriented. Then it all came rushing in. Her mind reeled, and she felt stuck. She longed for the comfort of prayer, though it had been hard to hear God's voice lately.

"God," Jenn said, welling up with emotion, "help me know what to do to protect my family. You know they're going to San Francisco. Show me what You want me to do. Holy Spirit, bind up any distractions so that I may hear Your will clearly. In Jesus's name I pray."

And then she listened. She focused on the question *What is Your will for me?* again and again. She slowed her breathing and kept her mind open. She listened carefully with all of her being for the voice of God. Clear as a bell, she heard, *Love My children*. Her heart filled with those words. A chill ran down her back. She felt full and tingling all over.

Love My children! Jenn was stunned. God had told her those exact same words last February. *His* message hadn't changed, but today she felt it entirely differently.

God had been sending her this clear and simple insight for months, but she'd been too stubborn to really listen. She had ignored all the markers He had put in her way because she had been so certain she already knew His plan.

Maya, Kyle, Sara, Josh—they'd all been telling her God loved Josh. She knew Lord Jesus wanted more love in the world. Rather than judge, she was meant to love her son.

Jenn felt energy from the Holy Spirit surge through her body. She was bursting to share her new understanding with Josh right now. She had an overwhelming and intense need to be with her family so she could tell *all* of them that she finally got the message: God loves Josh, just as he is!

"Thank you, God, for Your guidance today and all days. In the name of Jesus Christ, I pray."

Jenn turned on the ignition, opened the garage door to the bright light, and drove away. She was going to show the depth of her love somewhere that she never expected. At the BART station she got a round-trip ticket to Powell. Jenn had no idea where her family was, but she was going to find them, because she belonged with them.

Sitting on the train, she texted Josh, Steve, and Sara, *I'm coming. Where are you?* She pictured their surprise and joy when they saw her message.

At each stop many people got on. She tried not to stare but rather watched them out of the corner of her eye. Most were decked out in something festive. Mardi Gras beads, colorful hats, and rainbow paraphernalia were everywhere. People looked like they were going to a festival. Many of the women and some of the men wore sparkly fabric. Some couples had matching T-shirts. As they pulled out of the San Leandro station, a young man dressed in tight gold lamé shorts and a rainbow tank loomed over her from the aisle. He caught her glancing at his getup. She blushed and gave him a tight smile.

"It's OK," he said with a huge grin. Swishing his hips from side to side and waving his arms, he said, "Look all you want. I'm here to be seen today."

She was suddenly self-conscious about her clothes. She sure didn't look like she belonged with this crowd. Jenn was dressed for church, in a lavender linen shift and white patent-leather flats, not for a parade. Especially not this parade.

Leaning in close, the man said, "Love your necklace."

Jenn put her hand to the cross at her neck. He was making fun of her! Heat rose in her cheeks. Then he put his hand under his shirt and pulled out a simple silver cross.

"My grammy gave it to me when I graduated high school. She told me to keep Jesus close wherever I go. Her wise words have steered me well over the years. Not everybody understands." He nodded toward the crowd on the train, shrugged, tucked the cross back under his shirt, and then turned around to chat with his friends and other revelers on the train.

Jenn was touched by the interaction. There was something so sweet and innocent about him. Rather than making fun of her, he was showing her that they shared something in common. God had given her a sign that she was on the right path. Jenn smiled to herself—and checked her cell phone again. Still nothing from her family.

◆ ◆ ◆

By the time the train left West Oakland, the car was packed tight. Jenn felt a little panicky but took deep, slow breaths to calm her nerves. She reminded herself that, in a few minutes, she'd be off the train and away from the crowd. And that she really was fine right there in her seat.

She checked her phone, but still there was no reply. Lots of people got off at Embarcadero, but even more got on. Finally they reached Powell. The crowd pushed toward the door. Nearly everyone wanted off here. She waited until the car was almost empty, and then she stood up. As she exited the train, she was a little shaky, but determined.

The dense crowd pushed her along after she stepped off the escalator at Market Street, and fear rose in her again as she was carried along by the mass of people. She'd never, ever been in a crowd like this and had no idea this many people came to this parade. She forced her way to the edge and stepped out of the stream of people in front of a drugstore. Jenn looked around, uncertain where to go. She had no idea how she was going to find her family.

"Are you lost, honey?"

A very tall woman with dark skin and a lot of makeup was looking at Jenn with concern. Jenn suspected she was really a man.

She blinked back tears. "I'm trying to find my family."

"Oh, bless your heart. I feel so bad for the tourists who don't know what they're getting themselves into today."

"I'm not a tourist," Jenn explained. "I'm here for the parade."

Surprise registered on the stranger's face. She tilted her head and asked, "You are?"

"My family is marching...with PFLAG and a church. They left without me. Well...I didn't go with them, but suddenly I didn't want to be left out. So here I am. And they don't know it," Jenn explained, surprised to be blurting this out to a stranger.

"Want to use my cell, honey?"

Jenn pulled out her phone and said quietly, "No one replied."

"Well, then we just have to get you to the front so you can jump right in with them when they get here," the woman said enthusiastically. "I'm Orinda." She stuck out a large hand.

"I'm Jenn. Thank you." Jenn was so grateful for the help that she pushed aside any concern about the fact that she was being guided by a transvestite.

"I'm here to serve," Orinda declared.

Orinda grabbed Jenn's hand and walked down the sidewalk for a bit. Then she pushed her way through the crowd. It was two or three people deep, but somehow Orinda got them to the front, close to a corner, right at the curb.

"Here you are, dear," Orinda said. "This is a great view. You won't miss 'em. They'll be coming from down there." She pointed east.

"Thanks." Jenn was grateful and a little bewildered by this rescue.

"Who's your family marching for?" Orinda asked.

"My son, Josh." Jenn welled up. "He's…Josh…" Jenn's throat was tight. Then she blurted out, "Josh is homosexual."

"Your son?" Orinda looked surprised. "You don't look hardly old enough to have a grown son!"

"Josh is sixteen."

"Oh, bless his heart! It takes a lot of courage to come out that young. Good for you for raising him right—strong and proud. Bless you all, dear."

"God bless you," Jenn replied back.

"He already has!" Orinda said over her shoulder as she disappeared back into the crowd.

Raised him right? Because he was brave enough to be homosexual? Wow, that was an entirely new concept to Jenn—and yet a surprisingly nice thing to hear, even from a virtual stranger.

She took in the scene. Market Street was filled with marchers. The road and sidewalk were packed with people as far as the eye could see. Jenn looked west, but she couldn't see the beginning of the parade. It must have been going on for a while. Maybe her family had already gone past and she had missed her chance to join them.

"Excuse me," she said to the tall man standing next to her. "Has PFLAG gone by yet?"

"Nope." He shook his bald head, which was covered in rainbow sparkles.

Good. She hadn't missed them. She looked at her phone again. Nothing.

When she looked up from her cell, the street was empty because of a break in the parade, and Jenn got a good look at the people sitting on the curb across from her. Women with strollers interspersed between them lined the other side of the street. One stroller had a sign that said *I Love My Two Mommies*. Another was decked out with a sign that said *I Was Hatched by a Couple of Chicks*. The children kept looking at their parents and pointing. It reminded Jenn of being at the electric-light parade at Disneyland when her kids were toddlers.

"Did you get it?" Jenn heard the man next to her ask. She turned her head. He was talking to a boy who was maybe ten. The boy, accompanied by another man, held up three glow-in-the-dark necklaces with a big grin. They ripped open the packages and put the glowing tubes around their necks.

Love My children. Clear as a bell, Jenn heard God speak to her. *All My children.* She felt the Holy Spirit burst into her heart and move in her spine. *I have set My rainbow in the clouds, and it will be the sign of the covenant between Me and the earth.* Tears sprang to her eyes. She knew. Suddenly she just knew that all of these people—each and every one of them in this crowd, the old and the young, the homosexual and the heterosexual, the whole human family—were God's children. God loved them, and Jesus died for them. All of them. Her soul surrendered to this at last. All these months she'd been sure it was Josh who needed to be transformed by the Holy Spirit, but she was the one being tone-deaf to God's calling.

Jenn heard the crowd down the street cheer. The man nudged her and pointed. Half a block away, a large PFLAG banner rose up high above the parade.

"Why is everyone cheering?" Jenn asked.

"PFLAG! It means so much…" he said, his voice cracking. He cleared his throat. "It means so much to have your family with you in this. It's, you know…what we all dream of…our parents being proud of us."

Jenn nodded wordlessly and smiled. As the banner came closer and closer, tears streamed down her face. She searched for her family, quickly scanning each face. There were so many people, and the street was so wide. She could easily miss them. Then she saw a flash of purple. Jenn got on her tiptoes. Yes! That was Rachel's hoodie. Her family was right here, and she belonged with them.

Thank you, God, for this gift of transformation. She breathed in the Holy Spirit and stepped out into the stream of life.

EPILOGUE

Jenn woke up early to make breakfast. It wasn't Saturday, but she was making Grandma Mary Alice's pancakes. It would be a while before the five of them would eat them together again. She didn't flip on the news because she wanted the quiet for her own thoughts. She was teary but didn't fight it. It was only right to be emotional when your beloved child was leaving home.

She yelled up the stairs, "Breakfast!"

After everyone was seated, Rachel asked, "Can I say the prayer?"

Jenn nodded.

"Dear God, in Your name we pray. Thank You for this food and all of Your gifts that sustain our lives. Watch over my brother, Josh, as he makes his way to the big, bad city."

"Rachel!" Steve said.

Rachel laughed. "Just kidding, God. I mean watch over Josh in New York City. Keep him safe in his travels and give him a great roommate. In Jesus's name we pray. Amen."

"Amen," they all repeated.

◆ ◆ ◆

Before Jenn knew it, they were outside of security at SFO. Since 9/11 they couldn't go to the gate without a ticket, so they were saying good-bye to Josh right here. This was his first time flying alone. Jenn was scared for him and excited too. She knew he was ready for this challenge.

"Go right to the gate. Don't rush, but you want to be there when they start boarding. Make sure it says JFK," Steve instructed.

"I'll be fine," Josh assured them. "I'll text if I have any problems."

Josh hugged Rachel, Sara, and then Steve. Finally it was Jenn's turn to say good-bye to her son. They wrapped their arms around each other and squeezed tight. Josh blinked as he pulled away.

He walked up to the TSA agent with his driver's license and boarding pass in hand. He made it through the checkpoint and got into the long, twisting line. Steve put his arm around Jenn. She reached for Rachel. Sara joined on at the end. They stood in a row watching as Josh's head moved in and out of sight. Jenn saw him put his bag on the conveyor belt. He stopped at the scanner and then disappeared. Jenn got on her toes. She couldn't find him.

She scanned the crowd. Out of the corner of her eye, she saw Sara wave. Jenn followed Sara's gaze. There he was, looking at them with his bag on his shoulder and his shoes on his feet. He'd made it through without her. Josh waved at them. She waved back. Then he turned away and melted into the crowd, his brown hair bobbing along the crowd like a leaf floating away down a river.

They stood there in silence, none of them wanting this to be over. But eventually Rachel broke away. They started to walk back to the car.

"Should we stay until his plane takes off? Just in case," Sara asked.

"Sure," Steve said. "We can wait at Peet's."

Sitting at the café, Jenn sent Josh a text: *Text me when you're there safe.*

Josh: *Will do.*

A few minutes later, Jenn's phone vibrated.

Josh: *I love you.*

Jenn: *I know.* Then Jenn texted, *I'm proud of you.*

Josh: *I know.*

I'm grateful to:

The wonderful people willing to read drafts who helped me know where I was missing, and hitting, the mark: Sheri Prud'homme, Rinda Bartley, Darlanne Hoctor Mulmat, Andrea Goss, Em Kianka, Linda Hodges, Skot Davis, Dan Goss, Kathy Post, Carmen Tomaš, Lauren Poole, Read, Katrinca Ford, Sandy Grayson, Emma Delp, Anne Delp, Heather MacCleod, Susi Jensen, Lori Freedman, Hannah Freedman-Tsveli, Wendy Davis, Karen Scott, Cile Beatty, Jeffrey Dickemann, Rachel Ibrahim, Sarah Prud'homme, Kateri Carmola, Aria Killebrew-Bruehl, Melissa Levine, and Sophia Killebrew-Bruehl.

The coming-of-agers who challenged me to put their ideas in the story: Aria Killebrew-Bruehl (pigeon), Ella Jeffries (penny), Eliana Thompson (LEGO), Lydia Macy (sperm whale), Sara Leyser (spelling), Sophia Killebrew-Bruehl (dragonfly), and Wynnie Savageford (dog).

Deborah Cuny for sharing some of her painful and hopeful story with me.
Ori Tsveli for advice about medical issues.
Lorie Strelo for information about Dublin history.
Chris Williams for track and field information.
Catherine Shore and Andrew Shore for the NALT video.
Tiffany Yates Martin for kind, insightful, and honest professional feedback.
Joel (I wish I knew your last name) for awesome editing.
Jennifer (I wish I knew your last name) for awesome editing AND letting me know you liked this manuscript.

Hannah Eller-Isaacs, Ottilia Schafer, Marcus Liefert, and Sasha Hood for historic technology info.

Victoria Obonyano for valuable feedback.

For all the families hurt by conversion therapy.

Sam Ames for her work to end conversion therapy.

Skot Davis, Dana Forsberg, and Sheri Prud'homme for writing retreats.

Terry Goodman for taking my work to a whole other level.

My amazing family: Maya, Kalin, and Rinda. Down to the ground and up to the sky.

LIVING RIGHT DISCUSSION QUESTIONS

Has there been any situation that challenged your core beliefs? How did you respond?

Is there anything you care so much about that you might join a protest or write a letter to the editor?

Did you identify more with Jenn, Josh, or some other character? Why?

Who was your favorite character?

Did your feelings about Jenn change throughout the story? In what ways?

Jenn's physical location changes in the story, starting from her chair and ending on a public street. What are other examples of that change, and how does that add to the story?

Does this story parallel your life in any way? What did it feel like to read about this situation?

Living Right explores a major controversy in our society. In what ways does this book expand your understanding of the issues?

In *Living Right,* Laila Ibrahim explores the theme of children growing up to be different than their parents expected. Did she do it in a way that makes this a universal story of parenting adolescents?

Did you find yourself especially angry, sad, or hopeful in any scenes?

AUTHOR BIOGRAPHY

L aila Ibrahim is the acclaimed author of the best-selling novel, *Yellow Crocus*. The characters in *Living Right* came to her while she was on a road trip through the Sierra Nevada mountains a few weeks after she legally married her wife, Rinda. She imagined a scene in a hospital room with a young, evangelical Christian confiding to his sister that he had attempted suicide because he could not bear to tell his parents that he was gay. She wanted to know what happened to that young man and his family so she wrote this story. She's a devout Unitarian Universalist determined to plant seeds of love and justice in our hurting world. Laila lives in a co-housing community in Berkeley, California, and is a mother of two young adult daughters. She's grateful to be a full-time writer, and excited to be working on a sequel to *Yellow Crocus*. She loves hearing from readers and calling/ Skyping into book clubs. www.lailaibrahim.com

Made in the USA
Charleston, SC
20 April 2016